South Atlantic Soldier

To Marilyn

Stuart Pereira

Stuart Pereira 2018

The price of freedom

The consequences of war last long beyond the
duration of the conflict.
Since the end of the Falklands War many British
veterans have taken their own lives.

In the Second World War the British Merchant Navy
casualty rate was 17% This is almost double that of
the Royal Navy - 9.3%, or the R.A.F. - 9%, and
almost three times that of the Army - 6%.

This book is dedicated to those from both sides
whose wounds cannot be seen.

CONTENTS

ACKNOWLEDGMENTS

Cover design and Artwork by blueqube.org.uk

GLOSSARY

SAS	Special Air Service
Comms	Radio Communication
Basha	Shelter made from ground sheet
RV	Rendezvous, A rallying point
ERV	Emergency RV used if patrol separated
SLR	Self Loading Rifle (standard British issue)
M16	US Rifle used by British Special Forces
GPMG /Jimpy	General Purpose Machine Gun
LUP	Lying up position. Patrol daylight hide
SOP	Standard operating procedure
Cuds	The countryside
Rupert	An officer (Derogatory)
MI room	Medical inspection room
OG's	Olive green trousers
OC	Officer commanding
2IC	Second in Command
Tabbing	Walking: Tactical Advance to Battle
DZ	Drop zone (for parachuting)
LZ	Landing zone (Helicopter)
Boots DMS	Boots with rubber Direct Moulded Soles
Rubber Dick	Useless information, false rumour, a con.
Head Shed	Headquarters
Stag	Period on watch
LURRP	Long Range Reconnaissance Patrols
CQB	Close Quarter Battle (Unarmed combat)
TQ	Interrogation
RSM	Regimental Sergeant Major (God!)
NAAFI	Canteen/bar/club (recreational facility)

TONY

1

Rough Seas
RFA Princess Royal, Tuesday 18th May 1982

Blasted from my slumber by the blare of the Klaxon,
I struggled from the hammock, groping for my life
jacket. Pulling on my duvet coat, I sprinted to the
companionway taking the treads two at a time.
Turning sharp about at the mess deck, I galloped up
the next flight and out onto the boat deck; Yorkie
hard on my heels. Pulling on our anti-flash hoods, we
clambered up the ladder to our action station behind
the wheelhouse, gasping for breath in the thin, cold
air. Our machine gun was mounted onto the
starboard rail, protected by a makeshift wall of
sandbags and timber. I pulled the waterproof sleeve
from the gun, opened the feed tray and slapped on a
two hundred round belt. Yorkie snapped the cover
shut and yanked the cocking lever with a big-gloved
hand, before slowly pushing it all the way forward.
Scanning the sky for enemy aircraft, I saw only a
solitary albatross riding the wind. Recalling
Coleridge's 'Rime of the Ancient Mariner,' I prayed
that no trigger-happy gunner would mistake it for an
Argie aircraft. Bad luck we could do without.

Minutes ticked by and my eyes began to ache

from scouring the sky. The weather was hardly perfect for an attack, visibility fair to poor, the wind around force six. I stamped my chilled feet hard against the swaying steel deck, making it ring like a bell with a rubber clapper. Training shoes were hardly the most suitable footwear for the South Atlantic, but it sure beat sleeping in boots.

After fifteen minutes fruitless scanning, I looked to my immediate surroundings to relieve the strain on my eyes. The ship was crewed by civilians from the Merchant Navy, with a small Royal Navy contingent manning the anti-aircraft guns and helicopter deck. She looked tired. Rumour had it that she was due for the breaker's yard, but had been reprieved at the last-minute for the current crisis. Her paintwork was patchy, flaking through many layers. Everywhere, streaks of orange rust ran down the superstructure, staining her grey plates like nicotine on a sailor's teeth. Overhead, the rigging lines slapped tunelessly against the mast, while the radar scanner whipped around tirelessly, searching for any sign of attack. The bitter wind cut through my clothes while the steel deck sent icy fingers through the soles of my Reeboks. I pulled my flash hood tight and danced on the pitching deck to get the blood flowing.

'I'm supposed to be on holiday,' I shouted. 'Two weeks in Tenerife, booked and paid for.'

Yorkie gestured into the freezing wind skidding across the ocean. 'Not exactly a Caribbean cruise is it? Never mind, Tony, I'm sure Carol and the boys will send you a postcard.'

'Tenerife's in the Canary Islands, Muppet, off the coast of Africa.'

The starboard gunner yelled something but his

words were swept away by the wind as he swung the barrel of his Oerlikon cannon toward the starboard quarter. Yorkie saw it first. Following his gaze I spotted the faint glow, like a distant firefly, skimming across the waves towards us: a seven hundred mile-an-hour firefly with an explosive warhead. Yorkie locked the gun into his shoulder. A token gesture. Our gun was useless against a missile. I turned to my comrade. His blue eyes shone with defiance, lighting up a face as white as his anti flash hood, freckles apart that is. I turned quickly back to the missile. It would be all over in twenty-seconds; one way or another.

The Oerlikon opened fire, pouring high explosive towards the missile at seven rounds a second, the shells splashing into the waves, throwing up small white fountains well astern of the fiery threat. Time slowed to an agonizing crawl as we watched the fireball grow in size and intensity. The little white fountains chased the glowing missile, playing catch up, as the seventeen-year-old gunner frantically tried to nail his elusive target. Suddenly the firing stopped. My heart filled my mouth.

Our smaller gun burst into life. I began feeding the belt into the breach, as long bursts of copper-jacketed lead streaked across the water. Tracer rounds glowed orange, bouncing off the waves and rippling through the air as the steel deck rang to the music of brass cartridge cases raining down upon it. The pitching hull made accurate shooting impossible, but it was comforting to be in action. I began praying to God with all the faith I could muster. The Oerlikon resumed firing. The glowing ball closed on us. I held my breath.

At the last second my prayers were answered.

The missile flashed across our bows 300 metres ahead, trailing white smoke as it tore across the waves, disappearing as quickly as it had come.

'That was an Exocet.' I said.

'After bigger fish than us, thank God.'

'So much for this then.' I placed my hand on the gun. 'Might as well use a peashooter, for all the good it is.' I opened the ready-use locker, took out fresh box of ammunition and replaced the almost empty one on the mounting. Yorkie's grin, framed in the white circle of his flash hood gave me heart.

'I had to open up,' he said. 'I couldn't just watch.'

I nodded approval.

The rest of the alert passed without incident. After an hour we were stood down and we made our way back to our Spartan accommodation by way of the galley, where Yorkie charmed a couple mugs of tea out of the steward. Warmed through with the brew, we stripped off and hung up our wet gear, changed into tracksuits and settled into our pits. I began to feel a little seasick as the ship rolled in the swell.

'Christ, Yorkie, I thought the swing of the hammock was supposed to neutralize the rolling of the ship, not enhance it.'

'Stop moaning, you Welsh Dago. You'll get used to it. This is nothing to rounding the cape head on to a force ten. When I was on tankers...'

'Yeah, I know and you were only seventeen. I'm forty-two. Too old for this.'

'You're just a bairn.'

'I'm a soldier, not a bloody sailor, I trained to fight on terra firma.' I tried to stare into the distance to steady my stomach, only there was no distance to stare into in our cramped quarters. The jury-rigged 100 watt bulb swinging from the racking, cast crazy dancing shadows on the steel plates, adding to my nausea. Two yellowing caged bulkhead lights were our only other illumination.

'Don't worry, you're going to get your chance. We'll teach these Argie bastards not to mess with us Brits. Wait 'til the Paras get stuck in. They'll sort em out.'

'Don't forget the Marines.'

'Bloody cabbage heads.'

'Once a Para, always a Para. You're SAS now, remember?'

He let it go over his head.

'Cig?' I asked. He nodded. I lit two Bensons and passed him one. 'I'm going to have to replace this one of these days,' I said, idly flicking the Zippo's flint wheel.

'You've been saying that for years.'

'Look at the lid, the hinge is almost worn through.'

'Never mind. Treat yourself when we get home.'

When we get home! He seemed so certain we would return. I hoped he was right.

Our present home was very basic. We enjoyed exclusive use of the free space in a small storeroom in the bowels of the ship; room for one hammock, one camp bed, two white plastic garden chairs and our bergan rucksacks. A wooden crate served as a table. We were surrounded by steel racking crammed with ration boxes, batteries, sandbags and all manner of war stores.

Lack of natural light has a depressing effect so we took every opportunity to go up top, where, weather permitting, we spent two hours a day, running circuits of the deck. I say 'running,' but it was more of an obstacle course. The decks were packed tight with vehicles, crates and netted pallets loaded with equipment and munitions.

We kept up to date with events by listening to the BBC World Service on a small pocket radio rigged to a makeshift dipole aerial. Our main enemy was boredom. As the only Army personnel aboard and not being attached to any unit, we were forgotten to a degree; overlooked in the rush to get down south. Apart from lifeboat drill and our action station, we had no duties.

'Any idea what our position is?' I asked my companion, as much as anything to break the silence.

'I'd say our position is rather precocious at this time.'

'I think you mean *precarious*, my friend.'

'I know. Just winding you up. You bite every time.'

'Sure you were.' I said, humouring him, 'I was thinking, we can't be far off where my father's ship was sunk during the war. It's weird being here, all these years after he was killed.'

Just then a small white face appeared at the hatchway, like a weasel at the entrance to its burrow. It was the radio operator just coming off watch. 'A helicopter's gone down in the ocean with a load of regular SAS guys on board. Most went down with it. Sorry lads.'

I felt sick. Up to now it had been the Navy taking casualties. It had just got personal.

'Poor bastards.' I said.

'Occupational hazard' said Yorkie.

The news had thrown a heavy blanket of silence over our tiny grey storeroom. Swinging from side to side in my hammock, I stared at the naked light bulb, while reflecting upon my situation as I drifted away into the arms of Morpheus.

2
Briefing
R.F.A. Princess Royal, Tuesday 18th May 1982

Yorkie appeared at the door with a steaming mug of tea and a corned beef sandwich.

'Here. Get this down you.'

'You spoil me.' I said.

'Don't kid yourself, we've got a briefing in the sick bay in forty minutes.'

I rubbed my eyes and looked at my wristwatch. 09.20.

'Sick bay?'

'Only place with enough space, apparently. Rumour control says the Navy's going to transfer us to another ship.'

I did not answer, content just to chomp on my sandwich.

Spacious compared to our quarters, the sick bay smelled of rubber and antiseptic. The bulkhead shelves and cabinets were packed with medical supplies. Kit had been shoehorned into any free space. Boxes of saline drips, dressings and plasma lurked beneath the bunks. Yorkie nudged me and nodded to a large oilskin package lying on the deck like a beached walrus. Stencilled upon it in red just two words: Body Bags.

A Royal Marines Sergeant, with thick jet-black hair and a droopy moustache delivered the briefing. He looked like an extra from a spaghetti-western. This illusion was reinforced when he opened his mouth, to reveal a hoard of gold fillings, only to be instantly shattered by a stream of barely intelligible, broad Geordie.

'Right, bonnie lads, the situation on the ground. Enemy forces at company strength with heavy weapons and air support in your area of operation. Weather: Wind force 4, rain squalls and sleet expected next forty-eight hours. You will be transferred to a frigate by helicopter at 11.00 hrs tomorrow. You will get further orders there.'

The next few hours were spent cleaning weapons and packing and repacking kit.

'This must weigh fifty pounds,' I said, testing my bergan. Yorkie's was even heavier but he lifted it as if it was a lass's handbag.

'Thank God we're not carrying radios,' I said, stuffing emergency rations into my escape belt before shoehorning in my, as-yet empty, magazines and other survival kit should we need to ditch bergans and leg it. Gear stowed, we went for grub.

Wide-awake with fourteen hours to kill, I wrote a long letter home, trying to reassure Carol that the politicians would find a solution before we reached the Islands. I addressed it, but left it unsealed for the censor's benefit. Making a mental note to leave it with the officer of the watch before we disembarked, I stuffed it in my pocket. I tried to read but had trouble concentrating and in spite of having just eaten, I had an awful empty feeling in the pit of my stomach. The time to repay the British taxpayers' investment in me, was fast approaching. I must not let the Squadron down. I thought of my early days with the Regiment, when I got my SAS wings. I used to think I was real big time then; I didn't feel quite so big now.

'What's this place like then, Tony?' Yorkie asked.

'Bit like the Pennines: bare-arsed sheep country, mostly peat bog and rough grassland with rocky outcrops. Coastline's rugged like west Scotland.'

'Woods?'

'No trees at all worth the mention. The best cover, apart from the rocks, is gorse scrub from what I can remember, and not too much of that. It was twenty years ago you know.'

'A bit exposed then.'

'The wind blows all the time and we can expect snow any time soon.'

'Lovely.'

I was confident we would have no problem with the terrain or the weather. We were well equipped, well trained and experienced. The unknown, was the enemy. Argentina had not fought a major conflict in recent times and according to intelligence, the troops were mostly inexperienced conscripts. We would be isolated behind enemy lines and outnumbered several hundreds to one, at least until the main landings took place. This, however, was what we trained for. This was our job. I eventually dozed off.

The following morning, we made our way aft, to the

heli deck. The wind was moderate and visibility better than average. A fresh faced young rating signalled the pilot to start up as soon as we had squeezed our kit and ourselves in behind the two-man crew. The Rolls Royce Nimbus whined into life and the rotor blades began to turn, carving a thirty-two foot circle, in the cold, salty air. A twenty-year-old design, the Wasp, though small, was rugged and dependable and after a short flight we made our final approach to the frigate. The heli deck looked worryingly small, rising and falling alarmingly. My thoughts flashed back to the fate of the Sea King, as I fought to control my nerves. The pilot calmly manoeuvred into position, flaring above the pitching platform, before slamming us down with a bone jarring crunch, onto the frigate's heaving deck.

Shaken but grateful, we dismounted and crossed the swaying deck at a low crouch, dragging our kit behind us, conscious of the rotor blades whirling just above our heads. Yorkie kept one hand firmly clamped to his head, to prevent his thinning blond hair from being blown about. A rating waved us forward, verbal communication was impossible, owing to the noise of the Wasp's engine. Once inside the ship he spoke:

'Follow me please, sir.'

'*Sir?*'

I looked quizzically at Yorkie. A wry smile creased his freckled features.

'Let's not disillusion him,' I said, as we descended the steel ladder into the bowels of the vessel. We wore no badges of rank nor unit insignia, having discarded our berets in favour of more practical woolly hats. He was just playing it safe I guess, or perhaps our advanced years had something to do with it. The sailor stopped so suddenly that I collided with him.

'Sorry, lad'.

'My fault, Sir, er... Please make yourselves at home.'

He indicated the open doorway of a small cabin. 'Captain Michaels will see you shortly.'
Before we could reply he was gone.

'Well, "Colonel," what do you think?'

'Not up to our usual standard is it, "Major" Barnes?' I replied with a mouth full of plum stones. We burst into laughter.

'Do you think we'll get the pay to go with the rank?'

'No fuckin'chance.'

'I don't know, we're certainly getting the royal treatment. I mean the Captain wants to see us. You would have thought he'd have had his hands full running the ship.'

The cabin was luxurious compared with our accommodation on Princess Royal; twelve feet by eight with bunks and proper chairs upon which we sat, idly speculating about our immediate future, until the rating returned with a tall, young SAS officer.

'Don't get up chaps. Captain Michaels.'

'You muppet, Gomez.' I thought, *'Ship's Captain my arse. It's only a bloody Rupert.'*

The Captain sat on the lower bunk.

'Sergeant Gomez and Corporal Barnes, sir.'

'Yes, yes, alright. I'll fill you in on what has been happening ashore. Six days ago, one of our four-man patrols established an OP to watch the road to Stanley. The day before yesterday they snatched an

Air Force Major. We planned to extract him, but no helicopter was available. Since then Argies have occupied the immediate area, so extraction is no longer an option. We lost comms for some time but they have been re established in the last couple of hours. That's all the detail we have except that the patrol have established an RV, which will open today at twenty-three hundred hours. It will remain open for thirty-six hours. You have to get there by noon the day after tomorrow. We must interrogate the prisoner soonest. He could have vital information on the state of air power on the islands. He claims not to understand English. Probably a ploy. It's your job to get him to talk. You speak Spanish I understand?'

'Si, Capitan,' I responded.

He raised an eyebrow and gave me an old fashioned look.

'You will be inserted by Helicopter as close to the RV as is practical. Your job is to get as much information out of the prisoner as possible. The patrol will radio it back to us. Not ideal, but that's war, I'm afraid. It's now ten fifteen. Seaman Hughes will show you where you can get some scoff. Report here for an update at twelve thirty. Any questions?'
What about operational kit? We've no ammunition.'

'Corporal Slater's your man: Hughes will show you to his lair. That it? Good. Twelve thirty then.'

'Doesn't waste words, does he?' I said, after he'd gone.

'Nope,' replied a bemused Yorkie.

Seaman Hughes led the way to the lower mess deck and Corporal Slater's den. Perched on a crate surrounded by boxes of ammunition sat a small, wiry man in his thirties. Short cropped red hair, a face covered with freckles that looked as if they had been applied with a shotgun, Slater smiled warmly.

'Welcome to Slater's department store, gents. How may we help?'

'Ammo and rations, medic kit and batteries for a three one six radio please.'

'What calibre ammunition gents?' Slater asked. 'I have a special offer on mortar bombs. Buy one get one free.'

'Too heavy for us mate. We'll have all on to carry what we've got already,' I replied.

Yorkie chimed in. 'Seven point six two for my SLR and some little toy bullets for my friend's plastic gun,' he said, grinning like a lunatic.

Slater picked up a clip board and reached into a crate.

He placed three heavy cotton bandoliers on the counter. 'Three hundred rounds seven six two, grenades H.E. times four; smoke two; phosphorus two.'

'Pack mules,' I said, eyeing the growing mound of kit.

'Quit moaning your ammo's lighter than mine.'

'It should be I'm smaller than you.'

'Morphine syrettes, field dressings, ration packs, batteries. Sign here, gents.'

Yorkie scribbled across the bottom of Slater's form.

'Thanks, pal,' he said.

Waddling back to our accommodation, pockets bulging, festooned like Christmas trees, I wondered how I would manage such a load across country.

Distributing the extra stores amongst our kit was more of an art than a science. At the briefing we were issued maps, shown our flight path to the landing zone and route to the rendezvous. We ran through ditching drills with a Navy type and after the obligatory any questions? we returned to our quarters.

'Who would have imagined this then?' said Yorkie. 'Us off to war at the arse end of the world. It's a long way from the MI room.'

Our first meeting, just eleven years ago while waiting for our jabs in the Medical Inspection room did seem like a lifetime away.

3

Induction
West Yorkshire, February 1971

Life is like a journey along an unsigned road. At each junction, you have a choice – left or right. The one you take determines your future up to the next one and so on. The road that led me to the Falkland Islands, for the second time in my life at the ripe old age of forty-two, began in school, when I read Roy Farran's memoirs of SAS operations in Europe and Italy in the Second World War. I wanted to join the army but my grandmother insisted I *get an education*,' so I read zoology at Leeds university; you didn't argue with my grandmother.

I had no idea that the Territorial Army had an SAS Regiment, let alone that there was a squadron practically on my doorstep until I saw a small advert in the Yorkshire Post, aimed at recruiting young men for the unit. The headline read: *'Do you long for adventure?'* A week later I was standing in front of the officer commanding the unit. The major told me that joining the Squadron would not be easy, that the selection process was long and arduous and I would be frequently cold, wet, hungry and uncomfortable. There was, he stressed, a very high failure rate. He asked just one question. He asked me why I wanted to join.

Unable to think of anything more original I said that I liked a challenge. It seemed to do the trick, as he smiled, stood up and leaned across the desk to shake my hand. He wished me luck. I had a feeling I was going to need it.

At nine a.m. on Saturday I joined a queue at the stores.

The store ma looked me up and down and based on this brief scrutiny, issued me with two of everything – in someone else's size, the only exception being boots. Here, care was taken to ensure as good a fit as possible. No matter how fit or strong a recruit was, if he did not look after his feet he would fail. We were offered all kinds of advice how to look after our feet and boots, ranging from 'soak your feet in industrial alcohol to harden the skin' to the bizarre 'piss in your boots and leave them to soak overnight.'

The SSM (squadron sergeant major), a short, stocky man in his late forties, spoke softly but had such a commanding presence that a big stick would have been superfluous.

'Fall in in two ranks with your kit'

'Atten...shun!' There was a loud thud, as eleven pairs of boots hit the drill hall floor in unison, followed a second or so later by mine shuffling into place. I soon discovered that I was the only one with no previous military experience, which did nothing for my confidence. We were stood at ease and introduced to our course instructors. The sergeant was a real 'Jack-the-lad,' who had been there, done that and then some. Immaculately turned out with mirror gloss boots and creases in his trousers you could slash your wrists on, he looked about forty, with close-cropped hair and the lean body of a middle distance runner.

'My name is sergeant Fryer. You will address me as Staff. Am I Clear?'

'Yes, Staff' we replied in a ripple.

'Pathetic,' he said scrutinising each of us with piercing blue eyes. I felt suddenly uncomfortable.

'Corporal Samson they're all yours...and the best of British luck!'

'Listen in,' corporal Samson commanded. 'Pack all the kit you think you will need for a walking weekend in the Dales....go!'

I set to with enthusiasm, based on experience gained in the Boy Scouts. Sleeping bag first, spare water bottle, rations, and a change of clothes. I was halfway through the task when corporal Samson said in a quiet voice.

'Stop there and listen up. Which two attributes do you need to become an SAS soldier?'

No one spoke.

'Intelligence and strength, gentlemen. An SAS soldier needs a brain like Einstein and the back of a donkey. Some of you are obviously better equipped than others. Take Gomez here,' he picked up my bergan and held it out to the recruits. My chest swelled with pride. 'Gomez is half way there already. He has a back like Einstein and the brain of a donkey.'

I cringed.

'Gentlemen, this is your house, your home,' corporal Samson declared, holding a bergan aloft.

'There will be times when, in the interests of personal survival, you will find it necessary to leave home and leg it. If you are pursued by the enemy, you will not outrun him with sixty pounds on your back. That is when you will need your escape belt.'

He held up a canvas belt with two ammo pouches, two water bottles, a sheath knife and two small U.S. army pouches. What you carry in yours is up to you, but think hard. You may have to live for many days off the contents.'

He took a mess tin from one of the pouches and emptied out the contents. Emergency rations, waterproof matches, flint and steel for fire lighting, space blanket, water sterilizing tablets, stove, mess tin, it was a comprehensive list. There were fishing lines, a candle, nylon twine and among other things, a packet of Durex.

'What's the Durex for staff?' I asked naively.

'In an emergency one of these little beggars will hold enough water to last you several days and should you stumble across the wood cutter's daughter, it will prevent you getting the clap.'

Tuesday evening drill night following roll call, we climbed the stairs to the first floor and filed along a corridor to form a queue outside the Medical Inspection room. It was here that I first met Yorkie Barnes. He was standing in line in front of me when a sergeant came out of the MI room and playfully punched him in the ribs.

'Bruiser Barnes, what are you doing here?'

From the ensuing banter, it became obvious that they had both boxed together in the Parachute Regiment. Barnes was powerfully built and looked the sort you would not want to get on the wrong side of. When the sergeant went about his business I struck up a conversation with 'Bruiser.' We hit it off immediately, despite being complete opposites. He was blond, fair-skinned, blue eyed and clean-shaven, while I was olive skinned, with jet-black hair and a Pancho Villa moustache.

'You sound like a Rupert,' he said.

'What do you mean?'

'The posh accent.'

'I haven't got a posh accent, it's just my Welsh lilt.'

'Sounds posh to me.'

'What's a Rupert when it's at home?'

Barnes laughed. 'You haven't been in the army before, have you?'

'No,' I said, 'but I did try for the Royal Navy Reserve a few years back.'

'What happened?'

'I failed the medical.'

His face was a picture.

'You failed the medical for the RNR and you want to join the SAS. I do love an optimist.'

'I only failed on a technicality,' I said, 'admitted having hay fever. I didn't think it would matter. I pointed out the distinct lack of grass pollen on the high seas, but they failed me anyway.'

'Well, I wouldn't mention it in there,' he said nodding to the MI room.

'Don't worry, I've learnt my lesson.

'Well, the best of British, my Welsh friend.'

'Thanks, Bruiser, actually my mother was Welsh, I'm Spanish on my father's side. You still haven't told me what a Rupert is.'

'Rupert is a inflamatory term for an officer and forget the Bruiser bit, my friends call me Yorkie.'

'Oh, okay.' I said, noting his malapropism, but deciding it would be rude, not to mention unwise, to comment upon it. The line moved forward and we were at the open door of the M.I. room. The man in front of Yorkie was around six feet tall and muscular. He stepped into the room and was ordered to roll up his sleeve. When he saw the needle he went very pale and dropped like a stone.

'Next' shouted the orderly stepping over the body. Yorkie stepped up, took the jab, turned on his heel and marched out past me. I took my turn and then followed him. I was a bit of an embarrassment on parade again but as we were dismissed, my new found friend approached me.

'Don't worry about parade, I'll soon sort you out. Come for a drink in the bar.'

'I would, but I have to catch a bus.'

'I'll give you a lift.'

'You sure?

'No sweat'

'I'll need phone my wife first.'

'There's a pay phone in the bar,' said Yorkie steering me towards the doors. What are you having?'

'Pint of bitter please.'

'Ring your wife. I'll get them in.'

The bar was small and functional. Plain beech-wood tables with grey Formica tops and a mix of matching chairs and stools. Yorkie was sitting in a corner with two ex TA Paras, who were arguing about football, both being avid Leeds United fans with different views on the team structure.

'You into football?' Yorkie asked, handing me a pint.

'No interest at all I am afraid.'

'Me neither,' he said raising his glass.

'To Welsh Spaniards everywhere.'

'Cheers,' said I, 'had you been in the Paras long?'

'Ten years. My old man was in the during the war. He's 'Army Barmy,' expected me follow in his footsteps.'

'What about your mother?'

'Dead against. Wanted me to get a job in an office, not wind up driving a van like my old man. They were always rowing about it.'

He took a silver cigarette case from his pocket and offered me a Benson and Hedges. I took one and accepted a light from his Ronson.

'In the end I buggered off to Hull,' he continued, 'signed on a Dutch ship as cabin boy. I went back home at eighteen and got a job selling cars. Worked my way up to head salesman. My mother was happy because I was in a white collar job. No one in our family had done that before.'

'She must be proud of you.'

'Yes, I guess she is. Anyway I joined the TA Paras to keep my old man happy.'

'Another pint?' I enquired.

'Cheers'

I stood up and made my way to the bar. While waiting to be served I studied the photographs of the squadron from past years displayed behind the bar. I counted no more than forty-six men in any one picture. A very elite band.

'I got a couple of bags of crisps as well okay?'

'Thanks,' Yorkie said as he sucked the head from his pint. 'So what about you then? You've had my life story.'

'Never knew my dad,' I said, 'lost at sea in 1939.'

'Navy?'

'Merchant Navy: chief steward.'

'So you're the son of a Rupert,'

'I suppose I am. Don't really remember my mother, she was killed in an air raid when I was a kid. My Nan brought me up.'

'So what do you do for a civvy job then?'

'I'm a research assistant in the museum.'

'You must be clever then?'

'Not really, just lucky to have a university education.'

'I only managed a comprehensive school. I wish I'd been clever enough to go to college. What did you study?'

'Zoology, specifically Ornithology.'

'Did you have to study long?'

'Three years and two years post grad in the Falklands.'

'Where?'

'British Island Protectorate near Antarctica.'

'What the hell were you doing down there?

'Studying Penguins.'

'Sounds interesting' he said, his eyes glazing over.

'Piss taker,' I said. 'Another pint?'

'Cheers, I will'

One phone call, two hours and four pints later we were talking like old mates.

4

New Experience
West Yorkshire, February 1971

The following Friday, training started in earnest, with parade and roll call at 8 p.m. We collected 24-hour ration packs, signed out watch and compass from the stores, and walked out into the cold January night to climb into the back of a Bedford three ton lorry. The journey to the training area was an uncomfortable experience, chilling wind howled through gaps in the canvas cover, while exhaust fumes were sucked over the tailgate into the back. We de-bussed in the heart of the Wensleydale, surrounded by the steep dark hills of the Yorkshire Dales National Park. The night was clear, cold and sharp, a full moon washing the landscape with an eerie silver light. The only sound came from the River Wharfe, gurgling and rushing, somewhere behind the truck, as if in a desperate hurry to be somewhere else.

We were given the six-figure grid references of our location, and our objective. As soon as each man had satisfied the staff that he could locate both points on his map, we set off in single file. A member of the recruit training team took the lead. All through the night, our boots crunched their way up windy hill and down frosty dale. This 'gentle' introduction to the training area was designed to sound us out. We were constantly being assessed as to our physical fitness, appreciation of the terrain, map reading, and self discipline. We walked at a brisk pace along the road, crossing the swirling brown river by way of a humpbacked stone bridge. Climbing over a stile, we followed a vague footpath across pasture land. Our bergans weighed thirty pounds and my escape belt a further ten. With the bright full moon reflecting off our newly issued, off-white, windproof smocks, we looked like some giant ghostly serpent, snaking across the field, towards a towering rock-face with a prominent overhang. We began climbing quite steeply up a wide stony track to the side of the cliff, eventually curling around to the left of the feature, to reach a ridge level with the cliff top, some nine hundred feet above the road. My lungs were working overtime, my calf muscles screaming in protest at this sudden unexpected beasting.

We kept up the pace for over an hour, across rough sheep-grazed grassland laced with outcrops of pale grey Limestone, during which we climbed to fifteen hundred feet. Everywhere there were dry stone walls made from the same local limestone and almost every field in the valley below, had its own stone built barn. At last we stopped for a breather and I gratefully sank to the ground, leaving my bergan on as a backrest. Despite the cold, my back and hair were soaked with sweat and my first instinct was to reach for my water bottle.

'Go easy on the water, lads,' corporal Samson advised. 'Wait until your breathing is normal, then sip slowly. I don't want anyone with stomach cramp. We have a long way to go so no running out and drinking from the rivers without using the sterilizing tablets you were issued. Understood?'

I followed the advice and after a short wait, found that I wasn't quite so thirsty, which was just as well, given the size of my water bottle. I resolved to buy a second bottle to keep in my bergan and to invest in a thermos flask before next weekend. After a few minutes, the sweat on my back had turned cold and my legs began to stiffen, so I was more than ready to move when we got the order. We dropped down seven hundred feet to skirt around a large Tarn, my left cheek glowing with the icy wind that whipped across its inky black water. The path led us into a deep rocky gorge, with sheer vertical walls towering above us, throwing a deep black shadow which enveloped us in its darkness. The ground beneath our feet was strewn with boulders, logs and the roots of trees, exposed by years of constant flooding. The air was soon punctuated with curses, as shins and ankles suffered in the darkness. After an hour or so, we emerged from the blackness to find ourselves in a water meadow at the edge of a small village. We passed through a gate, the last man closing it carefully behind him, as we crept along the deserted main street past the only pub. Turning left at the church we crossed a stile into another field and began the assault on yet another hill. My bergan straps chafed my shoulders, causing much discomfort, but far worse were the new boots, which were giving my feet a really hard time, making every step increasingly painful.

It seemed as if we were always climbing and the only view I had was the backside of the man in front of me. When you shoulder a bergan, the natural instinct is to lean well forward to ease the load, so adopting the characteristic 'head down arse up attitude.' It is, in fact, physically impossible to walk upright. Any attempt to do so would result in you falling over backwards.

We had set off at midnight and by 04.00 hours I was feeling low, wondering what I had got myself into, when we stopped for a breather in a sheep pen. Leaning backwards against the wall to ease the load, I began to nod off, In spite of the cold. We were soon on the move again, however and after twenty minutes or so, we came to a stile which corporal Samson counted us over. Unfortunately we appeared to be one short and we were forced to about turn and retrace our steps. As we approached the sheep pen we heard the unmistakable sound of snoring. Steve Ellis was fast asleep on his feet leaning against the wall. I was sure he would get a bollocking, but was not prepared for what happened next.

'Drop and give me ten press ups, Ellis,' ordered Samson quietly.

'The rest of you give me twenty.'

We complied uncomprehendingly in silence.

'You will have only yourselves and each other to rely on in the Regiment. You will look out for each other at all times. One day your life may depend on it. Am I clear?'

He was.

As the sky began to lighten, I bucked up a bit. The sunrise was spectacular; worth all the effort so far, even my poor, blistered feet. We were descending our third fell when, as the sun's rays began to warm our tired bodies, we saw below us the three tonner in a pub car park at the bottom of the hill. Our spirits soared and twenty minutes later we reached the car park where we were told to get some scoff, and our heads down. Wonderful news.

While the water was heating in my mess tin, I removed my boots to examine my feet. Finding several blisters, most of which had burst, I cleaned them up and applied plasters, put on dry socks and my issue black pumps. We had been on the go for more than seven hours, straight after a week's work in the day job. I was knackered. Nobody said a lot: too busy getting a brew, a quick fag and kip. Sleep was precious, for we had no idea how much we would be allowed, or when we would get another chance.

After just five hours kip, we were roused and ordered to fall in at the back of the three tonner. Corporal Samson was in a relaxed mood as he stood before us, minus belt and beret, a mug of steaming tea in his right hand

'Afternoon gentlemen, I trust you slept well. I have a treat for you today. A pleasant stroll just five klicks there and five back. You can start when you like, but the sooner you start the sooner we return to barracks.' He nodded over his shoulder towards the towering mass of Pen y Ghent. 'Make a note of the number on the trig point at the summit.'

He turned and strolled away towards the cab, lighting a cigarette as he went. We were just about to get on with the job, when he fired a parting shot over his shoulder.

'Last one back buys everyone a beer in the bar.'
There was a sudden flurry of activity as we scrambled to get our gear. Three hours later, panting and

sweating profusely, I trotted into the car park to find most of the lads already back. Fifteen minutes later Thompson the medic limped in last, with the spectre of a heavy bar bill hanging over him.

5
Recruit Training
West Yorkshire, February – June 1971

Over the next twelve weekends, the distances increased and our bergans got heavier. These were weighed at random along the route. Anyone under forty-five pounds was given a large rock and ordered to do ten push ups...with the bergan on; after the rock had been added. I learned that an RV (rendezvous), was a prearranged meeting point, ERV was an emergency rallying point and that SOPs were standard operating procedures. I was issued an SLR (self-loading rifle). This and all other small arms, the Army did not call guns, but weapons. The exception that proved the rule, was the GPMG or general purpose machine gun, which could be referred to as either. Distance was measured not in miles, but kilometres, referred to as klicks or Ks. It was like learning a foreign language.

Yorkie became my mentor, guiding me through the idiosyncrasies of orders, procedures and routine. The Army has its own language and its own way of doing things. It was a language of acronyms and abbreviations, one of which puzzled me for very a long time. Each month we were sent a typed briefing through the post. This listed all exercises for the following four weekends, with timings and details of kit required. Always at the foot of the last page, after the last timing, was printed the acronym PUFO. Too embarrassed to admit my ignorance, I said nothing. To my undying shame, it was several years before I found out what it meant. I casually mentioned it to Yorkie, who accused me of taking the piss. Seeing that I wasn't, he looked me in the eye, shook his head and speaking slowly and deliberately, as if talking to someone with learning difficulties, he enlightened me. 'Pack Up and Fuck Off.'

The first weekend in March, we were ferried to a new training area and de-bussed in driving rain in a lay-by at the side of the A62 trans-Pennine road near the Lancashire border. We were sent off in pairs at intervals of five minutes with strict orders not to bunch up. It was exactly seventeen minutes to midnight when Yorkie and I set off head down, arse up into the wet black night across the worst terrain we had yet encountered. The ground was an endless stretch of sodden peat, covered in calf-high tussocks of cotton grass, which if trodden on would twist and collapse. A sprained ankle in our situation, would not only have meant an end to the exercise for both of us, but an extrication nightmare. The only way to progress was to tread between the tussocks. This entailed lifting our feet to knee height every step. Effective but very tiring it drained our energy reserves, at an alarming rate. The ground was crisscrossed with streams, tackled by sliding down the steep peat banks, squelching through ankle deep freezing water, then scrambling on all fours, three forward and two back, up the opposite bank. This heavy going slowed us right down and we began to drop further and further behind our estimated time to the next RV. To make it worse, Yorkie's knees began to cause problems, particularly on the downhill stretches.

'It's my cartilages,' he explained, 'all Paras suffer with them eventually. Too many heavy landings.'

'They sure know how to wear you down' I moaned, 'we must be barking mad, tabbing across this God forsaken place in the pouring rain. I am definitely going to Millets next week to buy some waterproofs.'

'The Army's too tight to issue waterproofs,' said Yorkie. 'Most of this kit is left over from World War Two.'

'Apart from my field dressing' I said, 'That's dated February 1939. Eight months before Hitler invaded Poland.'

Yorkie wiped the rain from his face with his stubby fingers. I suggested a breather. He nodded agreement and we moved into the lee of a large boulder and sat on our bergans. Yorkie produced his silver cigarette case. I fished out my Zippo and we lit up beneath our smocks. Under the onslaught of horizontal, icy rain, after just a few drags, my Benson & Hedges disintegrated into a soggy pulp. Yorkie delved into the rear pocket of his bergan and took out a Poncho. We huddled together beneath it and studied the map by the red glow of my torch, which, like my compass was small light and plastic. The issue ones were heavy and cumbersome and every ounce saved was worth it in gold. The RV was frustratingly close as the crow flies. Unfortunately we were not crows. Between us and the checkpoint was a deep valley sealed off by a massive concrete dam, forming a huge reservoir stretching way off to the West. On the 'dry' side of the dam was a steep sided rocky gorge, which would be difficult and time-consuming to negotiate. We were just below the ridge line, looking down into the dark, where we could make out the lights of occasional vehicles on the M62 motorway, which ran across our line of march, just in front of the reservoir. This glimpse of civilization raised our spirits somewhat and it was at this point that I had, what later proved to be, the dumbest idea of my military career.

'What do you reckon then?' I said, to my fellow drowned rat. 'Take a short cut over the dam? We should be able to make up for some of the lost time that way.'

'Just what I was thinking.'

The reservoir and dam were strictly out of bounds, but we were behind time and desperate to catch up. The rain was coming down steadily, as we made our descent and the terrain became a little more even. Before long we hit a stony track which led us through a tunnel under the motorway, built to allow the free movement of livestock from a nearby farm. Occasionally we could see vehicle lights, moving along the road on the far side of the water, as we approached the South side of the dam. Walking onto the huge concrete structure was simple; the top was wide enough to take a Land Rover and had chest high thick concrete walls on either side. The dam was around three hundred yards across, but despite the gloom I soon became aware that my short cut was not such a good idea after all; the centre section formed a convex topped sluice fifty yards across and less than a yard wide. The really bad news was that this was twelve feet lower than the level we were on and accessed by steel rungs set into the concrete. It was also totally exposed and there was nothing to hold on to.

'That's stuffed that idea.' I said, my spirits sinking.

'Has it bollocks! We can still get across.'

'Are you crazy? We'll get blown off the sluice to our deaths, we're too top heavy with these lumps on our backs.'

'We're wasting time Tony, Who Dares Wins, remember?' said Yorkie, quoting the Regiment's motto.

He was in no mood to be dissuaded and I knew if I did not go through with it, I would lose whatever respect I had gained to date. The prospect of falling two hundred feet to a grisly death terrified me. I had been terrified of heights all my life, indeed it was that very fear which formed a cornerstone of my desire to join the Regiment. I wished to confront my fear and to conquer it. I just didn't, expect the opportunity to present itself so soon. I had no choice but to test the theory. Appearing chicken in front of Yorkie was not an option.

'At least let's think about this,' I cried, 'what about the bergans?'

'You let me worry about them. All you have to do is get yourself across.' He climbed over the parapet and down the ladder to the sluice.

'Lower the bergans,' my comrade ordered from his precarious perch.

I complied. He held one in each hand to keep the centre of gravity as low as possible. The tricky bit was having to turn one hundred and eighty degrees on the narrow, slippery wet concrete, while holding the equivalent of a bag of cement in each hand. I was sick with fear watching him execute this manoeuvre, but all went well and he was off into the dark dirty night, hunched over against the rain driving in hard across the water, carrying our bergans as if they were hand luggage. I said a silent prayer, then against my better judgement, climbed over the parapet onto the ladder and began to descend. The steel rungs were freezing cold to the touch and wet and slippery under my rubber soled boots. My legs were shaking uncontrollably when I reached the sluice, my heart banging like a Bofors Gun.

With adrenaline pumping faster than a sailor with his first whore, I set off after my companion, now barely visible in the gloom almost half way across the sluice. With a sheer drop two hundred feet to the rocks on my right and the freezing water slapping hard against the dam wall, twenty feet below me to the left, I elected to lean towards the water. This was in the forlorn hope, that if I did fall, I would have some chance of survival. I was kidding myself of course. If I fell in the water I would just take longer to die. My rain soaked left side was numb with cold, as I shuffled across the concrete, my gaze fixed solidly on the top of the sluice, not daring to look down. Totally exposed to the freezing, driving rain, raw fear left me almost oblivious. Just three yards short of the ladder and the relative safety of the walkway, my right foot slipped on the wet concrete. I screamed, heart in my mouth, as I fought to maintain balance on my tiny perch before collapsing to my hands and knees, my life flashing before my eyes as I prepared to meet my maker. Miraculously I avoided toppling into space.

From somewhere above, a voice called my name through the black rain.

'I'm okay' I croaked, as I finished the last few yards on my hands and knees, leaving my dignity out on the sluice, where I had lost my balance. I had aged ten years.

'I thought you were going over for a minute.' Yorkie cried pulling me over the parapet. I collapsed in a heap beside my bergan, shaking with cold and shock.

'Come on, Tony. Get yourself moving and let's get some warmth into you.'

I was dragged to my feet and my bergan hoisted on to my back. Rain dripped from the end of my nose, as I struggled to tighten my shoulder straps with numb fingers. Shivering heavily and still in shock, I wondered if I had finally lost my marbles.

'Beats spending an hour climbing down the valley and slogging up the other side, eh, Tony?' Yorkie had a point, but I was too miserable to care, just concentrating on putting one foot in front of the other as we made our way across the walkway. We climbed over the gate at the end, squelched up the track to the main road and reported to the three tonner parked in a lay-by. We gave our position on the map and identified the next RV from the grid reference given by the DS staff. Minutes later we were off again, uphill as usual, with the rain still pouring down. It was quarter past three in the morning and we had at least another five hours of this savage amusement to endure. As it turned out, it was nearer six hours when we sighted the final RV The Land Rover was parked at a viewpoint overlooking

Saddleworth Moor, across which we were wearily slogging our way in the grey early morning, still soaked to the skin, even though the rain had ceased more than two hours ago. We had stopped to make some hot scoff in the ruins of an old barn and that had raised our morale somewhat, but nowhere near as much as the sight of the Land Rover and three tonner.

'Reckon that must be the final RV,' I panted.

'Maybe.'

'Maybe?' God I hope so, I thought to myself. I was convinced I could go no further, my back and shoulders were raw from the bergan straps and my feet sodden and blistered. We struggled up the last slope, quietly pleased with our navigation in such awful conditions, to find Brian Samson waiting for us. 'Well done lads, get yourselves onto the three tonner and get your heads down.'

Wearily climbing over the tailgate we were surprised to find only three sleeping bags, from one of which, a glowing cigarette testified to the owner's state of consciousness.

'Where is everyone?' I enquired, addressing the glowing ember.

'You're the third pair in,' answered a voice from behind the glow. I recognised it as belonging to Steve Ellis.

'Gordon and I got in an hour ago and Mick about twenty minutes since. Frisbee was pulled off at the last RV with an ankle injury.'

'We thought we were going to be last,' said a surprised Yorkie.

'There are six more pairs yet.' Steve replied.

With that happy news, I dragged my sleeping bag

out of my bergan and after towelling down and changing into dry clothes, I climbed in to join the other green 'maggits' to catch some Zs.

6

Test Weekend
Yorkshire Dales, July 1971

We trained hard; navigating rugged terrain day and night in all weathers, carrying fifty-five pounds of kit. We practiced weapon handling, until we could strip and reassemble blindfolded, spent hours live firing on the ranges and went through agonizing circuit training until our muscles burned.

By the beginning of June, of the seventeen original recruits, only five remained to tackle the test weekend, for a place on the next selection course. At the peak of physical condition and full of confidence, I was chafing at the bit. We had up to twelve hours to complete the twenty-seven mile course, which we each had to cover alone, buddying up being forbidden. I took Friday afternoon off work and spent the time packing and repacking my kit until I was satisfied with the weight distribution and accessibility of essential items. Finally I checked the weight on the scales – forty-eight pounds with another ten pounds for the escape belt. Carol stuffed me full of lasagne and drove me to the barracks, kissing me good luck at the gates, before driving away into the warm June evening. Four hours later I climbed out of a three tonner in the now familiar

Wensleydale landscape.

'Right lads, listen in.' Samson was in serious mood.

We were his babies and he wanted us to succeed. His promotion to Sergeant was riding on us.

'Reveille at oh five hundred, move off to start line at oh five thirty. You will be joined by recruits from the other Squadrons. I do not want to see any of them beat you round the course. Understood?'

We sang in unison. 'Yes Staff!'

'I suggest you get a brew and get your heads down.'

We used our ponchos to make lean-to shelters, or 'Bashas', against a dry stone wall, then brewed up and settled in our sleeping bags, to contemplate the morning. I stubbed out my Benson, carefully burying the butt in the soil with the point of my knife and settled down to sleep.

I awoke early, gagging for a brew and lost no time lighting the hexi cooker. Other bodies were stirring, lighting fags, brewing up, emptying bladders, each with his own private thoughts about the day ahead. I was quietly confident, but had a nagging fear of injury. So many before had lost out to leg and ankle injuries, just when victory seemed within their grasp.

My fears were unfounded, for, so familiar was the terrain, that we waltzed around the course. It was a bit of an anticlimax. We were at our peak, totally prepared for the task and so used to the geography and conditions, we had no problems. I arrived at the penultimate RV, which was the trig point on the summit of Pen y Ghent after eleven hours and twelve minutes. Waiting for me on the top was Yorkie, him being faster uphill than me, though I could always outdo him on the descents. He was having a last brew, before the descent into the final RV, in Horton in Ribblesdale. Accepting a quick swig of tea, I set off down the mountain with my companion. After five minutes we broke into a trot and in spite of the heavy bergans we kept it up until we hit a wide, rough track, strewn with limestone rocks and bounded on both sides by dry stone walls. At this point, we should have slowed down because of the risk of ankle injury, but we just did not care. We were elated, filled with the euphoria that only a body in peak condition can generate. We raced down the track oblivious to our sore, burning feet. Even Yorkie's cartilages were forgotten. Turning right into the village, I pulled up one hundred yards short of the RV. Yorkie was about thirty metres behind me and seconds later appeared at my side. Remarkably, our breathing was not too laboured, in spite of our exertions and our morale was sky high. We tossed a coin. I lost, leaving me to go in second, the rule being that each man should complete the course alone. I was checked in at eleven hours and fifty-six minutes.

'How are we doing, Staff?' I asked, barely able to contain my delight at my performance.

'You're the fifth and sixth, Ellis was first home twenty minutes ago. You did well lads. None of the other squadrons has shown yet.

7

Selection
South Wales, July 1971

We sat drinking bottles of Coke, gazing out of the window at sun-drenched fields rolling past beneath clear blue skies alive with swooping swallows. The weather was glorious and the long-range forecast was for more of the same but getting warmer. It was already seventy-two degrees and only ten a m, which gave us cause for concern. It made me particularly pleased with myself for having the foresight to pack salt tablets and spare water bottle. After changing trains at Birmingham, Yorkie and I eventually alighted at Brecon to find a corporal from 22 SAS awaiting us. After ticking us off on his clipboard, we loaded our kit and boarded the ubiquitous three tonner. Twenty minutes later the next trainload of hopefuls arrived and we set off. Nineteen of us.

In camp we were billeted in wooden huts which were to be our home for the duration, assuming we did not suffer the ultimate disappointment of being RTU'd – 'returned to unit.' This was the fate awaiting anyone failing the course or simply jacking it in. There was no shame attached to this in the eyes of observers, but many of those to whom it happened, were devastated and inconsolable after all the effort they had invested. Many other recruits were already at the camp. We had an hour to settle in before our first parade and used the time to locate the cookhouse, NAAFI, showers, etc., and to sort out kit. The huts were divided into small rooms. Ours had four bed spaces, each of which, had two bunks. I took the top and Yorkie the bottom. After claiming a locker each which we secured with padlocks brought with us for the purpose, we checked ourselves for any deficiencies in our appearance and then headed for the parade ground, eager to find out what we were going to be doing next. Thirty-seven recruits, paraded in four ranks were welcomed to the course, given a short pep talk and told the location and timings for the first briefing the following day.

We were marched to the armoury to draw our personal weapons, which we were ordered to carry with us twenty-four hours a day until further notice. The rifles had no slings and the manufacture of makeshift ones was strictly forbidden. The carrying handles had also been removed. From the moment we signed for them the weapons were to be within arm's reach at all times, which meant kipping with the weapon tucked up in your sleeping bag at night. Anyone caught more than an arm's length from his rifle was given twenty push ups, often carried out with a bergan on the back. Once dismissed, we headed for the cookhouse for the last meal of the day before turning in early.

We were roused from our slumber at oh six hundred on a clear sunny morning and following a hurried breakfast, headed for the parade ground. We were stood to attention, the roll was called and we were stood at ease. A bronzed hard-looking soldier with a back like a ramrod stepped out in front and addressed us in a clear, no nonsense tone. He was smartly turned out despite his camouflage windproof being faded from much exposure to the elements and his beret was sun-bleached to the colour of tropical sand.

'The honeymoon is over, gentlemen.' The RSM began, 'From now on, you will work harder than you have ever worked before. Some of you will not survive to the end. Some of you who do, may still be RTU'd if you are not considered SAS material. This is no disgrace, it simply means you are not suited to the work the Regiment is called upon to do. This is no reflection upon you as soldiers.'

The RSM withdrew and a Staff Sergeant took over.

'Listen in. We will move off from here at oh eight hundred hours with full kit; bergans will weigh no less than forty-five pounds. Dismissed!'

Yorkie was already doubling to the billet before I had moved a muscle. We had twenty minutes to get back ready to board the transport. This was to be the pattern for the rest of the course: Never enough time to do everything required of us it seemed, but somehow we managed it, albeit by the skin of our teeth. The worst was finding time to go to the bog and then having to force everything through at the double! Upon our return we were issued with one 24 hour ration pack, which we were ordered not to open as it was for emergencies only. We loaded our kit into the trucks and climbed aboard in the warm sunshine. Within minutes we were rolling through the beautiful Welsh countryside.

Our first test was easier than I had anticipated, it was a basic point to point navigation exercise, over some fairly tough, hilly terrain, but it only lasted about six hours. We were back in camp by four o'clock and just had time to change uniform, clean our boots and grab a quick bite before reporting to the classroom for a lecture on the history of the SAS followed by thirty minutes of pokey drill. This consisted of holding our rifles at all kinds of angles designed to make our muscles ache until we thought they would burst into flame. We practiced throwing dummy '36' grenades, the Mills bombs that our grandfathers had used in the trenches during the First World War and a more modern weapon of dubious effectiveness. The Energa rifle grenade was launched from the end of the SLR using a special cartridge, which increased the recoil dramatically. Any attempt to fire it with the rifle in the shoulder, would smash said bone and probably break the jaw as well. We were shown how to tuck the butt under our armpit, clamp it tight and squint through the sights on the launcher attachment by craning our head to the side as low as possible. Holding this position was very difficult, and extremely uncomfortable.

'Who designed this bloody weapon?' I moaned.

'A circus contortionist?' offered Steve Ellis.

Three shots each. Try as they might, few of my fellow recruits got anywhere near the target. Chance of success with this strange weapon were remote even in these calm controlled conditions; on the battlefield they would be zero.

When my turn came I went through the drill

and lined up on the target (an enemy machine gun nest I was told, although it looked suspiciously like a cardboard ration box to me) I held my breath and squeezed the trigger. An atomic bomb went off in my ear and a large horse kicked me in the ribs. Simultaneously, my grenade shot towards the target and my beret, blasted from my head, flew towards the instructor. To my utter astonishment, the grenade struck the target dead centre, shattering the plastic head and splattering the cardboard with bright blue chalk dust. (We were not considered safe to be let loose with live ordnance yet.) At the same time a muffled cry of surprise alerted me to the fact that my beret had also scored a direct hit on the instructor's face. Incredibly, my other two rounds also struck the target. Only three others had scored with one hit each. When I finally retired to my pit for a last smoke before sleep, my ears were still ringing.

I made up for my marksmanship with the Energa on the twenty-five yard pistol range. After expending countless rounds of nine millimetre ammunition from the Browning pistol, to negligible effect, the frustrated instructor approached me. With his face an inch from my nose and his eyes boring into mine, he let me have it both barrels.

'Gomez, you are the strongest argument that I have yet encountered for the fitting of a bayonet to the pistol.'

I was slowly making love with Carol on a clean crisp white bed sheet when a loud banging and a gruff voice yelling 'stand by your beds!' brought me crashing into reality. I rubbed my eyes and checked my watch - five a m. 'Bloody hell,' I exclaimed, dragging myself out of my green maggot just as the hut door slammed shut and a grinning corporal marched the length of the billet.

'Breakfast in fifteen minutes. Parade at oh six hundred, with full kit!'

A chorus of muffled curses and groans followed as we dragged our unwilling bodies off to the shower block and washed and shaved before heading for breakfast.

Sweat poured from me as I trudged along, stopping only to check the map and get as much water and salt into me as I had available. The beasting went on for ten hours and the next day another twelve hours. Then came a short lecture, after which we were driven out into the wilds for a night navigation exercise. This should have been simple, but we were all knackered, those of us that remained that is; seven had already been RTU'd and at the end of this exercise another two would follow. We were given a six figure grid ref which, when checked against the map, turned out to be just two kilometres away, but in the middle of featureless ground. I set the bearing on my compass and set off counting my paces as I had been taught in training, checking the compass every couple of hundred metres. The night was black as pitch with no moon and the boggy ground made progress painfully slow. By the time I reached the position where I reckoned the RV was, my feet were waterlogged and I had twice fallen into the bog. I strained my eyes into the darkness until they ached and I was having serious doubts about my navigation, when I saw the faintest glimmer of light ahead to my left. It was impossible to judge distance so I set off cautiously towards it and was surprised to find that after only ten paces a soft voice asked for my name and number. The sound came from a small one-man tent no more than three feet high pitched in a shallow depression in the ground. I was checked in, given another grid reference and sent on my way.

The weather was mild and the rest of the exercise went without too much trouble. Even so, by the time I reached the final RV I was well and truly worn out. I dozed all the way back to camp, finally getting my head down at one in the morning.

The following day, day four, was the big one, the endurance march, the infamous Long Drag. Last thing each day we were briefed on the following day's exercise. We had been progressively deprived of sleep, beasted over cruel terrain and subjected to constant pressure to jack it in. By the time we were driven out of the camp after less than four hours sleep, I was having difficulty convincing myself that I was still up to the challenge. We de-bussed at the side of a reservoir surrounded by the beautiful Welsh mountains rising majestically through the grey mist of early morning.

We were sent off one at a time at three minute intervals, with twenty four hours to cover the forty five kilometres, just under twenty-eight miles, over some of the highest peaks in the country. I wanted that winged dagger more than I had ever wanted anything.

I had been a sickly child, small and skinny. Constantly bullied at school, excused PT and rugby because of my chronic asthma, I envied the other boys who excelled at sport and attracted the girls in droves. Yorkie was the epitome of what I aspired to, an all round athlete, man of action, afraid of nothing. Although I had now filled out and built myself up and was, thanks to my father's genes not too bad looking I would have swapped all, including my education and qualifications, if I could only be like him. I was desperate not to fail.

Just after I had left the first RV I heard a familiar voice calling me.

'Wait up, you Welsh Dago.'

I slackened the pace and Yorkie was soon tabbing alongside.

'How is it then?' I asked.

'Piece of piss' he replied.

'You reckon?'

'Sure it is.'

We stayed more or less together for the next three hours despite the rule that we were to travel alone. Bunching was inevitable with so many guys on the course. Stopping to check the map on the summit of one of the many peaks, I could see below me at least a dozen humped backed figures slogging their way up the mountainside. Ahead on the line of march another four were clearly visible, snaking their way along the knife-edge ridge in bright midmorning sunshine.

The views would have taken my breath away had I any left after the long climb. I left the top and made my way along the ridge and was doing my usual running descent when I lost my footing and went arse over head just as the training major came jogging past me. To make matters worse, I had instinctively put my hands out to try to protect myself thus allowing my rifle to fly through the air like a javelin before burying itself, barrel first in the ground, right up to the gas regulator. I recovered from the fall in seconds, but my embarrassment took a lot longer to leave me. I slipped off my bergan, dug my rifle cleaning kit from my escape belt and set to work repairing the damage, cursing my luck and hoping that this would not be a fatal black mark against me.

Fortunately there was no damage to the weapon and I was able to clear the soil from the barrel and pull it through. In a matter of minutes I was back on track. The terrain was taking its toll on my feet and ankles, my back and shoulders were raw from constant rubbing, while the sun's rays beat down without mercy. Sweating buckets I soon ran very low on water, having to refill my bottles at every stream I came across.

I was on auto pilot and to pass the time as I slogged my way up and down the peaks I ran through the lyrics of some of my favourite tunes in my head. Half way up the dreaded three thousand foot Pen y Fan, I began to hallucinate, hearing the Beatles singing She Loves You. I stopped, shook my head to clear my ears and reached for my water bottle. As I drank, the music faded then disappeared altogether. I set off again, only to find that after ten minutes I could hear Joe Cocker's forceful rendition of The Letter. I stopped and sure enough it faded and died. I was worried that I might be suffering from sunstroke. The hallucinations persisted until I reached the summit and caught up with a Kiwi medical student on the course who had a transistor radio in the top of his bergan, which by now was banging out the Rolling Stones.

Half way down the mountain I again caught up with Yorkie, who was struggling with his cartilages. He was obviously in considerable pain.

'What the fuck am I doing here?' he joked through gritted teeth.

'Beats the shit out of me,' I replied as cheerfully as I could, 'we must be barking mad.'

That was the last time I saw him on the course. By late afternoon, in spite of the heat I was no longer sweating, my forehead bone dry. Clearly dehydrated, I poured as much water and salt into my aching body as I could and followed up with melted Mars Bars from my pockets. It was too little too late. I slowed up considerably and had great difficulty concentrating, especially when trying to read the map.

As the day wore on and dusk fell I made a serious error and walked over two miles in the wrong direction before I realized my mistake. Darkness fell and with it my spirits. My morale hit rock bottom and for the first time I doubted my ability to finish the course. I sat against a boulder and got a brew on followed by some curry and rice. I must have been there for well over half an hour; the first real break since setting off. It did the trick however and with my spirits lifted I examined the map and set a bearing to bring me back on course. The rest of the night was a blur, although I recall teaming up with three other guys at one stage who by their encouragement got me through the worst. We were approaching one RV when I announced that I was going to 'jack it in.'

When I got there and was given the next grid reference, so conditioned was I that I automatically pointed out the location on the map to the Staff and set off again. I was two hundred metres down the track before I realized and with an irrational reluctance to backtrack, I carried on. It was what saved me. The dawn broke to find me making my way down a minor metalled track, which wound downhill between stunted oaks bordering sheep pasture.

I was hobbling like a zombie, my rifle clamped to my chest for dear life and even though I kept nodding off to sleep, I kept moving and never slackened my grip on it. I had never been so tired in my entire life. As I rounded a bend I witnessed an astonishing event. No more than half a mile ahead was a three tonner and a number of figures moving around in front of it-the RV, the final RV, for surely it must be! At the same time I noticed a recruit sitting at the side of road ten metres ahead. He pulled his sleeping bag out of his bergan and crawled in! He was just too far gone, even though the end was probably in sight. I tried to persuade him to go the distance but he just said. 'Fuck it we're too late anyway.'

I looked at my watch: I had been going an incredible twenty six hours; the time limit for Long Drag was twenty four, but I was at least going to complete the exercise; time expired or not. I finally staggered down the hill to the truck, checked in and was told that this was indeed the final RV A 23 SAS sergeant I recognized as being from the squadron in Leeds, took me to one side and quietly told me to clean myself up as best I could, put his hand on my shoulder and said. 'Good effort.'

'How about the others?' I enquired.

'Ellis is okay, Thompson and Baxter jacked in, Barnes has been retired injured.' I was surprised at Gordon and Tommo and gutted that Yorkie was out, but had no time to dwell on it. I washed in a small spring at the side of the road, scraped my face with a razor, and sat down to remove my boots. My feet were a blistered and bloody mess, swollen so badly that I could not get my boots back on. After I had cleaned them up and dressed the blisters with plasters from my first aid kit, I put on clean clothes and my black issue plimsolls, just in time to get on parade before boarding the transport. I slept all the way back to camp and when we arrived, went straight to breakfast and then to the hut to sort my kit out. I was way beyond tired and just running on willpower, not daring to give in until I was officially told I had failed.

Some time during the morning I was summoned to the training Major's office. I knocked on his door and at the command 'Come' I entered, came to attention and threw up a smart salute. The Major, a tall wiry Scot with a shock of red hair resembling an exploding Brillo pad, looked up from his desk and leaned back in his chair with his hands clasped behind his head in the manner of a benevolent schoolmaster. He nodded towards a map of the exercise on the wall.

'Show me where you spent the night'

'I didn't stop for the night sir.' I replied.

'So what took you so long?'

I explained how and where I had lost my way and he seemed satisfied. Putting his hands together on the desk and sitting upright, he looked me in the eye for several seconds in complete silence. I was beginning to feel uncomfortable when he at last spoke.

'You have failed the course and will be returned to your unit first thing tomorrow.'

I knew it was coming but it was a terrible blow. I was gutted.

'I am offering you a recourse in November...

A what course? said a voice in my head.

'...we can teach you to map read, but we can't teach you to keep going for twenty-six and a half hours. Good effort. The Regiment can use people like you.'

I left the office in a state of euphoria. I had been given a second chance. Ten-seconds later, reality hit me with the impact of an SLR round. I had to go through it all over again from scratch. I stripped and cleaned my rifle, handed it in to the armoury, then packed my kit ready for morning. The next several hours were spent in the latrine, as a result of drinking water from the streams without using my steri tabs, another hard-learned lesson. Twenty-four hours later I was back at home. Carol dragged me to the doctor who put me on antibiotics for my diarrhoea and five pints of heavily salted water per day for a week for my dehydration.

8
Winged Dagger
West Germany, October 1971

I was soon back in training again and after three weeks Yorkie had recovered well enough to join me. From then on we were inseparable, vowing to look after one another and keep each other going, no matter what. By the time selection came round again, we were back at peak fitness, with morale and confidence at an all time high. This time selection was being run alongside annual camp. In contrast to Brecon, Germany was flat and covered with forest so dense that at times we had to crawl beneath the interlocking low branches of young conifers, dragging our bergans behind us. Winter had come early and we began Long Drag in freezing fog which conspired with the geography to make navigation a nightmare. Things deteriorated and by mid afternoon the fog had given way to freezing rain, which turned first to sleet, then heavy snow before returning to freezing rain again. The water froze in our water bottles and when we stopped to brew up we were shaking so much we couldn't light our stoves. In abject misery we plodded on, driven by willpower and an unspoken agreement that whatever the obstacles we would overcome them together. Nothing was going to stop us, we were bomb proof, tabbing along in atrocious conditions swapping jokes and taking the piss out of our miserable situation. I felt closer to Yorkie than I had ever felt to any man before.

'You should be used to being this wet' I said as we squelched our way down a firebreak, deep in a pine forest.

'How do you mean?'

'Well, you must have met rough weather in the Merchant Navy.'

'Yes, but at least we had oilskins and sea boots, not like the bloody army. The rain's gone right through my kagoule and cotton isn't waterproof.'

'Mine too. Bollocks to this let's get our ponchos on before we go down with hypothermia.'

We stopped at a small wooden shelter at the junction of the firebreak and a stony vehicle track. The only waterproof kit issued to us was our ponchos, cumbersome rubberized ground sheets with a hooded hole in the centre for our heads. They weighed a ton. Emerging from our shelter to do battle again with the elements, Batman and Robin the boy blunder, caped crusaders trudged onward. The humour of the farcical situation and the fact that the ponchos preserved what body heat we had left, saved us from serious trouble and we eventually reached the final RV after eighteen hours and twenty-two minutes. Conditions were so bad, the time limit was extended by two hours and of the forty-six runners, only fifteen had completed the course.

The second week we were introduced to SAS patrol skills we and spent much time on the ranges expending shed-loads of ammunition from all kinds of weapons, including US, Soviet and Chinese firearms. Formed into four-man patrols for the final exercise, we were tasked with crossing a river at night, meeting an 'agent' and retrieving a piece of vital military equipment, from an 'enemy' camp. Our final task was to ex-filtrate to a helicopter Landing Zone.

We set off at dusk into the cold and damp with Kenny and Spike, two Geordies from C squadron. Yorkie had been designated patrol commander for the duration of the exercise. The river was waist deep with a rough uneven stony bed and it would of course be very, very cold. Stopping just short of the bank in the lee of a hedge, we checked the map by shaded torch-light. There was no sign of a ford or bridge, but in spite of this, I suggested that we recce the river bank for a better crossing point. Yorkie was all for plunging in and wading across but with the Geordies' backing I persuaded him to look for a better crossing point. We split into pairs, Kenny and Spike heading upstream. We had covered less than two hundred metres downstream when we heard a whistle from the Geordies. We could not believe our luck when we rejoined them. A wooden footbridge not marked on our maps, emerged out of the darkness. Moments later as we set our dry feet on the far bank, we heard a commotion coming from upstream, followed by much splashing liberally punctuated with Anglo-Saxon in a heavy Glaswegian accent. Emerging from the freezing water to find our dry patrol brewing up on the bank really pissed off the Jocks. We shared our brew with them and then parted company.

The next leg was through dense forest. Walking in single file along a narrow track I was enjoying the scent of pine resin in the darkness. As tail end Charlie, I was following the standard operating procedure, visually sweeping one hundred and eighty degrees behind me every few paces. I became aware of two shadowy figures following us.

'Contact rear! Bug out! Bug out!' I yelled at the top of my lungs, at the same time diving into the trees.

All hell broke loose behind me, torches flashing, cursing, yelling, and the sounds of a struggle. Thin branches whipped painfully across my face as I ploughed into the undergrowth. After only a few metres I hit the deck and crawled around to face the noise, breathing heavily and pumped full of adrenaline. I lay still for several minutes, absorbing the smell of damp earth and pine needles, senses on full alert, my heart pounding like a steam hammer.

The hullabaloo subsided and silence descended. It was black as pitch under the forest canopy and I was forced to rely on my ears alone for signs of danger. Having heard no sound for twenty minutes I cautiously crawled away on my stomach the smell of damp earth and pine needles. Progress was difficult owing to my bergan snagging on low branches, forcing my face into the ground. Trailing my rifle in my right hand I wriggled my way in a wide arc to approach the track back along the line of march. Moving at a low crouch, parallel to the track I reached a point I estimated to be fifty metres from the contact according to standard operating procedures. I cached my bergan and crawled to the edge of the trees where I lay watching and listening. After ten minutes, I sensed movement on the far side of the track. I was about to challenge the movement with the password, when a voice close to my right called out softly and was answered. We stepped out into the track together; myself and the two Geordies.

'Any sign of Yorkie?' I asked.

Neither had seen him since the contact. I retrieved my bergan and returned to the others. We agreed to wait another thirty minutes and settled into all round defence. He turned up in twenty.

'You okay?' I asked. 'What happened?'

'Had to ditch my bergan and go back for it later.'

He had nasty cut over his right eye but refused to have it treated.

'Let's get going lads' Yorkie urged, 'we have a lot of ground to cover.' We set off cautiously and some two hours later we made contact with the agent, who turned out to be one of the directing staff. We retrieved the *military equipment* (a bucket of coal) and carried it to the LZ. The helicopter bore an uncanny resemblance to a Bedford three ton truck, a truly masterful piece of camouflage. That said, the whole affair was treated deadly seriously, for we knew we were under scrutiny every minute. Taking great care to follow our SOPs we completed the exercise with no further problems. Reaching the final RV tired and hungry, I was looking forward to a brew and a bacon bap; I got a hood and handcuffs!

We were led into a long single storey brick building, ordered to remove all clothing, thrown a pair of old denim overalls each with our own boots, minus laces. Our wrists were handcuffed behind our backs, sandbags pulled over our heads and we were led away separately. I was unceremoniously thrown in a heap on a concrete floor to the sound of a slamming door. We were about to sample the delights of Tactical Questioning, TQ for short. I got to my feet and carefully began to explore my surroundings, working my way around the walls feeling my way with my hands. This was not easy with them handcuffed behind my back, but with practice, I managed to establish that the room had no discernible windows and a wooden door with no knob on the inside. The only furniture was a metal bed frame covered with a damp musty smelling mattress. The coarse dusty hessian irritated my skin and made my eyes water and though I could not see through the sandbag, I could make out light and dark, observing a single concentration of light above my head in the centre of the room. I sat on the floor with my back against the wall, facing where I knew the door to be. The silence was total. There was nothing to do but wait to see what would happen next.

After fifteen minutes or so, the silence was broken by the sound of a beating. The cursing and swearing of the ones dishing it out acted as counterpoint to the cries of the unfortunate victim. I felt very vulnerable with my hands behind me and tried to work them to the front by pulling my legs through, but it proved impossible. Rationalising that the apparent violence was a pantomime designed to scare us, I decided to adopt a mental resistance to my tormentors. I had always been a keen gardener. I pictured my plot in my head and began to completely redesign it, digging up plants and replacing or moving them, building a pergola and pond and putting up new fences and gates. I was in the middle of erecting a trellis for a Clematis, when the sound of approaching footsteps caused me to stiffen with apprehension. I heard the sound of the key turning in the lock then a loud bang as the door was flung open. Grabbed roughly by the arms I was dragged into the corridor and along to another room where I was ordered to stand on one leg. When discomfort turned to pain, I lowered my foot, which earned me a painful jab in the side with something sharp. This went on for some time: first one leg then the other. When they tired of this game, my handcuffs were removed and I was spread-eagled against a stone wall, arms stretched and spread wide, my weight supported on my fingertips. The guard kicked my feet wide apart about three feet from its base. My legs soon began to shake and cramp spread to my arms.

Gritting my teeth, I returned to my garden, digging, planting and pruning, concentrating hard on the detail to distract myself from my predicament. This kind of treatment continued for hours; the only relief being when I was dragged to the showers and hosed down with freezing cold water. When my turn came for interrogation I was exhausted and viewed it as a welcome relief. In the interrogation room, I was pushed onto a wooden chair and my hood removed. I shut my eyes to the blinding light.

'What is your regiment? I could feel his breath on my skin. What is your mission?' The voice behind my head, so close, hissing in my ear, spattering spittle on my neck.

'I am sorry sir, I cannot answer that question,' I replied, just as I'd been taught. I fought hard to concentrate on training my imaginary Wisteria sinensis up the trellis on the garden wall.

'Question? Question?' he yelled, 'that was two questions. Can't you count, you moron?'

I braced myself.

'Name?' he shouted in my ear so loud it hurt. 'What is your name?'

'Gomez, Trooper, 24216742.' I replied parrot fashion, reeling off the only information I was obliged to give.

'Name! Just your name cretin! Don't you understand English, you bloody Spick?'

He carried on, alternately berating me and bombarding me with questions. He tried racial abuse, calling me a 'queer,' a coward and many other things in an attempt to get a reaction, but I clung to my mental garden, determined not to rise to the bait. The bullying tactics became almost comical at one point, as in the back of my mind I knew that all I had to do was hang on for twenty four hours or so and it would end. However, for the most part it was extremely stressful, physically painful and totally exhausting. Hooded again, they dragged me back to my cell. Waiting for me were two other prisoners, neither of whom I was able to recognise from their voices. They were apparently from the previous course, but had returned to complete the interrogation phase. I was so knackered I almost fell for it. I told them it was not a good idea to speak as the cell might be bugged and moved away to sit in a corner, retreating to my garden again, marvelling at the power of the human mind. Sleep was difficult in spite of the exhaustion, but I did manage to doze, though not for long. I was hauled out for more cold shower treatment followed by the propping up of walls. I began hallucinating and had to struggle to hold the vision of the garden in my mind. The guards eventually hauled me into a room where my hood was again removed. I had lost all sense of time and found it very hard to concentrate. When my eyes adjusted to the light, I saw a desk behind which sat a man in his early fifties, wearing a white coat. I noticed the stethoscope around his neck. He was charming and friendly in a fatherly way and he set about examining me.

'Any aches and pains?' he enquired. 'General health okay? Any complaints about your treatment?'

'Room service needs improving,' I replied.

'Yes, not exactly five star, is it? When did you last eat?'

'I...,' my voice trailed away as the worm of doubt began nibbling at my conscience. 'I do not remember,' I lied. Crafty bastards! I very nearly fell for this one. Desperately, I searched my immediate memory for any sign I had given anything away. I concluded I had not. Relieved, I returned to my garden ceasing all conversation with the 'doctor.' They sent me back to my tormentors for further beasting. I did the only thing I could; I gritted my teeth.

Paraded in front of an empty desk at the next interrogation, my hood and handcuffs were removed and I was ordered to take off my overalls. My minders took my clothes leaving me stark naked and alone, in the small room. There was a door behind me and in the corner of the wall to my right another behind the desk. Also behind the desk was a window, which was not barred and opened easily. Unfortunately there was a guard immediately outside. The door behind the desk had a key in the lock. Could they be testing me to see what I might do? I opened it. Unfortunately it went nowhere, just a room full of stationary and other office stuff, a desk and chair. No way out.

I crossed to the door behind me but it was locked. Seconds later it opened and in walked the interrogator. She, yes, she, was in her early forties, attractive in a worldly way and dressed in civilian clothes. She wore a well cut, grey business suit, the skirt just above the knee, her feet in calf-length black leather boots. Beneath her unbuttoned jacket a white blouse was fighting a losing battle trying to contain her more than ample breasts. I felt a mixture of curiosity, embarrassment and vulnerability. The door behind me opened and I was aware of someone entering. The woman spoke in an authoritative voice to the interloper.

'Find anything?'

'Nothing Ma'am,' a man answered.

'Very well. Carry on'

The door closed again and I began shivering with cold. She lit a cigarette, filling her lungs then blowing smoke in my face, she walked around me shaking her head slowly from side to side tutting to herself. She looked me up and down like a farmer at a sheep auction. She stopped in front of me, perching casually on the edge of the desk taking care to reveal that, yes, those were stockings and not tights. At last she addressed me.

'I do wish they would stop wasting my time' she sighed, 'SAS indeed, I ask you, as if a sorry specimen like you would be even be accepted for training. You wouldn't pass the medical. Those are real men. Look at you. Hung like a hamster,' she sneered, prodding my poor shrivelled manhood with a Biro. 'Who do you think you are going to pleasure with that?'

'Me?' I suggested, already bored with the game. Before she could capitalise on her opening I clammed up, diving once more into the cover of my mental shrubbery.

'Bend over, worm!' she snapped at me. As I complied with the request I couldn't help thinking that some men would pay good money for this kind of treatment. Head between legs I observed one of the guards standing silently against the wall beside the door. He had not left when it was closed after all. His uniform was that of a Russian infantryman. In his hands he held an AK 47 assault rifle. They were nothing if not thorough!

'Spread your cheeks, worm,' she demanded.

Head down, looking through my legs straight at the guard, I inserted the index finger of each hand into the sides of my mouth and pulled my cheeks apart. The guard cracked and was forced stifle a chuckle.

'Spread your cheeks!' she screamed at me, unaware that I was doing just that.

The guard started grinning.

'What is your problem corporal?'

That did it, he could not stop himself.

'Nothing ma'am, nothing,' he giggled.

'Get out! Dismissed!' she ordered, struggling to regain her composure.

We were now alone. Seizing the opportunity I

ducked around the desk, grabbed the key from the lock and dived through the door, slamming and locking it shut. I jammed the chair under the door knob. There was a small wash basin and a kettle, next to which was a brew kit and a tube of condensed milk. I was not going anywhere, but at least I had bought myself some breathing space. While the corporal hammered on the door I squeezed the tube of sweet sticky milk into my mouth. Breaking down the door would be a piece of cake for my captors but damaging MOD property and the subsequent embarrassment of explaining the situation made that seem unlikely. I could not go anywhere. Ignoring the clamour and threats beyond the door, I searched the filing cabinets and found a packet of chocolate digestive biscuits. Hanging on the door was a combat jacket, which I quickly put on while I waited for the kettle to boil. Using one of the mugs on the desk I made myself a cup of tea, ignoring the cursing and threats from without.

By the time they had persuaded me to leave I had scoffed all the biscuits and drunk two mugfuls of hot tea. This small victory had raised my morale considerably, helping me cope with the rest of my time in custody.

After twenty-four hours in the pen I was released, shattered and exhausted. Yorkie and I were reunited in the back of a Land Rover.

'You look like shite,' we each said in unison, immediately bursting into laughter. We had come through everything they had thrown at us and we were intact. Tired, hungry, disoriented but intact.

The final exercise over, we returned to camp when the last patrol reported in and after our first hot meal in almost thirty-six hours we assembled in the classroom for a debrief. About halfway through the proceedings, two Corporals stood up in front of the class to give an account of their attempt to snatch prisoners from one of the patrols in the forest. They were tough looking individuals, which made their appearance all the more remarkable. The taller of the two had a nasty bruise on his right cheek and a badly swollen lip, while his companion sported a beautiful black eye. They were forced to admit that they were unsuccessful as the patrol was alert and had good SOPs. They had caught one man but were unable to hang onto him. They looked more than slightly embarrassed. I glanced across at Yorkie. He gave an almost imperceptible shrug of his powerful shoulders.

'If they can't take a joke they shouldn't have joined,' he whispered.

The following morning as I stood on parade with my fellow survivors, I was struck by how few we were. The course had begun with forty-six hopefuls. Just seven of us remained to be presented with our winged dagger badges. We wasted no time in sewing them on our berets. So it was, that nine months after my interview in the OC's office, I had finally made it into the Regiment. Now the learning would really begin.

9

'Knowledge Dispels Fear'
Abingdon, Berkshire April 1972

I grew up close to fields and woods, in the suburbs of a large city and major European seaport. An only child, I spent most of my spare time wandering alone in the woods and hills around my home. Like most young boys I liked to climb trees, but my fear of heights made me careful not to climb too far from the ground. It was therefore with some trepidation that I passed through the main gate of RAF Abingdon, home to Number 1 Parachute Training School, one sunny April day in 1972. After reporting to the guardroom, Yorkie and I were allocated accommodation and sent to the stores where we were issued with bedding and heavy Denison Smocks the size of two man tents. Yorkie promptly relegated his to his locker, preferring to retain his new light weight camouflaged windproof SAS smock. The only British troops issued with camouflage clothing were Airborne and Special forces and our smocks marked us as SAS soldiers. Fearing discipline for contravening standing orders I stuck with the one issued.

We took a stroll to familiarise ourselves with the camp. The first thing we came upon was a tall tower with a metal crane jib at the top. A steel ladder ran from the bottom up to a large platform sixty feet above us. Hanging from the crane jib was a parachute harness. My stomach began a series of slow somersaults while my legs lost their rigidity. (I was not a happy bunny.) This was the one part of training I had been dreading since the beginning.

The RAF ran the course and all the PJIs (Parachute Jump Instructors) were RAF Sergeant physical training instructors. Admin and discipline was handled by the Parachute Regiment. All parades were taken by a no nonsense, Staff Sergeant wearing a faded red beret, that had obviously seen many years service. The first few days were crammed with PT until all thirty-four course members were a mass of aching muscles. This was followed by jumping from low ramps, to practice the technique of rolling on landing. Next we were introduced to the fan, a steel drum around which was wound a cable, much like the winch mounted on the front of some vehicles. At the end of the cable was a harness. Attached to the drum was a steel bladed fan. The whole assembly was fixed on a high catwalk just below the roof of the aircraft hangar. Climbing the steel ladder and on to the platform my knees became spongy. I strapped on the harness and stepped to the edge. The theory was that when I stepped off the platform, the cable would turn the fan and the air resistance would slow my descent to deposit me safely on the ground. The fan looked way too small to do the job. Heart in mouth I launched myself into space. I landed standing up, amazed but unhurt, only to get a bollocking for not rolling as I had been taught. Most of the day we spent on the fan, but despite easy landings I could not dispel my anxiety.

Next day we moved outside to the tower, where we practiced dangling sixty feet in the air before plunging earthwards to hit the ground with a thud. Somehow I managed to control my nerves and get through it. Whenever serious doubt threatened, Yorkie was there with a wink, a joke or some other small, but significant gesture of support. He carried me through.

The exit trainer, more commonly known as the knacker cracker, I can only describe as a shed on stilts, accessed by way of an external wooden staircase. It had an opening representing the aircraft door, from which a steel cable sloped down to the ground some forty metres away. Queuing on the staircase, anxiously awaiting my turn the man in front of me turned around looking green about the gills. Before I could react, he deposited his last meal over the front of my smock. By the time I had strapped on the harness I was in a sorry state. Launched into space with a jerk, while reeking of vomit and feeling sorry for myself, I was thinking things couldn't get much worse when the two steel harness buckles under my crotch slammed together like blunt secateurs leaving me in no doubt why it was called the knacker cracker. Thrown around like a rag doll, the smell of vomit invading my nostrils, the chaotic ride ended with a bollocking for a bad exit. I was ordered to the back of the queue to try again. My next attempt was slightly more graceful but just as painful as the first, bringing tears to my eyes once more. The one saving grace of the course was the food, which was varied, plentiful, and appetising.

Unlike the SAS, the Parachute Regiment was big on bullshit and we were subjected to random kit inspection without notice. A high standard was demanded with fines and other petty punishments for failing to measure up. Despite being an ex-Para, Yorkie was irritated by the regime and things came to a head when one morning we were given the task of clearing litter from the area around our accommodation. We formed up in line abreast and walked around the huts picking up fag ends, paper, etc. As we rounded a corner we just caught sight of a Para Corporal scattering said litter from a bin that he was carrying. Yorkie set off after the man and grabbed him roughly by the shoulder.

'What the fuck is the idea?' he demanded.

'Don't blame me I just follow orders.'

'That's what the Nazis said at Nuremberg

Trying to regain composure and establish some authority he turned on Yorkie. 'Show some respect for rank, or I'll put you on a charge!'

'I'll put you on your back! We're Special Forces, not park keepers.'

I intervened before it got out of hand, using my diplomatic skills to smooth things over. It seemed the RSM had given orders that we were to be kept occupied as the wind was too high for jumping. The camp was clean as a whistle so the Corporal had been ordered to distribute rubbish so we would have something to pick up. We agreed to return to our billets in return for which the corporal agreed to take his bin home.

The following afternoon my diplomatic skills were

again required; this time to stop Yorkie being thrown off the course. Marching in three files towards the Salvation Army canteen we were about one hundred metres from the hut when two RAF lads cantered across the grass, bent on beating us to the front of the queue. Yorkie, who was in charge of the squad, barked. 'Double time!'

Responding enthusiastically, thirty-four pairs of boots pounded towards their goal. The RAF types broke into a gallop.

'Break ranks!' bellowed Yorkie. It was every man for himself in a mad dash. The two groups collided at the corner of the building as the RAF blue crumpled beneath the mass of camouflage and khaki. Undeterred the disheveled Airmen marched past us. Big lads they went straight to the front of the queue. Told to get to the back, the tallest, a well built lad of around twenty began arguing the toss. Getting nowhere, he stormed out sticking two fingers up at us. I had to admire his guts. Yorkie put his hand on the man's shoulder. He spun around and spat a stream of invective at my buddy. What happened next was so swift it took me completely by surprise. One-second the RAF guy was standing on the ground and the next he was airborne, his feet inches off the ground as he was held against the wall of the hut by Yorkie's left hand around his throat. The right hand was drawn back, fist clenched ready to leave the launch pad. I grabbed the arm with both hands hauling down on it with all my might.

'Leave it! You'll be RTU'd. Leave it! For Christ's sake put him down!'

Slowly he complied and a very frightened

looking Airman was lowered to the ground. His face blue, he was coughing and wheezing fit to bust as he sloped off towards the end of the line.

'Cheeky bastard.' Said Yorkie.

The next day we were bussed out to Weston on the Green for our first descents; two balloon jumps from eight hundred feet. We filed through the large pantechnicon which served as parachute stores. At the counter I was handed a main 'chute and reserve, by none other than the guy that Yorkie had almost slotted. Yorkie was next and upon seeing him the Airman addressed him.

'I have saved a good one specially for you,' he said with a glint in his eye as he reached deep under the counter. Pulling out what looked like a bundle of dirty laundry, he grinned as he handed it over. Of the three visible ties holding the canopy in the pack, one was broken and the other two though intact looked a little frayed. We were entitled to refuse a chute with two visible ties broken, but not this dodgy looking pack. As we were fitting our chutes, Yorkie turned to the rest of us.

'If this 'chute doesn't open lads, promise me you will kill the bastard.'

As one we vowed so to do. We were divided into 'sticks' of four men, then when our turn came we shuffled into the balloon cage, in drizzling rain. The plywood box just large enough for five men, had sides about chest high, one of which had an opening in the centre, with a single steel bar across it at waist height. The cage was suspended from a Second World War barrage balloon, a huge silver gasbag.

'Up eight hundred. Four men jumping,' the instructor called out. The winch started and the balloon rose skywards. A sudden jolt and the cage followed.

'You gentlemen are about to discover that adrenalin is liquid and brown,' announced the PJI with obvious glee. The motto on his overalls read 'Knowledge Dispels Fear.' I concluded that I had much to learn.

'Listen in lads. I have a joke for you' our kindly PJI said smiling. He was having a great time.

'There was this Yank from the 82nd Airborne and one of your Paras having a chat and the Yank says: One of our officers had a bad landing when his chute didn't open fully and he landed on a fence and ripped his belly open and spilled his guts on the deck. He just stuffed his guts back in and pinned himself together with safety pins from his first aid kit and was back on parade the following morning.'

We were now at around two hundred and fifty feet and with the cage swaying in the slight breeze, I was beginning to feel sick. I glanced at Yorkie who seemed in his element. With over forty jumps to his credit this was just a refresher for him. The PJI continued his tale.

'We had another officer who smashed his skull on landing and spilled his brains on the deck. He just scooped them up, stuffed them back in and put his helmet back on. He too was back on parade the next morning. 'So what,' said the Para, all our officers have no guts and no brains and they are on parade every morning.'

No one laughed.

75

Suddenly, we stopped with a sickening lurch, swaying beneath the great silver balloon. The only sound the erie moaning of the wind blowing across the cable. My heart was in my mouth. I felt as if it was about to be joined by my breakfast. Yorkie winked at me and smiled. *'Doesn't he ever get nervous?'* I thought. The cage lurched again as the winch kicked in and we began descending. I looked nervously towards the PJI

'Don't panic lads. We are just dropping down a bit to get un der this cloud.'

We finally came to rest at six hundred feet at which point I most unwisely looked over the side. I tried desperately to will myself home by sheer force of mind over matter. My companion, showing no trace of anxiety looked me in the eye and enquired 'Nervous?'

'Nervous? Me? I'm not nervous, I'm bloody petrified!'

He just grinned. 'See you on the ground.'

The PJI called Yorkie forward, checked his static line was securely hooked up to the overhead bar and suddenly he was gone. My turn came next. I shuffled forward, just in time to see Yorkie's parachute billowing below. Legs like molten lead, I went through the checks. My stomach was harbouring the Gordian knot, my mouth as dry as the Kalahari Desert. I had never been this scared before.

'Ready.'

I heard the command in my ear

'Go!'

A firm hand struck my shoulder and I stepped into space, aware of the rushing sound of the air funnelling past me as I plummeted two hundred feet like a stone. I was really starting to have serious misgivings, when suddenly the parachute streamed out above me and began to deploy, jerking me up sharply to what appeared to be almost a stop. At this point I ceased to function altogether. Several seconds later a distant voice began calling from the ground with increasing urgency.

'Check your canopy, number two. Number two check your canopy! Number two!'

Hang on: Number two – that's me isn't it? I'm number two. I looked up, but could see nothing. Panic gripped me momentarily. *Where is it?* At this point I realised I had my eyes clamped shut. By a great show of willpower I forced them open and there was a perfectly deployed canopy. No holes or other malfunctions, thank God. I turned my attention to the ground. It seemed close – very close and getting closer by the second... *elbows in, chin on chest, knees bent...* I ran through the drill in my head as I got myself into what I thought was a good landing position. The ground rushed up to meet me. I made what was to be my best ever landing. The descent lasted just forty-five seconds. We were sent back up the minute we had fitted new chutes and successfully made our second and last balloon descent of the course.

I had faced my fear and got away with it, but it was still with me and I knew then, that it would have to be to be faced again many times in the future.

The worst part by far was the waiting. Much time was spent hanging around waiting for the wind to drop, then, when conditions were right, we would fit parachutes and line up to emplane, only to be stood down again. By the time we finally got airborne, my legs were like jelly.

Our subsequent descents were a complete contrast to the silence of the balloon. The noise from the Hercules' four engines was deafening, with the bone shaking scaffold pole and webbing seats magnifying every vibration. Inside the fuselage, the testosterone charged air was heavy with the smell of aviation fuel and stale sweat. On my sixth descent we jumped with equipment for the first time. On the order to stand I strapped my ninety pound equipment container to my leg, clipped my reserve 'chute onto my chest and faced the rear of the aircraft. No easy task, squeezed in as we were like sardines. Each move had to be timed to perfection, like a well choreographed ballet.

'Hook up!' shouted the Dispatcher.

I reached up and clipped the hook on my static line onto the steel cable running the length of the fuselage. Simply standing was difficult, loaded with one hundredweight of kit.

'Check equipment!' the Dispatcher yelled.

We were flying straight and level one thousand feet above the Oxfordshire countryside. Through the open door I could see cars on the roads below.

'Sound off for equipment check!' The Dispatcher boomed.

'Twelve okay.'

'Eleven okay...'

'Four okay.'

'Three okay I croaked, my eyes glued to number two's parachute six inches from my nose. 'Two okay.'

'One okay. Port Stick okay!'

The aircraft lined up with the DZ (Drop Zone).

'Red On!' Yelled the dispatcher as the bulb next to the exit door came on, bathing Yorkie's face in its crimson glow.

I swallowed hard.

The green light came on.

'Go!'

Sweating profusely under layers of kit I shuffled forward as fast as my encumbrances allowed. Suddenly the parachute in front of my nose was gone. I took one pace; turned ninety degrees to my right and crossing my arms on my chest I launched myself into space. Still travelling forward at over one hundred miles per hour with the momentum of the aircraft, I was simultaneously blasted backwards by the slipstream from the propellers. My right foot swept up past my face, while the left, weighed down with my container, tried in vain to follow. The slipstream caught my legs sending me spinning, twisting my rigging lines like a skein of wool, hard down onto my helmet, forcing my head into my shoulders. The 'chute was deployed by the force of the slipstream giving little sense of falling. I tried to force my head back to check my canopy but the twisted rigging lines made it impossible. I checked below, pulled the safety pin and tripped the hooks.

The container fell from my leg, stopping with a jerk at the end of the fifteen foot rope, attaching it to my harness. I began kicking furiously to unwind the twists, my heart hammering in my chest. At last they were free. Look up, *canopy okay,* down, *ground closing rapidly,* two hundred and fifty feet? One hundred feet.

Drifting right. Fifty feet, coming in fast. *Oh God!* Elbows in, knees bent, thummmpp! Container down, thuddd! Roll: Check for damage: Wiggle toes; nothing broken.

I was in one piece. I gathered my equipment and hobbled off the D.Z. The final jump was again with equipment the same afternoon. I went out the door like a sack of shite, twisting and spinning with my rigging lines twisted down to the top of my steel helmet again. I was euphoric, having got through the course without injury or refusing to jump. I received my wings. Tony Gomez had entered the world of Special Forces. Acutely aware that I had only passed through the door, I was eager to get stuck in to the real learning.

That evening a crowd of us went into Abingdon and embarked upon a monumental pub crawl. Yorkie and I teamed up with Pete Ferris, a lad from HQ company, 4 Para in Bradford, to form what we loosely referred to as the 'Yorkshire Volunteers.' Somewhere around seven or eight pints into the marathon I went down with a dose of sentimentality, letting my guard down with Yorkie.

'Remember what you said about me wanting to get in the Regiment so bad?'

My mouth was now slipping into overdrive as the clutch dipped and my brain slid into neutral. 'I just want to say I couldn't have done this without you, mate.'

'Don't talk bollocks.'

'I know I'm a bit pissed but I know what I'm saying. No listen, it's true, I swear to God. Ever since

I was a little kid I have been surrounded by women. Smothered by them. I love 'em mind. My Nan, bless her, she was great. You see I never had a male role model. No father, no grandfather not even a big brother to look up to. They made me soft you see. Soft like a bloody girl. I was shit at sport, weak as a kitten 'cause of asthma and hay fever. My Nan, my aunts, they all expected me to go to university and become an academic. I'm not really all that clever.'

'Fuck off.'

'No honest, I only just scraped through my exams. I've been so scared I wouldn't make it, especially this course. I am shit scared of heights. They don't bother you at all.'

'Nothing to be ashamed of. You've got your wings and no one can take them away. I'm just too thick to be scared.'

Then my mouth went into free fall. 'I wish I was like you. You're the brother I never had, you are. I wish I wasn't so scared of stuff.'

'For fuck's sake, shut up, you daft twat. I'd swop muscle for brains any day.'

The mood was suddenly broken by a voice in my ear. It was Pete Ferris 'When you two love birds have finished licking each others arses my glass is empty. It's your round, Tony.'

'On my way already' I replied, getting unsteadily to my feet and weaving my way towards the bar.

The next morning I woke up with the mother and father of all hangovers. I was not the only one.

10
Learning Curve
Yorkshire/Europe, May 1972 - May 1982

In the autumn of 1972, I witnessed Yorkie's skill in the ring at first hand at annual camp in Germany. We had just finished a joint exercise with the Paras that morning, and had been stood down for the next twenty four hours. A bunch of us were walking through the camp to the MT section to get a lift into the town for some R and R (rest and recreation) when we came across the Paras, crowded around a boxing ring at the edge of the parade ground. They were taking part in the ritual of milling. This involved two recruits of similar weight standing toe to toe in the ring trying to knock seven bells out of each other for one minute. A minute does not sound long, but when someone is using you for a punchbag it can seem an eternity. We stopped to watch.

The first pair were evenly matched and traded blows by the book. The second pair had to be pushed together. Neither wanted to hurt the other. It seemed they were best mates. That cut no ice with the Paras. The name of the game was aggression. It wasn't boxing. You had to show you could fight and fight hard. Pair number three lasted forty five seconds before a gloved fist flattened an opponents nose in a welter of claret to the cheers of the crowd. Four more pairs and it was over, well almost. A brick latrine wearing boxing gloves and shorts was remonstrating with the referee. It seemed he did not have an opponent. There was no one in his weight class. Yorkie's voice boomed above the crowd.

'Give us a pair of gloves. I'll take him.'

The guy's eyes lit up like beacons. A Para held out a pair of gloves.

'Hold these a minute, Tony,' he said, passing them to me. He removed the jacket from his Austin Reed suit, took off his shirt and tie and swapped them for the gloves I was holding. The Para corporal referee held up the rope and Yorkie climbed into the ring. The Paras were sniggering in anticipation of the interloper's destruction at the hands of their heavy. Yorkie was giving away three inches in height and about a stone and a half in weight. The brick bog had a longer reach too, by the look of it. I hoped my pal knew what he was doing. He winked at me from his corner, a broad grin creasing his features.

'Doesn't he know any fear?' I asked.

'If he does he never shows it,' one of the lads replied.

We watched the two antagonists glaring at each other from opposite corners, waiting for the bell to ring. The bell went and with it went Yorkie - right across the ring like cheetah. The brick was hardly off his stool when the first punch landed in his solar plexus. Two more swiftly followed, doubling him over. Before he had a chance to recover from the onslaught the look of stunned surprise was wiped from the big man's face by a bone-crunching uppercut which lifted him off his feet and switched all his lights off. You could have heard a pin drop. The Paras could not believe what had happened and I must admit it impressed the hell out of me. I was well aware of Yorkie's reputation but I had never seen him in action before. I wouldn't have missed it for the world.

Yorkie returned to his corner, to be helped off with his gloves. Stunned silence from the Paras. I handed our champ his shirt and jacket.

'They never learn,' said Yorkie. 'The big 'uns. They think it's all brute strength. Speed. Aggression. Surprise. SAS that's what it's all about.'

He knotted his tie. The brick bog was now sitting up, supported by the referee and a couple of others. He looked like he had no idea what planet he was on.

'Come on then lads,' said Yorkie. 'Let's go and get us a steak and a cold German beer.'

Over the next ten years I absorbed the skills vital to an SAS soldier. I spent hours tapping on the Morse key, until my fingers were numb. My ears ached, bombarded by endless streams of dots and dashes hammering in my headphones. There was much to learn: antenna theory, codes and cyphers, jamming, the list went on and on. On my first exercise as a qualified signaller, I put these skills into practice, crouching over a radio set on the North Yorkshire Moors. With a flimsy groundsheet anchored to a wire fence my only shelter from the howling wind, I tried to pick out messages for my call sign from a skip load of audio garbage. I could find none. My transmissions drew no response either. Sixteen hours huddled in the heather and no reply. I began to despair of ever getting through. My patrol commander, an experienced signaller just grinned.

'Stick with it. It'll come.'

I was not convinced. We were almost ready to pack in for the weekend when I heard my call-sign — Delta One Five — faintly in my earphones. I was ecstatic. I replied 'message received.' Base confirmed receipt with 'delta one five roger, out.'

Overcome with emotion I cried out to the rest of the patrol.

'I've been Rogered! I've been Rogered!' My outburst was met by raucous laughter.

Signalling is the most valuable of all SAS Skills; it got me my first stripe.

Lance Corporal Gomez's next training course was in the art of demolitions. Blowing things up with plastic explosive and improvised devices, was something I really took to, although it involved a lot of maths; not my best subject! My introduction to the world of demolitions will stay with me always. There were just seven of us on the course, much of which was 'hands on' on the ranges.

'I am Sergeant Willis. Welcome to my world of big bangs' was our instructor's opening line. A lean lanky Royal Engineer in his mid forties, with prematurely greying hair and heavy horn-rimmed spectacles, Willis had an easy laid back manner. He held up what looked like a couple of pounds of jumbo sausages wrapped in greaseproof paper.

'This, gentlemen, is plastic explosive, PE to you.

This particular PE is Nobel's eight oh eight,' he said holding it up for us to see, 'invented by the Alfred Nobel of Peace Prize fame. Take a close look,' he urged, removing the greaseproof wrapping. We passed it around, gingerly examining the sticks, which looked like pale green, oily plasticine.

'What's this oily stuff ?' I asked wiping the liquid from my fingers in the grass.

'Good question,' Willis answered. 'It is glycerine, which sweats out of the explosive when it gets past its sell by date and becomes unstable. That is why you have ben given this batch to play with. We shall render it harmless by detonating it.'

It went very quiet.

'Notice the aroma, gentlemen,' Willis continued, 'the distinct smell of marzipan, just the thing for icing the mother-in-law's birthday cake. Talking of cake let's have a brew. Anyone got any Hexi?'

Someone volunteered a couple of blocks, which the sergeant promptly lit before placing two sticks of explosive on the flames. That certainly grabbed our attention! Placing a mess tin of water on the fire he carried on.

We all watched the fire, totally mesmerized. Willis continued with his patter.

'PE is a solid material, which when detonated burns at around four and a half miles per second at which point it turns from a solid to a gas and expands several hundred times its original volume in the blink of an eye. Am I boring you, Gomez?'

'No, Sergeant.' I answered, my eyes still glued to the explosive, now burning away merrily beneath the mess tin.

'Good, then I shall continue. In order to detonate the explosive, we need a shock wave or intense heat.'

I was beginning to feel uncomfortable, as I watched the water in the mess tin start to boil, while the flames licked up the sides. I was not alone.

'Relax, gents. We would have to burn a couple of boxes of PE, to generate enough heat to detonate it.'

I wanted so hard to believe him.

Having made his point, Sergeant Willis detailed one of the course members to make the brew, which was past around the group. Next, we were introduced to detcord, which looked very much like white plastic washing line, but was in fact high explosive. There followed an introduction to various kinds of detonators, both electrical, and mechanical. Next came fuses, time pencils, pressure and pressure release switches, mercury tilt switches and all manner of other weird and wonderful devices.

On the fifth day of the course we got to set off some real explosions, blowing holes in steel girders and cutting railway lines. We used specially shaped charges to blast holes in the roof of a concrete pillbox and sent a spectacular ball of fire fifty feet into the air when we blew up an oil drum, half filled with petrol. The course favourite however, was the cutting down of a telegraph pole by wrapping a length of detcord around it. We initiated the explosive electrically, by command wire, from the regulation safe distance for 'cutting' wood. With a loud bang, the pole jumped five feet and landed upright in a muddy

Stuart Pereira

crater a few yards away to cheers all round.

While I was working up these skills, Yorkie was following his instinct with an advanced course in small arms. He followed this with a sniper course at which he excelled. Lance Corporal Barnes qualified as a small arms instructor, later completing a CQB (close quarter battle) instructors' course, achieving one of the highest pass marks ever recorded. He became the Squadron's new Unarmed Combat instructor. He won the Regimental Pistol Championship four years in a row, a unique achievement which helped him get his second stripe, a few months before I too made full corporal.

Through regularly working in the same patrol over the next few years we each got to know what the other was thinking. We learned to trust and rely on each other totally, and although we did not always agree, we respected each other's position. We never fell out. I helped him with his Morse, which he found a struggle. In return he taught me to shoot. We practised live firing with all the weapons we had in our armoury, especially the SLR and nine millimetre Browning pistol.

We rehearsed 'shoot and scoot' skills. My introduction to this manoeuvre was as frightening as it was exciting. The rush was up there with balloon jumping, and Dam crossing. We were taken on the ranges one patrol at a time. The instructor was a Staff Sergeant from 22 SAS He was good.

'Right lads this is the drill,' he began, 'you will advance up the range at a slow walk for four hundred metres in a diamond formation. Corporal Barnes will lead; five paces behind to the left, Trooper Biggs; same to the right, Sergeant Stone. Corporal Gomez in the rear ten paces behind Corporal Barnes. Any questions?'

Silence reigned.

'Patrol...weapons unload,' the Sergeant barked. 'For inspection, port arms!' We removed magazines, unloaded our rifles and presented them for inspection. After checking the weapons our instructor continued with the briefing.

'At any point during your advance, targets can and will appear anywhere within one hundred and eighty degrees. You will engage targets and the break off contact by the following method. Two men nearest targets will turn, withdraw through rear pair, stop, turn and re-engage. Next pair will then do same and repeat until I give the order to stop. Clear?'

We advanced up the range.

After fifty metres five man size targets popped up out of the grass to our left. We followed instructions until ordered to stop. I felt a bit silly shouting 'Bang! Bang! Bang!' as ordered but as we constantly had to swing our rifles across the backs of our mates, simulating shooting past them within feet of their heads using live ammo was obviously out of the question. Obviously.

'Right, lads,' our hard-nosed instructor said. 'Listen up.'

With a magazine of twenty live rounds...load!'

We complied without thinking.

'Take your positions. You know the drill. Ready!'

I cocked my rifle

'Apply safety catches,'

Click!

'Advance to contact.'

We started forward. My mind was racing through the drill, rehearsing the sequence in my head.

'Remember safety catch I repeated to my self over and'...Three targets appeared one hundred metres away at 11 o'clock. I dropped to one knee swinging my SLR across Yorkie's back, vividly conscious of my finger alongside the trigger guard. Bang! Bang! Yorkie's rifle barked. Our three joined in, my rounds zipping down range between Biggs and Yorkie. Seconds later they were haring past me towards the rear. The increased noise level told me they were firing again. I stopped, thumbed the safety catch, turned and sprinted towards them, their live rounds fizzing past my head on both sides. Running towards two guys firing in my direction was surreal but exhilarating — such an adrenalin rush. It felt so real, the noise of four SLRs in close proximity deafening. We were moving fast, but my brain was moving even faster. My life and that of my mates depended upon it.

'Cease firing!'

We stopped and applied safety catches, keeping our weapons pointing down range.

'Unload!'

It was over. We did it.

'Good effort,' commented our instructor.

We all agreed it had been an excellent experience and that we had performed well. No amount of practise however, will tell you how good you are until someone is shooting at you with deadly intent. I wondered if the time came for real, I would do the business or bottle it? Would training carry me above my fear? I hoped so.

Despite his boxer's build, Yorkie was an accomplished gymnast. It was natural for him to complete an APJI (Assistant Parachute Jump Instructor) course, which got him promoted to Sergeant. He unfortunately got busted back to corporal a year later, after giving our new 2 IC, a blunt appraisal of his competence for the job of second in command of an SAS Sabre Squadron. I completed a medic course, which involved a four-week attachment to a hospital casualty unit and was promoted to Sergeant in October 1979. By the time of the Falklands invasion in 1982, we were both coming up for retirement after an exciting and eventful ten years. I had changed a lot. My early days in the squadron as a green civvy with no previous military experience were left way behind. My confidence as a soldier increased with every training course I was sent on, and they were many. I no longer felt like a part time soldier, but a professional. I lived for the weekends and had, in essence, morphed into a part time civilian. We had been privileged to operate some of the latest military hardware, much of which was on the secret list; kit which many regular soldiers knew nothing of. We no longer carried canvas bergans that doubled their empty weight whenever it rained. Our new ones were larger, lighter and waterproof, as were our poncho groundsheets. Gone were the vintage puttees of Kipling's era, along with the Second World War radio equipment, now replaced by high ankle boots and classified communications kit.

I always knew that I might one day have to go to war, but thought it only a remote possibility. War, if it came, would be against the Russians and the 'Warsaw Pact.' We would be deployed in northern Europe, where for ten years we had studied the tactics, weapons and capabilities of these forces until we knew just about everything about our cold war enemy. No one predicted the present scenario. My ignorance of the Argentine military, meant learning on the job. There was one bonus: our training. We had spent most of our time in the limestone landscape of the Yorkshire Dales or the peat bogs of the Pennines. This ground was as close to the Falklands landscape as you could get in the UK.

So it was that as I sat upon my bergan, in the bowels of a Royal Navy Frigate, reality set in. Excited and apprehensive, the old familiar feeling that I had experienced on the edge of the balloon cage returned. I was going into action, my free ride was over.

RAMON

11
A Sting in the Tale
East Falkland
Monday 5th – Tuesday 18th May 1982

Major Ramon Ramirez surveyed the bomb damage.

'How could this happen, Carlos? It must have taken a massive effort to launch a raid like this?'

'This bomber did not come from any aircraft carrier, amigo,' his wingman replied, turning up collar of his Parka against the biting wind, 'not with that payload. Have you counted the craters? Twenty-one Twenty-one bombs in a single stick. The only British aircraft able to carry that many bombs is the Vulcan.'

Ramon looked out across the airfield, eyeing the row of craters with a sneaking admiration for the perpetrators.

'But where did it fly from? The nearest British airfield is on Ascension Island. That's four thousand miles away.'

'They must be using a base in Chile. Pinochet and that she devil, Thatcher, are as thick as thieves.'

'I cannot think how else. At least the damage is slight, just one crater in the runway and the engineers will soon have that fixed'

'The physical damage is slight,' Ramon agreed. 'but the damage this could to morale is something else.'

The raid was a statement of intent. The message was clear. The British were resolved to reclaim the islands.

Two days later Carlos found Ramon alone in the briefing room sat at one of the tables, his head in his hands.

'What is wrong, amigo?'

Ramon gave a start. 'Carlos, I did not hear you come in.'

'What is it?'

'I've just received this signal,' said Ramon, holding out the communications form. 'They have sunk the Belgrano. The flagship, Carlos. All thirteen thousand tons of her, at the bottom of the ocean.'

'How?'

'Torpedoed by a submarine. Raoul is on board. My baby brother, Carlos. He is only seventeen.'

'I am sure he will be okay, amigo. He will be picked up, you see.'

'I pray to God you are right.' said Ramon, sounding less than convinced.

The following day, when Ramon stood up to deliver the morning briefing, there were dark circles below his eyes.

'Gentlemen,' he began, his voice a hoarse whisper. 'You will have seen the enemy's pathetic attempt to destroy our runway. They have achieved nothing. It is business as usual. Today we begin combat patrols throughout the hours of daylight. Do not be fooled by the fact that the British fleet is miles out to sea. We have intelligence which suggests that British special forces have been landed by helicopter and are hiding in the mountains. They are there to gather intelligence on our troop dispositions and movements. It is imperative we find them. The mission is to seek out the enemy and destroy him. Seek and destroy gentlemen!'

There was a murmur from the aircrews but whether it was approval or apprehension was unclear to Ramon. He tried to push thoughts of his little brother to the back of his mind as he continued with the briefing, but it was a constant battle.

He was kept busy in the following few days as the squadron flew constant patrols at low altitude, scouring the barren, windswept, landscape. They found no sign of the enemy.

During the brief periods he was off duty, Ramon went to the chapel to pray for Raoul's safe deliverance. Three days later, a signal sheet clutched in his hand Ramon shed tears as he learned his prayers had not been answered. Raoul, who loved football and ABBA. Raoul, was gone. He thought of his Mother working behind the bar in their restaurant on the quayside, while his father prepared the food for hungry sailors fresh from the voyage. He wondered how they were coping with the news. Ramon shook his head, swallowed hard and forced himself to concentrate on his duties.

Despite being a member of the armed forces of Argentina, Ramon had never seriously considered a situation where he might be obliged to take a life. It was against all the Church's teaching and he was a good Catholic. His passion was for flying. Anyway

Argentina had not fought a war against a foreign power since beating the Anglo - French fleet at Vuelta de Obligado in 1845. This was not just schoolboy history to Ramon, for he grew up on the banks of the Parana River where the battle took place.

On May 17, Ramon and Carlos took off on another routine patrol. Twenty minutes into the flight Carlos broke radio silence. 'Sweeper one, to sweeper two. Acknowledge.'

'Sweeper two, receiving. Do you have a problem, Carlos?'

'I'm losing oil pressure. Port engine'

'How bad, Sweeper two?'

'Down forty percent and falling.'

'Return to base, Carlos.'

'And you?'

'I shall carry on.'

'But standing orders?'

'To base, Carlos. That is an order.'

Despite the rumours of British Special Forces operating on the ground Ramon knew his chances of finding a target were slim, but he found it easier if he kept busy. When the opportunity to avenge his brother presented itself, barely an hour later he struggled to believe the evidence before his eyes at first. A large helicopter hugging the contours, heading west. A Sea King! It had to be British.

Quickly scanning the sky around and behind, Ramon satisfied himself he was alone, then turned in pursuit. Easing the Pucara down to six hundred feet, he lined up on the helicopter's tail and switched on the reflector sight. The Sea King gave no indication of being aware of his presence as he
reduced airspeed to avoid overshooting. Switching the

two 20mm cannons to armed, Ramon cast a last quick look around for any threat. Closing to three hundred metres he fired a four-second burst. The helicopter shuddered as the explosive cannon shells tore through its cabin. The stricken aircraft ploughed into the ground and disintegrated. Pulling up to twelve hundred feet Ramon flew a wide circle around the crash site to survey the smoking wreckage.

'That is for Raoul,' he said aloud in a burst of excitement. No sooner had the words left his lips, however he began to feel regret. It was job well done. He should be pleased, but he just felt flat, saddened at the death of fellow aviators. He assumed that there would have been at least three on board; perhaps more, if they had been carrying troops. He had never killed anyone before. It was not a good feeling.

The first indication Ramon had that anything was wrong, was a loud bang and something kicking him hard in his legs. The aircraft refused to respond to the stick and airspeed began dropping dramatically. He wrestled with the controls. *If I don't get her nose up in the next few seconds I'm in trouble.* Smoke poured into the cockpit. *Time to get out. The firing handle...* he reached above his head and pulled down hard. Nothing could have prepared him for the force of the ejection. Mercifully he lost consciousness.

'Spanner, you jammy bastard. Brilliant mate, just fucking brilliant!'
Spanner watched the Pucara disappear over the ridge line trailing white smoke, amazed by his own actions. He had never fired a Stinger before, indeed he had never even seen one until a few weeks ago.

'Nothing to it. Just switch it on, point and

shoot. Good old Uncle Sam. The Yanks are spoilt with all this hi tech kit.' He patted the missile launcher as you might a favourite dog.

'Nice of them to lend us one though, eh?' said Wheels, raising the binoculars and trimming the focus wheel. The pilot's down on the edge of the creek. Alive, I think. Let's go see.'

'Stay put.' Jock ordered from his hide in the rocks. His tungsten-tipped Glaswegian accent prompted instant compliance. Jock only spoke when necessary. When he did, you listened.

'Back in your hides.'

The two men crawled back under their camouflage netting.

Jock lay perfectly still, so well hidden that a hawk would have trouble spotting him. However, it wasn't hawks he was concerned about, but aircraft. They usually flew in pairs. He watched the prone figure for several minutes then put down the Binos. Thirty years of soldiering wouldn't allow him to risk giving their position away. The pilot wasn't going anywhere. They would pick him up after dark if his own side hadn't collected him: assuming he was still alive.

Ramon was lying on the ground, enveloped in parachute canopy, his head swimming. His legs were wet and cold. At first he thought he must have landed in a pool or stream, but on examination realized it was not water, but blood. He stood and tried to walk, managing a couple of steps only, before his shrapnel riddled legs gave way under him. After two more unsuccessful attempts, he collapsed with the effort. He drifted in and out of consciousness, hallucinating. *A Grumman Goose amphibian, was landing on the Parana River. He was just four years old, standing in front of his parents' bar, in Rosario. One day he would fly an aeroplane.* He struggled to focus, his head hurt. *He was older now. His mother was scolding him for not applying himself to his studies.* The blackness descended. He was slipping into the void again. *He clung to his mother's image for dear life. He promised her he would work hard. His mother was crying. It was graduation day. They were happy tears, Aeronautical Engineering, a good degree, she was so proud.* Darkness again.

When he finally came around, it was dark and he was unable to move. His body was cocooned in something soft. He strained his eyes, eventually making out stars and a cloud-covered moon, hovering above his feet, at the end of what appeared to be some sort of tunnel. He was aware of a presence close to him in the dark and called out. '¿Dónde estoy?'

'Silencio!' A voice with a strange accent rasped in a hoarse whisper, inches from his face.

'You are my prisoner. Comprende? Your war is over. You will be fine, but no noise. Silencio. Comprende?'

Ramon was wide-awake now and although disoriented, he was aware enough to pretend not to understand English.

'No hablo Inglés.'

A face thrust its way out of the dark, an inch from Ramon's nose, while at the same time a finger was placed across his lips. 'Shh!' The face breathed at him in the darkness reinforcing the command with point of a knife an inch from Ramon's eye. 'No noise. Comprende?'

'Sí sí. Entiendo sí.'

Ramon gradually became aware that he was inside a sleeping bag and that someone had bandaged his wounds. He felt dizzy and a little sick. His legs hurt. It seemed that the rumours of British special forces operating on the islands were true. Who else could his captor be?

Another voice spoke from somewhere near his feet.

'Jock wants you, Spanner.'

'Okay. Watch speedy Gonzales. He's awake.'

Ramon watched the new arrival carefully replacing the camouflage after taking Spanner's place in the hide.

'Spanner, Jock and this one makes at least three of them.' Ramon observed, filing the information away in the back of his brain. Ramon regarded the new man in silence. It was difficult to see much in the darkness but he had the impression of a small, slightly built man despite his multi layered clothing.

Spanner crawled across the escarpment to Jock's position in a fissure between the rocks. It was just wide enough to turn around in, roofed with a poncho stretched over chicken wire and topped with turf and limestone fragments.

'How's the Argie?' Jock enquired, his grey teeth in clear contrast his grimy, cam-creamed face. A face adorned with a thick droopy moustache and several days stubble.

'Woke up a few minutes ago. He'll be fine, for now.'

'They're going to casevac him soon as a chopper's available. We'll have to relocate.'

'That's a pain in the arse,' Spanner said, his Cockney lilt a distinct contrast his patrol commander's Glaswegian.

'No choice.'

'Yeah' Spanner acknowledged. He was still a little in awe of his patrol commander. Jock's exploits in the Regiment were legendary. Just two years previously he had a starring role on the TV news as he abseiled from the roof into the Iranian Embassy in London, to rescue hostages. Over the past twenty odd years, he had fought in most conflicts that had made the Six O'clock News: and a lot that didn't. Spanner had heard that Jock had been decorated for bravery, not that acts of gallantry were uncommon in the Regiment. Their recognition, however, was, as most SAS activities were politically highly sensitive and took place in secret.

'I'll get back,' Spanner said, sensing that the brief conversation was over.

Jock nodded, barely noticeable in the darkness. He settled back into his routine. A soldier from the age of seventeen, he was in his element. Jock took everything in his stride. Growing up in a tough Glasgow tenement, had prepared him for anything life threw his way, and it had heaved bucket loads in his direction.

12

Visitors

East Falkland, Wednesday 19th May 1982

Ramon awoke to the sound of rotor blades. His trained ear recognised the twin rotor Chinook, but was it friend or foe? As Ramon's eyes got used to the light he could make out the features of his new minder. This one took the tally up to four. He was young, twenty-two or three maybe, with sharp features and thick eyebrows that fused above an aquiline nose. He removed his woollen hat and passed a grimy hand through thick, dark, hair, unusually long for a soldier. He looked as if he had been on the island for some time. Hanging from green nylon parachute cord around his neck was a pair of binoculars. He lifted them to his face and looked out at the landscape.

Sixpack scanned the land and sky through the observation port between the rocks. He sucked in a noisy breath. Not one, but two Argentinean heavy lift helicopters were circling an area between the stony track that passed for the road to Stanley and the sea shore. He watched mesmerised as they landed and with their rotor blades still turning, disgorged heavily armed infantry, who immediately set up a defensive perimeter. They were less than a mile away. His first thought was that the hide had been compromised and that this was an assault force sent to neutralise them. The Chinooks took off again and ten minutes later, a small helicopter flew in landing in the centre of the perimeter. Sixpack recognised it as a Huey, so familiar from the Vietnam war films.

The area was busy for the rest of the day as the Hueys and Chinooks came and went, landing stores and finally bringing in a battery of light anti aircraft guns. The smaller Huey utility helicopters had machine guns in the doorways. It was apparent that the Argentines establishing the Helicopter Base and had no idea of the patrol's presence. Radio traffic flew between the patrol and H.Q. throughout the night and at 03.00 hours Wheels, the signaller, handed Jock a message. It read: *2 x 23 enroute your location. R.V. Grid Ref. 427 605. T.Q. prisoner your loc.* He could not believe that anyone would be stupid enough to try something like this under the enemy's nose. *23, what did that mean?* He showed the decoded sheet to Spanner. 'Tell me this '23' doesn't mean what I think it does, Jock.'

'Can't be anything else, mate.'

'Jesus, Jock, 23 SAS Weekend warriors. We really are scraping the barrel. What are they thinking sending us a couple of part time wannabies? Who you sending to RV with these TA tossers?'

Jock looked at Spanner without a word.

'Don't do this to me.'

'No option. I have to run the OP Wheels has to man the radio, Sixpack doesn't have the experience. You're it.'

Spanner crept away muttering under his breath. *'Baby sitting. Why me? I gave up Sergeant's pay to join the SAS. For some real soldiering, not to wet nurse a pair of weekend warriors.'*

TONY

13
Preparation
HMS Antrim, Wednesday 19th May 1982

The oppressive atmosphere in the rope locker was not helped by the constant rolling of the ship. The three of us were practically on top of one another. We spread the map against the bulkhead and fixed it to the steel plate with black gaffer tape. There was no room to sit and nothing to sit on.

'Gentlemen,' Captain Michaels opened.

'Ground: Undulating sheep grazed pasture running to upland moor and mountain. Enemy: One hundred and twenty plus airforce and army personnel, five helicopters and four light anti aircraft guns located here.'

He stabbed the map with his finger. He stabbed again showing us the route into the RV and the emergency RV

'Password is the sum of ten. Apart from the patrol no other friendly troops in the area. Weather: Snow flurries, wind south easterly force four. The task is straightforward, providing your navigation is good. Any questions?'

'What about night sights?' I asked.

'None available I'm afraid.' I glanced at Yorkie.

He just shrugged.

'How long is the password valid for sir?' I had been caught out on exersise with out of date passwords. Once in Denmark I crawled along hedge in the dead of night and came face to face with a Trooper from our Scottish Squadron. The password then was also the sum of ten. I challenged him with Six, expecting the answer Four, six plus four equals ten. Simple. Unfortunately he was working on the sum of twelve, the previous day's password. The reply I got was Six. Fortunately we knew one another and no harm was done. Had it been for real someone could have been killed. This was the real thing and I did not want to get shot by one of my own because of a basic error.

'Password is live until you make contact.' Our young officer answered. 'However long that takes. That it? Right chaps, report to the flight deck at fifteen twenty. Take off at fifteen forty. Good luck!'

We made our way back to our bed-spaces and went over the information.

'These maps are years old.' Yorkie complained.

'It won't matter. This place hasn't changed in decades', I said. 'Intel's patchy too. Nine K night march to the RV About seven hours, moving tactically, with all this kit.'

'Another eleven to the patrol location. We'll have to do better than that. Only fifteen hours of darkness.'

'Two K an hour at least, to be safe.'

'That's doable but we'll have to compromise tactics.'

'No choice have we?'

'Nope.'

The LZ was on East Falkland alongside Malo Creek, an inlet on the South coast of Port Salvador, the largest sheltered stretch of water on the island. We would need to make maximum use of the terrain to minimize the risk of being picked up by the enemy night sights.

'Navigation shouldn't be too bad, I said pointing to the map. Once we locate the creek, follow it South until it forks, then follow this tributary for five K. Take a compass bearing to the two small ponds and we've cracked it.' The RV, was far from ideal, being very exposed. It was, however, the only clearly identifiable point in the area and as such would have to do. We were not taking any radio sets with us and thus would be on our own, with no possibility of backup until we reached the patrol. Being a trained signaller, I was uneasy at this, but at least I would be spared the extra weight. We ran through our contact drills, emergency procedures and 'actions on' until we were satisfied we had covered all contingencies. Lastly we picked our own emergency RV on the map and satisfied we could do no more, we went to see our friend Corporal Slater.

'What can I do for you lads?' he said cheerily

'Ammo. We need another fifty rounds each.

'What for?'

'To zero and test fire our weapons,' said Yorkie. 'Any ideas?'

'Test firing is no problem, just shoot over the side. Zeroing is a different matter altogether. You will have to clear it with the Navy. Give me half an hour to work on it.'

'Cheers. Come on, Yorkie let's go on deck and get some air.' I was longing for something to take my mind off the impending operation and a breath of salt air was just what I needed. Stopping briefly to pick up our duvet jackets we headed up to the deck amidships. The sea was relatively calm, the sky grey and overcast. Leaning on the rail, I turned to my companion.

'This is it then. We are finally going to earn the Queen's shilling.'

'It's about time, all that training going to waste all these years.' Yorkie was raring to go. I was not so eager.

'Yeah, we'll soon know how good it really is' I replied, trying to sound enthusiastic.

'It's the best training in the world,' said Yorkie. 'We are the best in the world.'

'Certainement, mon ami, mais je suis seulement TA.' said I mimicking someone half way between Charles Aznavour and Sacha Distel.

'What are you burbling about now you foreign fusilier?'

'It's French, you Royal Irish Mudguard.' I replied.

'Of course it is, but what does it mean? We poor secondary modern boys didn't learn languages. Too busy getting a proper education learning practical skills.'

'Like what?'

There was a long pause until at last he offered....

'Woodwork...?'

'Woodwork! You can't knock a nail in straight.'

'Who wants poncy French anyway? We were too busy developing our bodies on the sports field. Why don't you stick to Spanish, or better still

English?'

'Just demonstrating my superior intellect, allow me to translate. It means, but I am only TA.'

'What's this only TA? Look at the patrol competitions we've been in over the years. Look at all the shields in the bar. We've pissed all over the French Paras, the Dutch Marines, Danes, Belgique Para Commando; you name 'em we've beaten them. NATO's best. And as for the Yanks...'

'I know we pissed all over them too.'

'They can't touch us and you know it. When the shit hits the fan you'll be fine. We both will, so stop worrying.'

I still couldn't shake the feeling that I was going to be a casualty of this unforeseen war. I was worried I would let the side down. 'I'm going inside,' I said, as the cold ate its way through my hollow fibre quilting.

'You're going below, you ignorant grammar school landlubber,' said Yorkie.

'What do you think lads?' Corporal Slater was holding an improvised kite with a five litre white plastic Jerry can hung beneath it by nylon cords. 'Just run it out from the stern rail to one hundred metres. The Navy will tow a fifty gallon drum behind the ship to get you started.'

'Great! We will be able to see the strikes in the sea to make our adjustments' said Yorkie.

'I don't get it. Why the kite?' I enquired.

'The drum will be bouncing all over in the wake but it
Should, give us enough to get the sights somewhere close then we can fine tune them on the jerrican,' explained Yorkie patiently.

'Okay let's do it.'

'Hold on lads, the Navy will set up the drum in about half an hour. They'll call me when they're ready. Fancy a brew to pass the time?'

'Excellent idea, you're a star, Slater!'

'Bob.'

'Me Tony, he Yorkie' I responded.

'Pull up a ration box and take the weight off your feet. I'll put the kettle on.'

The tea was hot, strong and sweetened with condensed milk; most welcome, as was the distraction of idle conversation.

'So what made you blokes want to join the SAS? Thirst for adventure was it?' Our host asked.

'Glamour of the uniform,' I replied. 'Thought it would attract the women.'

'Did it work?' Bob enquired.

'We were conned. Sold a big fat rubber dick,' interjected my fellow super-soldier.

'How come?' said Bob, leaning closer, his curiosity aroused.

Seeing his opportunity for tale telling Yorkie launched himself into raconteur mode.

'Most people think SAS stands for Special Air Service. Actually it stands for Silly 'at Service.'

'How's that then?'

'It's like this. Someone in the MOD decides that the Army needs a special unit to take on dirty, boring and dangerous jobs. Jobs that no one in their right mind would touch with a barge pole. The problem is how to persuade soldiers to join, because no squaddie worth his salt is going to volunteer for anything. They need a carrot and this is where the silly hat comes in. They create a selection course and make it hard enough to have a high failure rate, so that anyone who passes will think he is the dog's bollocks. Now, for the really clever bit! The prize for passing, is a different coloured hat, with an interesting badge that marks you as an élite unit. What they don't tell you, is that apart from the passing out parade, which is only attended by your fellow soldiers in identical hats, you will not be allowed to wear your coveted beret outside barracks once you have earned it, except on very rare occasions when travelling in uniform.'

'Even then it's pointless,' I chipped in. 'Remember platform four?'

'Very well as it happens,' said Yorkie

Corporal Slater was now totally hooked

'What's that all about then?'

'You tell him Tony,' my companion pleaded, 'I can't bear the embarrassment.'

'Yeah go on' urged Bob, 'let's hear it.'

'Not that much to it really,' I began. 'It was just after we had passed our selection course and Yorkie was waiting for a train on a platform at Leeds railway station. He was in his uniform and wearing his brand new SAS beret. With him was this recruit who was hoping to transfer from the Paras. Anyway, there was this elderly couple on the platform. The old lady turns to her husband and says, 'Who are those soldiers George?' And he says. 'Well, you see the one in the red beret, he's a paratrooper.' At this point, Yorkie here, sticks out his chest and pulls himself up to his full five feet nine inches'...

'Six feet' if you don't mind' said my companion, adopting a wounded tone.

'Dream on short arse.' I continued. 'Anyway

this old guy points to Yorkie and says to his wife, *I think he must be a cook*.' Bob pissed himself laughing.

Slater's contraption worked better than expected and after expending forty rounds a piece, we were satisfied that we had achieved the best we could and returned the kite and cord. Back in our pits we cleaned and oiled our weapons, then emptied, cleaned and reloaded our magazines. If we got into a firefight, we did not want any stoppages; especially with our limited firepower. In the last hour before kick off, I wrote a woefully inadequate, final letter to Carol and the boys: to be sent only if I did not make it back. Finally we checked that we were sterile, that no personal papers, photographs, etc., were on our person. I took one last look at the three pictures which I had carried so carefully halfway across the world. Carol smiling radiantly from a park bench, the boys posing for the school photographer and finally my mother and father on their wedding day. I carefully slipped them into my wallet, put it into my kit bag and climbed into my hammock to snatch some much needed sleep.

I awoke after two hours to find Yorkie raring to go. We primed our grenades, smeared our faces with camouflage cream and at fourteen forty we donned our webbing and hauled our kit up to the Heli Deck. The Wasp was in the hangar and the empty deck, cold, wet and windswept. The sound of the Wessex approaching through the gathering gloom caused us to look across the grey Atlantic swell. The drab grey Royal Navy workhorse clattered its way across the waves towards us, like some giant alien insect hunting for prey.

14

Infiltration
East Falkland
Wednesday 19th – Thursday 20th May 1982

Communication inside the helicopter was by hand signals, as it was impossible to make ourselves heard above the clamour of the engine. The noise was so loud that if we came under accurate small arms fire, holes appearing in the fuselage would be the first we knew of it. The aircraft raced across the icy black ocean at two miles a minute, skimming the waves to keep below enemy radar. From our position on the floor of the cargo compartment we could see through the open door. There was nothing to see but black night punctuated with snow flurries. We had our backs against the rear bulkhead, bergans at our sides, weapons between our knees. The air was heavy with the paraffin smell of aviation fuel, damp canvas, oil and rubber. The seats had been removed to improve carrying capacity: an operational necessity, given the shortage of available helicopters. Many layers of clothing topped off with our quilted jackets made us look like green Michelin men; life saving kit given the weather, which was worsening by the minute. We had declined the bulky immersion suits normally required for long flights over water, reasoning that if we did finish up in the ocean we were dead meat anyway. Looking across to the big open doorway on the starboard side, we could now see a white curtain of snow flashing past towards the tail as we sat buffeted by the wind howling through the opening. We could do nothing but pray that the pilot knew his job and that the aircraft had passed its MOT

Thankfully, our Wessex was equipped with radar, enabling it to operate day or night in all weather. Despite this, the pilot needed all his skill and experience to keep the aircraft from finishing up in the drink. We reached landfall without incident and for the next fifteen minutes or so we flew a winding course hugging the terrain. The winch-man tapped my shoulder and held up three fingers. Three minutes to the LZ Yorkie removed the magazine from his SLR, checked that the rounds were seated correctly and replaced it on the weapon. He pulled the cocking handle to the rear, allowing it to fly back under the pressure of the spring before applying the safety catch. I followed suit. We exchanged a brief glance as we prepared ourselves for action. Our civvy coats were essential to combat the freezing weather and would come into their own when we got to the RV and had to lie up in what ever cover we could find. We would keep warm enough as long as we were on the move, but in a static location on hard routine (no cooking, no hot food or drink), we would need to preserve every ounce of body heat

The winch-man held up one finger just as the Wessex lost airspeed and gained altitude, indicating that we had reached rising ground. One minute to go. My senses were wired in adrenalin - fuelled anticipation, my guts churning, while my mind raced through the possible dangers and 'actions on' drills, should any occur. The aircraft shuddered and slowed dramatically to a hover, buffeted by the wind. The winch-man was lying on the deck, head and shoulders out in the howling blizzard looking for the ground. He was in communication with the pilot through his headset intercom and coaxed him slowly down until we must have been as close as he was prepared to risk. The ground may be too soft to land; it was impossible to tell in the prevailing conditions. Our eyes were glued to him for the signal to move.

When it came, we acted instantly, dragging our kit to the door. The ground was around six or eight feet below. We pushed our bergans out and jumped after them. I hit the ground and sank ankle deep in peat before rolling to the left and crashing into a bergan. I quickly scanned through three hundred and sixty degrees and was comforted to see Yorkie doing the same a couple of metres to my right. The noise of the wind was gentle on my ears after the battering they had received in the Wessex, which was fast disappearing into the night towards the warmth of the Frigate.

I felt suddenly quite alone and exposed after the comforting interior of the helicopter. Visibility was better than I had expected, but still only fifty metres or so. I pulled my wooly hat over my ears. The good news was, I could just make out an inlet ahead to my left, with the creek running in from the coast and away into the interior behind us. If this was the right creek, then the pilot deserved a medal.

We shouldered our bergans and checked the

direction of the watercourse against the compass. It matched expectations. It appeared we were in the right place. Turning inland, with the water now on our right, Yorkie led the way upstream. The wind was howling in from the Northwest, which was a blessing as it was at our backs, making it easier to see. Beneath our feet, the ground was spongy under the grass and the landscape undulating for as far as we were able to see. This was the type of terrain we had trained on in Yorkshire for years; we were in our element. Struggling under the weight of equipment, I was soon sweating despite the cold, my shoulders hunched and bowed under the load.

Every few metres Yorkie checked behind to see that I was still with him, while I in turn swept my gaze across both flanks and checked behind to see that we were still alone. It was so like many of the winter exercises in the Yorkshire Dales and Pennines, that I had to keep reminding myself that this was a live operation with a real enemy.

Counting my paces I estimated that we had covered almost two kilometres in the first hour; not bad going in a tactical situation with full kit. Yorkie stopped suddenly and dropped to one knee, staring ahead for what seemed an eternity. All I could do was to stop, drop and observe. Trouble was, I could see nothing at all except my bodyguard and I would have been hard pressed to hear anything above the wind noise. Eventually, he rose to his feet and moved off, turning briefly to make eye contact and signal thumbs up, to show all was well. The cold was beginning to bite into my face and the gap where my gloves did not quite reach the elasticated cuffs of my coat. The snow had eased some, but visibility in the dark night was not noticeably affected. We maintained our distance.

Following the creek was a Godsend. Navigating across this open landscape, in these conditions, would otherwise have been extremely difficult and have slowed us down considerably. As it was, we were making good progress with no problems, apart from the strain of peering constantly into darkness so black it could hide an Argentine regiment. Four K from the LZ, the creek turned sharp left just before looping back on itself. It was here that a smaller creek just about fifteen feet wide joined it a couple of hundred metres after passing under the road between the settlements of Teal Inlet to the Northwest and Estancia to the East. We needed to follow this stream.

Gingerly approaching the gravel track, we settled down to observe. There was no sign of activity so Yorkie went ahead to recce. He was back in a few minutes and waved me forward. I followed him onto the gravel road surface as quietly as I could and we crossed the small stone bridge over the creek melting into the landscape on the far bank. After a brief check for signs of life, we set off, away from the road as fast as was tactically sensible before turning south, parallel to the road until we picked up the smaller creek. Following the watercourse upstream we headed towards the mountains.

The constant fear that we could be clearly seen in the enemy night sights long before we would ever see them, served only to heighten our senses. We strained eyes, ears and nostrils for any sign of life in the darkness.

I wondered, *How many weapons might be trained on us now,* while trying to concentrate on counting my paces, check my arcs, watch my companion for any sign of trouble and sweep the ground in front for obstacles. My watch showed 20.43. We had been on the move since 18.00 and covered six klicks, give or take. I was well pleased. (All this was about to change, however as I found another creek by stepping into it!) The time was now 00.25 and we still had three klicks to go, but at least we were back on track and had not been compromised by the enemy. The wind at our backs again at last, I was feeling very cold and stiff, but otherwise in good spirits, confident we would achieve our objective. After another seven hundred metres along the bank, we reached the tributary, found the sharp bend, and were able to take a bearing to the lake. We had to wade the creek, but it was only calf deep at this point and our feet were already soaked. *Thank God I brought four pairs of socks.*

Yorkie was looking strained from constant staring into the blackness, with nerves taught as as strings on a banjo, waiting for the bullet from nowhere. Lead scout is nerve wracking enough on exercise. On operations it is total stress. You are the first target. The enemy is more likely to see you first, so you have to be wired every step of the way, ready to react instinctively, with deadly force and then withdraw, under covering fire from the rest of the patrol. All this before the enemy can bring effective fire to bear. Being our first experience of operations made it harder still, but Yorkie would not let me relieve him, insisting rightly that it was his job to get me to the RV in one piece. Following the compass bearing was not easy. On top of the darkness and the weather, the ground was devoid of any significant features. We were forced to semi leapfrog: Yorkie would move ahead to the limit of my visibility and I would check that he had stayed on the bearing. As soon as he was happy that it was safe for me, I would the advance to join him. He would then move forward, while I watched him. When he stopped I would adjust his position to the left or right by hand signals. We would then repeat the laborious performance over and over again. By this means and by counting our paces, we reached a spot we calculated as two hundred metres from the RV at the lake.

Visibility had improved substantially, while the snow had turned first to sleet, then finally stopped leaving no more than a light dusting on the ground. Cold, wet and tired we lay shivering between the grass tussocks keeping as low a profile as possible while we worked out our next move.

'Soon as we get close enough to see the shoreline go to ground, back up, crawl ten metres left or right and observe. Okay?'

'You're the scout.' I replied.

'Good. If we're happy the RV isn't compromised, I'll make first contact.'

'Hang on a minute, you're the best shot, and you have the most powerful rifle. You are best qualified to give covering fire.' He reluctantly conceded. Scoffing a Mars Bar each we shared a cup of coffee from my flask, the warm liquid giving a welcome boost to my morale. We agreed that our present position would be our emergency RV if we got bumped and that it would remain open for twelve hours. It was at this point, it occurred to me, that we had no plan for withdrawal or extraction if we failed to link up with the patrol. We would be effectively abandoned with no means of communicating with our forces and no idea where the nearest British troops were. It was not a comforting thought. I decided not to share it with my companion, although I suspected that he had come to the same conclusion.

We set off cautiously towards our goal, Yorkie in the lead. We had advanced just thirty metres when he stopped and gave the thumbs up to indicate success and then placed his hand palm down on the top of his head indicating that I should join him. As we lay surveying the landscape from the top of a grass bank about two feet high, we could make out the edge of the lake, just visible by the light of the moon filtering through the clouds. The grassy slope ran gently down to the water's edge around one hundred and twenty metres away. I could not believe our navigation had been so accurate. Twenty metres away to the left, was a patch of low scrubby vegetation half the size of a tennis court; the only significant cover. Instinctively crawling away from this bullet magnet we lost ourselves in the featureless ground. Hide in plain sight was our policy. It had worked before and we saw no reason why it should not work now.

After ten metres I stopped and allowed Yorkie to get into a good position for covering the RV He slipped off his bergan and cached it behind him before settling in a small depression and covering himself with his one-man cam net; a few small adornments from the local vegetation and he had all but disappeared. I took out a length of Para cord from my pocket, tied one end to the D ring on my webbing and passed the roll to Yorkie. I moved off a further five metres and followed his example, lying facing his position rather than the RV This gave me the ability to watch the ground behind him as well as the RV, while he in turn could watch one hundred and eighty degrees covering the RV and the ground behind me. There were inevitably blind spots which, had we been a standard four-man patrol would have been covered. It was the best we could do with two of us. If our contact was on the ball, he would be here already and may well have us under observation with an image intensifier. This would not be a problem, it would assist in making the contact. After watching for twenty five-minutes, I convinced myself that it was safe to approach, but I waited another thirty minutes to be on the safe side. I untied the Para cord and attached it to my bergan tugging gently on it twice to tell Yorkie I was about to move. The last thing I wanted was to be mistaken for an Argie, given his marksmanship.

I began to crawl very slowly, in belt order, rifle at the ready, towards the rendezvous point weaving between the grass tussocks. After twenty-five metres I rose slowly to one knee scanning three hundred and sixty degrees. My heart was beating so loudly I was worried the enemy might hear it in Port Stanley. Despite the bitter cold my palms were sweating inside my gloves. Adrenaline flowing, senses alive to the slightest sound or movement I stood up and walked slowly towards the inlet, each step a nerve twisting experience. Filled with the expectation of sudden, lethal violence, I scanned the ground for any available cover. Nothing happened. I made it to the RV. Standing with my back to the lake I waited; constantly scanning all around. From somewhere close to my right side a voice spoke softly but clearly.

'Nine'

I nearly jumped out of my skin and for a moment forgot the appropriate response.

'One,' I replied at last staring into the ground at the other side of the small stream, amazed that I hadn't soiled my slacks.

About three metres away a clump of grass tussocks rose, as the chicken wire to which they were attached was raised. A shadowy figure crawled from beneath the camouflage, his rifle pointed directly at me. I would have been impressed except I had done the same thing many times on exercise. I lowered my M16 and introduced myself. He was a couple of inches shorter than me, probably mid thirties but difficult to tell under all that camouflage. He was well

padded in a parka and quilted trousers.

'You can tell your mate to come down now,' he said in a business like tone, tapping the image intensifier hanging around his neck 'And get a move on!' he finished in a hostile tone.

Smug bastard, I thought. It really hit home how vulnerable we were to the enemy, knowing they were similarly equipped. I was sure we had made a good tactical approach and we had followed SOPs I headed across to Yorkie's position while our guide rolled up his 'hide' and stowed it away in his bergan. I retrieved my kit and within a few minutes we were all together at the inlet ready to move off. I was put in the middle with Yorkie at the rear and 'Mr. Grumpy' leading the way.

'ERV' he hissed, indicating the inlet as our point to regroup if we got ambushed or separated by some other drama. He moved off south along the lake shore. We fell in behind, keeping well spaced, watching our arcs for any sign of trouble. The wind had picked up again but at least the snow held off, if not the cold. It was good to be moving as I had really stiffened up and my joints were quite painful until I got my blood to circulate some warmth around my body. It was not long before I began to fall behind, much to the annoyance of our leader. It occurred to me that he would have only brought essential kit with him and this was borne out by the size of his bergan, which must have weighed less than half mine. He was not a happy bunny but he cut the pace when it became obvious that we were going as fast as we could. As he swept three sixty to check we were still with him, I caught his gaze. The face was all concentration on the job in hand, but the eyes spoke to me. They said 'TA wankers' loud and clear, even in the dark. Maybe I was paranoid; somehow I did not think so.

After two hours of gently but steadily rising ground we reached a limestone pavement reminiscent of Ingleborough in the Yorkshire Dales. We stopped and adopted all round defence.

'Stay' our host commanded by hand signal, before disappearing into the dark. I felt like someone's least favourite dog.

'Real charmer isn't he' I whispered to Yorkie.

'Remind me to save a couple of rounds for him,' was the reply.

The minutes ticked by and stretched to half an hour. I was just beginning to get pissed off lying in the freezing grass with no idea what we should do if our guide did not return, when Yorkie tapped my boot with his and pointed his rifle towards the area where we had last seen our guide. There was a slight movement and then a figure emerged from the gloom framed in our rifle sights.

'The LUP is five hundred metres. Get in and get cammed up. Make it good, by day the Argies are all over us.'

'What about the prisoner?' I enquired.

'That's up to the patrol commander.'

'I want him with me' I said firmly, quite surprising myself. 'Any delay getting information out of him could cost lives,' I emphasised with unnecessary drama.

He was not impressed and turned away in the direction of the LUP Having no alternative, we followed in silence exchanging bemused looks as Yorkie made a 'dickhead' gesture with his fist to his forehead. I silently concurred and hoped the rest of the patrol would be more amenable. We climbed through the rocks reaching the LUP without incident. It was just a jumble of rocks on the side of a slope, but there were a number of fissures which were deep and wide enough to conceal a man and all his kit. The patrol had made overhead cover with chicken wire and hessian, topped off with moss and small shards of rock. The patrol commander was a hard looking Scot, around forty something, his weather beaten face adorned with a prominent moustache. Deep set piercing grey eyes were topped by thick eyebrows which indicated the hair beneath his thick woollen hat must be red He wore a camouflage smock and a custom-made waistcoat with dozens of pockets crammed with a mix of deadly ordnance.

'Jock' he said simply. 'The Argies are fifteen hundred metres that way,' pointing with his rifle.

'They're not flying at night just now, but that could change. Hard routine, no smoking or cooking, no unnecessary movement. Get settled in and I will introduce you to our guest. Take the right flank and cover our back door. Questions?'

We shook our heads.

'We brought you some batteries for the radio. Oh and a medic pack.' I said, then set off. We had little time before first light and got to work settling in. I selected a gap between two rocks which were near the crest of the slope, about five metres from the nearest patrol member's hide. With only moonlight to see by, I set to work in silence. It was relatively easy to rig overhead cover, as, although the fissure was three feet wide at ground level, the rocks were less than two feet apart at the top. Half way along the left hand side there was a miniature cave in the rock big enough to take my bergan and escape belt. Above this, ran a ledge around four inches deep which was ideal to take my M16. Wedging bungee cords into cracks in the stone I stretched them across to form a framework. Covered with my poncho, this formed a roof a foot below the tops of the rocks, creating a cave eight feet long by three feet high and wide, tapering to two feet near the top of the ridge. I plugged the gap at the ridge top with loose rocks and moss until I was left with a 'rabbit hole' which would give me a reasonable view down to and beyond the road in daylight. Even now, the moonlight was bright enough for me to just make out the line of the road. The rabbit hole was camouflaged with a face veil to complete my hide. With my high-density sponge carry mat lining the floor topped with my sleeping bag I was quite comfortable. My personal cam net concealed the entrance. Doing this in a confined space in the dark is far easier to describe than to execute, but I had been practicing for ten years, longer really, if you take into account all the childhood dens I created in the woods near my home.

Swallowing the last of my coffee from the flask I stripped and cleaned my M16, removed my boots, cleaned my feet with a flannel and towel I had brought for the purpose, and dusted them with foot powder. The simple act of putting on clean, dry socks and trainers greatly increased my comfort level raising my morale. I left my boots to dry out a bit. It was still dark as I moved stealthily across the rocks to Jock's lair, taking care not to expose myself above the skyline. I was looking forward to my first glimpse of the enemy.

15

Interrogation
East Falkland, Thursday 20th May 1982

The prisoner was blindfolded, his hands secured behind his back with plastic handcuffs. Bandages swathed his lower legs and he was in obvious discomfort. In spite of these impediments, we moved him across to my LUP (Lying Up Position) without too much difficulty, after first gagging him with masking tape. Subdued and cooperative, he was in no fit state to escape, which should make my job a little easier. He was shoved into the corner of my lair and I squeezed myself in behind him.

Jock handed over a small black poly bag.

'Prisoner's personal effects. No Intel value.'

He secured my camouflage before disappearing into the darkness. I switched on my torch shielding the red lens with my gloved hand and settled in with my captive. It would not remain dark for long. I spoke to my charge.

'¿Es usted habla Inglés' I asked. He did not respond.

'Ho hay problema hablo español.' He stiffened slightly. 'Fluido!' I added emphatically. I continued in Spanish.

'I am going to remove your gag. You may speak quietly but if you attempt to shout I will silence you. Do you understand?'

A slight nod was followed by a wince as I ripped the tape from his face. 'Excellent. We understand each other. Your name is Ramon Ramirez and you are a Major in the Argentine Air Force.'

'My name is Ramon Ramirez and my rank is Major, my serial number is...' I cut him short by jabbing him hard in the chest with my boot knife.

'Save it Major. You were seen ejecting from a Pucara. We know you are a pilot and that you are a squadron commander.' This last was a shot not entirely in the dark, given his rank and the fact that he was a pilot.

'Besides the uniform is a bit of a give away don't you think?' I added sarcastically.

'I am not obliged to answer any questions and I am to be treated with the respect accorded to my rank,' he stammered.

'I agree, but we are playing for high stakes here and I do not have time to concern myself with niceties. My job is to get results. Let's cut the crap, I promise not to insult your intelligence if you promise not to insult mine, okay? Have you been mistreated since your capture?'

'No.'

'Your wounds have been attended to, you have been given morphine, food and water. Why do you think you have been well treated?'

'Because you British are a civilised nation'

'Wrong, amigo, you were looked after so

that you would be in a fit state to answer my questions.' He stiffened again. 'We are a civilised nation, but when dealing with people who launch unprovoked attacks on British civilians and invade British sovereign territory, we are inclined to overlook civility. My friend has a brother in the Royal Marines. He was at Moody Brook barracks when your army invaded. Your Special Forces. They beat him up.' (I was lying, Yorkie did not have a brother but I needed him to believe we had both a motive and the desire to physically harm him.) 'My friend is eager to meet anyone from the Armed Forces of Argentina.'

He was becoming anxious, fidgeting and stiffening when I spoke. Outside, dawn began to break but my prisoner was unaware of this, owing to the blindfold and anyway the light had not yet penetrated inside of my little den. I made no attempt to ask him any questions at first, as it was unlikely that he would answer them truthfully, if at all, in fact. I concentrated on giving him grief for attacking British subjects and generally instilling into him a belief that I hated all things Argentinean. I played on his isolation and vulnerability.

'The war is going badly for Argentina. The fact that we are so close to the capital and have remained undetected is testimony to the professionalism of our forces. Victory will inevitably be ours, you must see that.'

An educated man, he was not easily intimidated, but he was just a man, a man who was lost, alone and fearful.

I reached for the bag with Ramon's personal effects, leaving him to think on what I had said. Some loose change, a Tag Heuer pilot's watch, small pocket compass, Swiss Army Knife, comb and a Prayer Book. He was tired and disoriented. In this he was not alone. It was now 10.20. I'd had only two hours sleep in the last forty-eight and was running on empty. My stomach was giving me gyp from being deprived of hot food and drink in this cold climate. I was running out of steam and I knew it. Some years ago, as part of an experiment to test soldiers abilities to function after sleep deprivation, I had taken part in trials run by the Ministry Of Defence. I had been kept awake for seventy-two hours, during which time I was given a number of routine tasks to perform while boffins monitored my performance. By the end I was a total zombie, incapable of tying a shoelace. I was not keen to repeat the experience.

'This war will be over in a matter of weeks,' I told him 'the outcome is a forgone conclusion. We have a very powerful fleet and we will win, but it will cost many lives. Many young men will not return to their wives and mothers. Many who do will be maimed physically and mentally, all because of the whims of politicians. You can help to shorten this war and save the lives of your countrymen. Just give me the information I need. You know the war is lost. We have superior numbers', I lied. 'Your flagship has been sunk and your Navy is nowhere to be seen.'

'Murderers!' he exclaimed suddenly.

I had touched a nerve somewhere.

'Your Airforce has fought with great courage, but it is not enough. Your president has duped you. He started this war to take attention away from his troubles at home.'

'That is outrageous! It is you who have been duped by Margaret Thatcher. She is a warmonger who has used Las Malvinas to boost her popularity. She does not care for the people here, nor does she care for her soldiers.' He spoke with great passion and his point was not missed. I was well pleased. I had cracked his shell; he was entering into dialogue.

'All politicians are the same, Major, not one of them is to be trusted, regardless of party or country. It is always the soldier who suffers.' I said, trying to establish a common.

bond and win his trust. We spent the next hour arguing the toss and generally discussing the current situation and although he put on a brave face, it was becoming apparent that his morale was sinking.

'We all want to see our families again and get on with our lives, Ramon,' I said softly using his Christian name for the first time. 'We are pawns on a chess board, we each have our job to do even though it is often distasteful to us. We are soldiers, we will do our duty.'

'Duty to whom?'Ramon asked. 'To our country? What about our duty to God?'

'I, like you am a Catholic. I try to be a good Christian. I will answer to God when my time comes.'

'If you are what you say you will understand how much my faith means to me and perhaps you will do me a kindness as one Catholic to another.'

Asking for a favour now, was he? That's progress.

'What would that be?' I asked.

'My prayer book, they took it. It would be such a comfort to me in my last hours.'

'Don't be such a drama queen, you are not

going to die.'

'You do not lie so good. We both know that without medical treatment the infection in my wounds will spread. It is just a matter of time.'

We both knew he was right. It would have been simply humane to comply with his request. My heart was ready to comply, but training took over.

'Tell me what I need to know and I will see what I can do, I said.'

He hung his head his hopes dashed.

'I can say nothing'

'Suit yourself, but cooperate and I will not only give you your prayer book, but I will remove the handcuffs and blindfold so you can read it. See I have it here.' I removed the book from the bag and pressed its cold embossed cover to his cheek.

'I do not have time to waste. If I do not get the answers I need, my orders are to let my friend with the brother in the Royal Marines take over. He has already killed three of your soldiers: two with a bayonet, just two days ago. If you wish to see your family again it would be best to talk to me now. The sooner you cooperate, the sooner we finish this war and we can all go home.' I paused to let my words sink in.

'What is your squadron strength? Where are you based?' I asked.

Before he could react, fate intervened. There was a roaring sound overhead and the earth shook violently to the sound of exploding ordnance, followed by the sudden banging of several heavy guns from close by. Ramon curled into a ball and I pressed myself into the ground as hard as I could, trying to burrow deeper with every concussion. The cacophony of noise was terrifying. The roar of fast jets screaming in at low level was closely followed by a whooshing sound, punctuated by rippling explosions, overplayed with the crackling of small arms and the steady hammering of cannon fire. The ground shook with bone-jarring violence. It seemed to go on forever. In reality it lasted only a few minutes.

The attack was followed by ghostly silence. I did not realise it straight away, but this was largely because I had been deafened, albeit temporarily. I looked up and around at my surroundings. Incredibly my poncho was still in place, as was the cam net. The face veil had been blown in and peering through the 'rabbit hole' I witnessed an awesome sight. The Argentine Helicopter Base was a total shambles. I reached for my binos and focused them on the scene of devastation. Two Chinooks were wrecked and burning fiercely; an ammunition dump was ablaze, with bullets exploding all over the place in complete silence, to me at least. It was a great firework display. Men were running around in confusion, arms waving in the air. The anti aircraft guns were silent. At least one of them would never again fire a shot in anger. The place was wrecked. I was shaking quite violently, whether with fear or excitement I knew not – probably both. My ears began ringing as I surveyed the awesome destruction that man had wreaked upon his fellow man. I had never witnessed the terrifying power of an air strike before. I was impressed and frightened at the same time. A cold chill ran down my spine, as I realized that next time it could be us. Something was pushing against me. Ramon was wriggling against the rock trying to dislodge his blindfold. I put my hand on his shoulder.

'It's okay. Take it easy,' I said, pulling off the blindfold. My ears were still ringing, but some hearing was beginning to return. I could hear him asking what had happened. He looked like a frightened rabbit, caught in the headlights of a car, a split second before the collision. My first thought was for Yorkie, but reasoned that he must be okay, as he was only a few metres away. I forced Ramon's head into the rabbit hole so he could see the devastation.

'Your airforce is no match for the RAF. Look! You can stop this madness.'

The RAF had just destroyed much of his country's military hardware and in all probability sent some of his comrades to meet their maker. I pressed home the advantage and questioned him relentlessly while he was still shaken. He let go. He had had enough. The crash; ejecting; his wounds and the sight of the airstrike had conspired to rob him of his will to resist. For a fleeting moment I felt sorry for him, just a brief moment. Back to work.

'See that?' I said, forcing his face back towards the rabbit hole. 'See what happens when you do not cooperate. We will strike without warning, when and where we choose. This is your doing. You made the rules when your army set foot, uninvited, on our islands. Now answer my questions and stop further unnecessary loss off life. I pulled him back down slamming him against the hard rock. He let out a gasp. He was a sorry sight. All the fight seemed to have left him.

'I love to fly, I have always wanted to fly. It is

not in my nature to kill. I hate war. All war. I just want to see my family again. I will cooperate, but only because I am a humanitarian. If that is what it takes to save lives, then so be it.'

As he began to talk, I wrote down the details in my notebook. When I was happy that I had enough to send, I gave him some water and half of my last Mars Bar. He was grateful beyond reason for this small kindness. 'Poor bastard' I thought, 'there but for the grace of God...' I looked through the 'rabbit hole' and saw that the enemy, although fully alert, were too busy to be sending patrols out and as far as I could see, they had no serviceable aircraft to send up. I decided it would be safe to leave the hide and pass on the information I had gained.

Picking up my weapon, I crawled out through the opening, across the cold rocks and down to Yorkie's position. I was relieved to see his broad grin.

'That stuffed them.' He whispered.

'Sure did. Watch the prisoner will you?'

He nodded and slid out and over the rocks, rifle in hand. I turned and crawled towards Jock's position, taking care to stick to the limestone so as not to leave a trail. The light dusting of snow had been blown from the rocks during the night by the wind, which had now subsided to a moderate breeze. It was still bitterly cold, despite the watery morning sunlight. My joints and muscles ached from lack of exercise. I approached Jock's Basha cautiously, and called softly through the entrance camouflage.

'Speak!' commanded a low voice from within. I passed my notes under the net. After a short silence the net was eased to one side by a large gloved hand, as Jock's grimy, stubbled face appeared inches from mine. The strain of operating close to the enemy for so long showed in his eyes.

'Is this Kosher?' he quizzed.

'I reckon so. He's had it, that little firework display finished him off. I take it that was at your request?'

'We just report the targets. The head shed decides what to hit.'

'Good job just the same,' I said.

Jock was unmoved.

'Sort out stags between you and your oppo to cover the rear.'

I nodded.

Moving back towards my basha, my spirits rose at the prospect of getting some sleep. Ramon was already either asleep or unconscious. It was hard to tell which. His ghostly grey face and shallow breathing were not good. I checked his pulse and made him as comfortable as I could. Yorkie insisted on doing the first two hours stag. I didn't argue. I handed him a ring pull from an old thirty-six grenade to which was attached a small reel of nylon fishing line. He attached this to his wrist with a short length of Para cord and headed for his lair, trailing the line behind him as I paid it out. I checked Ramon's handcuffs and settled into my sleeping bag.

My last waking act was to secure the fishing line to my wrist by passing it under my watchstrap, ensuring that there was enough slack to avoid my inadvertently alarming Yorkie with a false signal if I moved in my sleep. I closed my eyes and then opened them again a nano second later, or so it seemed. A quick look at my watch revealed the truth; two hours had passed and it was my turn on stag. I tugged twice on the nylon to acknowledge and shook myself from my slumber. Ramon was in the land of dreams and looked pale, but strangely peaceful given his circumstances. I took a boiled sweet from my pocket and with some difficulty removed the soggy sticky wrapper and put it into my mouth. I began to suck, savouring its sugary, sharp citrus flavour, while manoeuvring myself into a position where I could watch the approach to the rear.

Through the camouflage screen across the entrance, I began scanning the ground, at first unaided and then with the binos. All was peaceful. Light snow patches still showed here and there and the grass stirred in the strong breeze. I watched a white-chinned petrel gliding low across the tundra and wished that I too could fly. I wondered what the immediate future held. Apart from 'watching the back door,' I was now effectively redundant, my main concern being to stay alive. Vital member of the team one minute: cannon fodder the next.

My stag passed without incident and after the two hours had elapsed, I tugged on the fishing line to wake Yorkie. Seconds later the line jerked his reply. Ramon was awake and asking for water. I took the bottle from my belt and held it to his lips. He drank slowly and then spoke for the first time in perfect English. 'I need to piss'

'So you speak English after all.' I remarked without surprise, as I reached into the depths of my bergan. 'Okay, hold on.' I pulled an old aluminium water bottle, with PISS in bold capitals written on it with black marker pen.

'Give me your word not to attempt to escape and I will remove your handcuffs'

'I cannot walk and I have no desire to be shot. I give you my word of honour I will not try to escape.'

'Thank you,' I said, reaching for my Swiss Army Knife. I cut the plasticuffs and massaged some life back into his wrists. He looked like death and was obviously much weaker than when I first saw him. He took the bottle and with some difficulty attended to his need before passing the bottle back. I replaced the cap, taking care to screw it on tight, before stowing it away in my bergan.

'Your Spanish is very good,' he croaked.

'Thank you. So is your English.'

'In Argentina we learn English at school and my parents are bilingual. Did you learn Spanish at school?'

'My father was Spanish' I replied.

'Was?' Queried Ramon.

'He was killed in the war. I was brought up by his mother, so I too am bilingual, well, trilingual. I speak Welsh also. It's the land of my birth.'

'Your mother is Welsh?'

'Was. She was killed in the war also.'

'I am sorry. You must have been very young.'

'Yes, I was two.'

'My mother was born in a small town in the Andes called Esquel. Welsh and Spanish are both spoken. There are other places in Argentina where

Welsh is spoken.'

'Yes, I know, in Patagonia. Welsh sheep farmers settled there in the eighteen sixties, if I remember my history,' I replied, surprising myself with my ability to recall facts, from some far off, almost forgotten, history lesson.

'Your parents, they were killed in the bombing, yes?' He seemed genuinely sorry.

'My mother was killed in an air raid but my father was lost at sea before I was born.'

'War is a very bad thing,' remarked Ramon, with an air of resignation. 'I do not think I shall see my family again.' His voice tailed away to nothing.

'You should not think like that. You must be positive.' I said, trying to be encouraging as I warmed to my captive. He had a look of distant resignation on his face as he lapsed into silence, retreating deep within himself. His face was the colour of putty and his breathing laboured as he drifted into a trancelike state, hovering between sleep and consciousness.

'My prayer book?' he murmured, 'por favor.'

I turned away to reach for his effects and picked out his prize, but too late. He had lapsed into unconsciousness. He did not look good, but truth to tell we were all living on borrowed time. It was just a question of when. Some of us might die in bed at a ripe old age, but chances were that some of us would not see our homes again. It was a sobering thought. I slipped the prayer book into my pocket.

16
A Cruel Twist of Fate
East Falkland, Thursday 20th – Fri. 21st May 1982

During the night the Argentineans pulled out what was left of their force by road. Yorkie and I discussed what we should do, now that our primary task was complete. and He went across to Jock to seek clarification. He returned unamused, having got no change out of our patrol leader, who had bollocked him for leaving his position.

'Bastard won't say anything. Thinks he's God. It's clear they don't need us and they sure as hell don't want us.'

'They don't know what to do with us either. We've been dumped on them. They don't think we're up to the job.'

'We could piss all over 'em,' said Yorkie.

'Too right, pal' I agreed, in awe of his self confidence.

I might have been exaggerating, just a tad. We two were a tight team forged in training hard together for ten years: An average of almost three days a week, including courses. Their advantage was that they could in theory train seven days a week. In practice this was unlikely and three of them were under thirty, two probably no more than twenty-two at most. This would give them an average of perhaps seven years military service each and no more than three years in the Regiment. Like us, they might have no experience of combat, except for Jock, of course. Jock was different. You only had to look at those world-weary eyes to know that he had been, seen and done it all. His T shirt collection would be something to behold.

'Well,' I said, 'we are well and truly redundant at the moment and my Spanish is not doing our cause any good here. Watch the prisoner. I won't be long.' I picked up my rifle and slipped out of the Basha, making my way to Jock's, cursing for not going myself, in the first place. Taking extreme care not to leave traces of my passing I picked my way across the rocks. He was not amused at my appearance.

'Are you trying to get us all killed?' he hissed at me. 'You will have the whole Argie Army down on us.'

'They have their hands full at the moment and we are going to have a problem with the prisoner.'

'He's not going to make it?'

'I doubt it'

'Tough shit!' Jock's remark was no surprise 'Anything else?' Jock demanded.

'Re-tasking; our job here is finished.' I replied, still annoyed by the man's lack of compassion for our prisoner.

'The request has already been sent. When I get any news you will be told. Until then, keep out of sight.'

I made a tactical withdrawal to give Yorkie the good news.

The rest of the day was very much routine, sleeping, eating, scanning the ground for trouble and cleaning weapons.

Friday dawned with driving sleet and a further drop in temperature. The lack of hot food was making it difficult to maintain body heat, in spite of the many layers of clothes, woolly hat, etc. Ramon did not look good and was delirious for most of the time. If he did not get medical attention and hot food soon it was going to be too late. The morning passed in the usual routine of two hour stags. The hardest thing of all was the cold, which cut through to the bone. I was shivering almost the whole time and in spite of my covering him with all the spare clothing I could find, I could not keep Ramon warm. His condition continued to deteriorate. Despite all my training and experience I gave him my sleeping bag. Humanity is a strong emotion, with a long pedigree. Around noon he stirred slightly and spoke lucidly for the first time in ages.

'Por favour, amigo. I am not going home, I will not see my family again.'

'Of course you will.' My voice carried no conviction.

'You are a good man but a bad liar. We both know I shall to die soon. I ask a favour, as one soldier to another.'

'Of course.' I replied, guessing what was coming.

'Will you write to my mother and tell her that I love her and that I did my duty?'

'You have my word it will be done.'

'Gracias, amigo'

'Forget it, pal' I replied, looking at his exhausted form huddled in my sleeping bag.

I wrote the address down in my notebook and after satisfying Ramon that I had taken it down correctly, I stowed it in the breast pocket of my windproof smock underneath my duvet coat. We huddled together against the cold and after a few minutes he was asleep. I had developed a bond with my captive, the kind you only find between men who share hardship in close proximity.

I didn't want him to die, he was my country's enemy not mine. I had no personal grudge against him, I wished him well and a safe return to the bosom of his family, all I wished for myself. I watched him slip away into sleep.

17
Ex-filtration
East Falkland, Friday 21st May 1982

Some time after dark, Spanner appeared at my Basha.
I derived immense pleasure from being ready for him,
despite his stealthy approach. Instinct alone warned
me of his coming; I had become tuned in to my
surroundings and sensed changes as they occurred.
He crawled to the entrance. I could feel the hostility
as the air seemed to crackle with tension. To say that
we did not get on would be a colossal
understatement.

'Exfil. one hour, TA' he sneered. 'Be ready to move in
forty-five minutes.' He made no attempt to conceal
the hostility in his voice.

'What about the prisoner?'

'Fuck the prisoner! That's an order, you TA tosser!'
He spat back at me.

'He's too sick to be moved and I am not leaving him'
I replied, anger welling up inside me. Spanner looked
as if he had been smacked in the face with a shovel.

'You will do as you are told' he hissed. 'The Argie's
dying anyway.'

'Not alone, he isn't' I replied, rage clawing it's way up
from my breast. 'Now fuck off!' I hissed.

His hand shot through the entrance and gripped my collar, twisting it, forcing his gloved knuckles into my throat. Expecting some such response, I was not caught off guard and counter attacked by smashing my binoculars onto the bridge of his nose. His grip slackened as my rage boiled over. I struck him again with all the force I could muster in the confined space. Before he could recover from his surprise at being struck by a 'TA Tosser,' I pulled the binocular strap over his head and yanked hard. I tightened the ligature around his throat, putting every ounce of my anger into the effort. My forearms were on fire with adrenalin and the red mist curtains drew across my eyes. Time stood still as I hung on to the cord pulling it ever tighter.

A voice was calling from far away. 'Stop! Stop or you will kill him.' It was Ramon.

I noticed the now limp form in my grip and came to my senses. At the same time as I released the cord, Jock and Wheels appeared and went to Spanner's aid. The colour came back to his cheeks and he slowly came round, coughing for air.

'What the fuck are you playing at?' demanded Jock.

'I don't like being called a TA Tosser.' I replied.

'The enemy is the Argentine army. If you try anything like this again I will cut your bollocks off, is that clear? That applies to both of you.

'I am not leaving the prisoner' I said defiantly.

Jock's blue eyes bore into mine. 'You'll do as ordered.' He said emphatically, 'There's a chopper on the way to pick us up – all of us. Be ready to move in thirty minutes.' With that the three of them dissolved into the night.

'Nice one,' said a voice in the darkness.

'Yorkie. How long have you been there?'

'Long enough. He had it coming, but I didn't expect you to do it. I thought that pleasure would be mine. You must have been really pissed off to kick off like that.'

'The twat's been on our backs from the start, he just wound me up a notch too far' I replied. 'I must get Ramon ready to move.'

The moon was up and the weather had improved significantly by the time the chopper was due. Ramon had rallied a little at the prospect of being evacuated to a hospital ship and his morale climbed higher than it had been for a quite a while. It took all of twenty minutes to dismantle the Basha, pack our kit and sanitise the area. All our rubbish was double bagged and would go with us. The LZ was only eight hundred metres away at the foot of the reverse slope away from the gravel road. Yorkie took my bergan and hoisted it on top of his with a little help from me and I knelt down so that Jock and Wheels could get Ramon on my back. This achieved, Jock led the way, ahead of Wheels, with Yorkie and me in the middle followed by Spanner. Sixpack brought up the rear as tail end Charlie. I was sweating from the exertion despite the intense cold, but the night was light enough to make the going reasonably easy. We made the LZ without any problems. I laid Ramon down on my carrymat with my bergan for a pillow, while the others went into all round defence. I did what I could to make my prisoner as comfortable as conditions would allow and settled down to wait for the helicopter. My eyes and ears strained in the gloom for any sign of our ticket out of this freezing, windswept, wasteland.

The pick up time came and went, with no sign of our salvation. For four hours we suffered in miserable silence, lying on the perishing damp ground with no protection from the elements. Just as I had about given up hope, the sound of rotor blades beating air reached my frozen ears, faint at first but getting steadily louder, heralding the approach of our saviour. The menacing black shape of the Wessex loomed out of the darkness and a red light was briefly flashed by one of our patrol as it flared for landing. I was never so pleased to see an aircraft in my life. It took three of us to get the unconscious Ramon into the cabin, which, by the time we had all climbed aboard, was filled to overflowing with tired men and equipment. The engine noise was tremendous and the icy wind whipped through the open door as we clattered across the landscape at low altitude into the inky black night, towards hot food and a steaming hot brew. After five minutes flying time, the engine noise got louder. It began to pop and bang as it misfired. I glanced at Yorkie who simply mouthed 'Oh shit' I could not hear him of course, for the noise, but you didn't need to be a lip reader to understand. Bracing himself against the bulkhead the Winchman gave us 'thumbs down' indicating that we were going down. We hung on to anything we could and prayed. Our descent became increasingly rapid, the engine continuing to emit bang after loud bang. I began to pray out loud and hung on to Ramon with one arm while clutching the airframe with the other. Funny, I thought to myself, here I am praying to a God I was cursing only hours ago. It was as this thought crossed my mind that we hit the ground. The landing was hard but we were upright and, as far as I could tell, I was unhurt. Seconds later, Jock spoke briefly to the Winchman, ordered me to stay put and then jumped out, followed closely by the rest of his patrol. Ramon was still unconscious but appeared to be breathing okay. It was then that I noticed the silence. The engine had stopped and although the rotors were still turning, the relative silence was an eerie contrast to previous few minutes.

'You okay Tony?' Yorkie asked.

'I'm fine. But he's not so good,' I said nodding towards Ramon.

'I think you two should get married,' he said, looking at the prone form cradled in my arms.

The crew disembarked and began removing the engine access covers to investigate the trouble.

After what seemed a lifetime sitting on the cold metal floor of the cabin, the crew climbed aboard and Jock appeared at the door. 'Sorry, lads. You'll have to get off.'

'What's the score?' Yorkie asked.

'They think they can get off again but with limited power so they can only take the Argie. We're waiting for the next one.'

My morale dropped like it was jumping from a balloon onto a waterlogged DZ. I turned to Ramon's pathetic unconscious form for a brief moment and then jumped to the ground with Yorkie hard on my heels. We joined the patrol. They had moved off a few yards and were poring over the map, lit by the glow of a red filtered torch.

'Where are we then?' I asked, not the least surprised by the lack of response to my request. After a few moments, Jock responded by indicating the position which turned out to be the middle of nowhere on low ground to the north of Mount Simon in the centre of East Falkland. The silence was shattered as the Wessex fired up and the rotors began to turn. Sounding like a bag of spanners in a spin dryer, the aircraft lurched uncertainly into the air and in a moment was clanking erratically, away into the cold black night. There was a lot of cold black night – sixteen hours out of every twenty-four. It gave us the illusion of a safety blanket, despite the uncomfortable truth that the enemy were well equipped with night vision aids that would show us up as if it were daylight. We had no idea how long it would take to get another helicopter out to us and no choice but to stay where we were, in the middle of nowhere. Wheels set up the radio and tried to raise base while the rest of us remained in all round defence. He fiddled with the dials and cursed under his breath.

The problem was, there wasn't anything we could hoist the aerials up. No trees cliffs or masts, and that made reception and transmission very hit-and-miss. He appeared to be an experienced operator in spite of his youth, but what he needed was luck. A lot of luck.

I glanced at my watch. It was just past midnight and still no comms. Wheels continued tapping the Morse key. I guessed it was more in hope than expectation.

18

Contact
East Falkland, a.m. Saturday 22nd May 1982

After thirty minutes, Jock decreed that three of us could get our heads down, myself included. Yorkie joined Jock on watch, while Wheels tried in vain to get a response from the radio. After two hours fitful sleep cocooned in my 'green maggit,' I crawled out of my bag and let Yorkie into it. No sense in getting his out when mine was all warmed up. The cold numbed my face as I grudgingly dragged my aching limbs from my bag to lay in the rough grass.

Scanning the moonlit landscape down the barrel of my M16 I dreamed of bacon, eggs and hot tea. The night was cold and clear with the ever-present biting wind, but visibility was good. I rummaged in my pockets and managed to find a boiled sweet. It took some time to extricate it from the sticky mess gluing it to the waxed paper wrapper, which I folded tightly before putting into my pocket. The freshness of lime was a joy to my taste buds, a pleasant respite from the dry metallic taste that haunted my palate.

About twenty minutes into my stag, I was startled by

a row of orange lights twinkling at the edge of the darkness to the accompaniment of a crackling sound like burning tinder. Simultaneously, the ground some five metres to my front erupted in sudden fountains of peat. At first, my brain did not register what was happening. It was outside it's realm of experience. Seconds later the whip crack of bullets passing over head brought enlightenment. My heart jumped, kick started by adrenaline as my brain processed the information.

My senses relayed a sharp report blasting my ear. It was not until several more blasts that I realised it was the sound of my own weapon. The training really did work; I was on autopilot returning fire with no recollection of releasing the safety catch. The noise level increased dramatically as the others opened up a fierce fusillade. A hand grabbed my shoulder. I turned. Yorkie's face seemed to glow at me in the dark. He thrust my bergan at me, the sleeping bag still hanging out where it had been hastily stuffed in. He jerked his head towards the rear. I nodded, grabbed my kit and took off, dragging it behind me for thirty yards or so before stopping and turning to give covering fire. Two of the others had dropped back at the same time and we three now began firing at the muzzle flashes to cover the withdrawal of the rest of the patrol. Moments later Yorkie and the others passed through our position and did the same for us. The enemy fire grew ragged and slackened off, allowing us to successfully disengage.

We regrouped three hundred metres from the original contact and after establishing that there were no casualties, we took off at speed, Wheels in the lead, with Sixpack hot on his heels, Yorkie, Jock and me in the middle and Spanner as tail end Charlie. When we finally stopped and took up all round defence in a shallow depression, I had time to reflect on the action. It was not at all like I had expected it to be. I had not had time to be scared; the training had just taken over. Now I was scared, conscious of the narrow escape and acutely aware of my own mortality. My heart was pounding, my mouth was dry and in spite of the cold I was sweating profusely. The firefight had lasted no more than a few minutes and we were unhurt, but the accuracy of the enemy fire had a sobering effect on me.

'Can't understand why I didn't spot them,' I said apologetically.

'Night sights,' said Jock. 'No sweat, no casualties' and almost as an after thought he added, 'You did okay.'

Praise indeed I thought.

'You are a lucky bastard having me to look after you,' said Yorkie.

'About time you earned your keep you tosser.' I beamed back at him. I had survived my first fire-fight and I was in a state of high excitement.

'Okay listen in!' Jock's authoritative voice broke in. 'We need to move ASAP.'

He opened his map and we gathered around under a poncho, as he shone a red lens torch on our position, shielding it with his black gloved hand. We tab one K east, then one K north and a final leg west, to the high ground here on the lower slopes of Ball Mountain. That should confuse them. He indicated the position with the point of a butterfly knife.

'Questions?'

'What about the mountains? I asked. The Argies are sure to have OPs (observation posts) up there.'

'Aye, but they will be able to see us wherever we go and if we stick close to the base and use the ground we stand a good chance at night.'

Yorkie and I exchanged brief glances.

'Then what?' My companion asked.

'We call Navy and order a taxi. Saddle up.'

We set off at a cracking pace, with Yorkie and I in the middle, cracking on, pausing only to check the compass whenever we changed course. We eventually reached the lower slopes of Ball Mountain where we found cover in a rocky outcrop on a small knoll. With good defensive potential and an escape route up the mountain if we were attacked from the front or flanks, it was as good as we were going to get. Any threat from the mountain and we would have to take our chances across the open ground or stay and fight. Spanner began to unreel the aerials over the rocks, while Wheels set up the radio, tuning the dials as it crackled and hissed with static. We were in a saucer shaped depression around fifteen metres across, edged with sharp-featured rocks, offering good cover from view and small arms fire. The position gave good views down the slopes to three sides and up along the ridge towards what we had to assume was enemy-occupied ground above. Hardly ideal, but we were stuck with it for now. Movement had to be kept to an absolute minimum.

We hastily erected our personal camouflage nets

and tried to make ourselves as invisible as possible. Yorkie and I shared a gully between two crags about four feet apart and some three feet high, providing a good field of fire down the slope to the South and southeast. Jock covered the danger zone north along the ridge to the summit while Spanner took the West and southwest, leaving Sixpack the eastern slope. Yorkie looked across from his position and called softly 'Tony, here, catch!' He threw me a small parcel not much bigger than a cigarette packet. I flashed a puzzled look at him and he mimed opening it, which I did. It was a cig packet wrapped in a small manila envelope, but it was too heavy for cigarettes. Inside the packet was a brand new Zippo lighter engraved with one word. 'Brother.' Yorkie mouthed 'Happy Birthday' while grinning from ear to ear. May 22nd, my forty-second birthday. I was choked. He remembered, even with all the stuff going on around us these last weeks. 'Brother' it said on the stainless steel, 'Brother.' Bless him, it was touching. I mimed raising a glass as if to say 'cheers' and he responded similarly.

Wheels was fully occupied with the radio but had not managed to raise anyone. At eleven twenty a Chinook flew a northerly course across the open ground to the East, too far away to identify as either friend or foe. This was the only event of note until the Argentine army showed up around noon.

19
The Grim Reaper
East Falkland, p.m. Saturday 22nd May 1982

I was floating on a Lilo in sunny Tenerife with the boys trying to capsize me into the hotel pool, when urgent tugging on the fishing line jerked me back to reality. Pulling the zip down I forced my stiff upper body out of the sleeping bag, pulling my rifle with me. I peered through the cam net towards Yorkie's position. He gave me one of his serious looks from beneath the edge of his cam net and pointed down the slope to the South. I eased myself into a position where I could see down the hill, taking care not to do anything to give our position away. About two kilometres away, a Puma was hovering just above the ground, its rotors whipping up snow from the patches among the grass and rocks. It settled onto the ground as I watched, figures tumbling out of the side to disappear into the landscape.

I eased myself into a firing position, removed the magazine from my M16, and tested the spring action with my thumb. Satisfied that the weapon was ready to fire, I replaced the magazine, applied the safety catch and laid it beside me. Reaching into my webbing, I took out all my magazines except one, placing them on the rock beside me. The Puma was fast disappearing towards the horizon. Using my binoculars, I scanned the area where the helicopter had discharged its human cargo and soon picked up the shapes of several infantry in line abreast, advancing steadily towards our position. I counted at twenty-four: odds of four to one against. No problem. We were in a good defensive position, holding the high ground with clear fields of fire.

'Bloody amateurs,' I thought. 'If they try a frontal assault uphill without artillery support, we'll murder them. Why in God's name didn't they land on the mountain and attack us from above?'

That is when it occurred to me that maybe they had done exactly that and that the troops below could be merely a diversion. Not a happy thought to conjure with. I prayed they would not find us. A forlorn hope for it was obvious that they knew where we were. It stood to reason that they would have at least an OP on the mountain above us. Still I clutched at straws, my stomach knotting itself tightly as my bladder nagged at me to empty it. I watched transfixed as the line of soldiers moved inexorably closer to confrontation. When they were still six hundred metres away the troops stopped and took what little cover they could find in the bleak windswept landscape. 'Strange,' I thought. 'We had no weapons which could present a serious threat beyond four hundred metres. But then they wouldn't know that would they? Perhaps they were just taking a breather or maybe taking orders for the assault which must surely come.'

I lowered the binos and turned towards Yorkie's position, somehow managing a weak grin.

He grinned back and winked at me. It helped; not a lot, but it helped. I looked around the LUP but apart from Yorkie, I could only see part of Jock's cam net stretched between rocks some ten metres directly behind us. I glanced back at Yorkie and nodded in the direction of our leader's lair. He shrugged his shoulders, made a gesture like squeezing a trigger and turned his attention back towards the enemy. We had no way of knowing if he heard the aircraft from his position and no way of communicating without risking giving our position away. Yorkie was right. He would know when the shooting started.

Well, this is it then, I thought, turning my attention again towards the enemy. 'This is what I came for, the grand adventure. I'll soon see if the training is as good as I believe, if I can do the job and justify all the tax payers' money that's been invested in me.'

Thinking of Carol, I remembered that last kiss on the station platform. My sons wrestling with me on the back lawn while the smell of Sunday roast wafted out from the open kitchen door. A lump came up in my throat and I struggled to swallow. My mouth was dry and in spite of the cold, my palms were sweating again inside my thermal gloves. Through the binos I observed that the Argentineans had made no attempt to move forward. I was surprised to find that this irritated me. The waiting was playing on my nerves. I wanted activity, something to occupy me and bury the fear rising inside me.

When it did come, my fear turned first to dread and then to resignation. I felt a sense of foreboding that started with a small speck just above the horizon.

Another Puma? More troops? A plume of purple signal smoke rose from the Argentine positions as I watched the speck grow in size. My stomach churned as the frightening reality dawned and the speck assumed the mantle of death, the grim reaper. I had always been a mad keen lover of military aircraft since I was a kid. I'd filled my bedroom with Airfix kits and read every reference book I could lay my hands on, soaking up statistics like a sponge. If there was ever a time I wished I knew nothing about aeroplanes, that time was now. It was the weapon I dreaded most, the Pucara; an aircraft specifically designed to annihilate ground targets. It had two twenty millimetre cannons, each loaded with 270 rounds. One single shell could literally blow a man's head off. Four machine-guns each with 900 rounds. Add six bombs and seventy-six rockets and you have the complete bowel opening experience. Four thousand two hundred and twenty-two individual pieces of ordnance; 4,222 separate lottery chances to win a place in heaven or hell.

I watched mesmerised, like a Cobra under the spell of the snake charmer. We were six mortal souls all together in our LUP, Yorkie being just spitting distance away and yet I had never felt so totally alone. So frightened. It was no longer death I feared, for I now accepted that as a certainty. It was the manner of my death. I was terrified of the pain that I felt sure would accompany it. I prayed to God to be merciful and make it swift.

Tearing my eyes from the hypnotic Pucara, I clawed my way into the earth, screwed myself into the smallest ball humanly possible, held my breath and prayed. There was a sudden roar of aircraft engines and then nothing. No explosion, no bullets no screams of pain, just silence.

The aircraft roared overhead, banking to the right, then swung away to the North in a long, lazy arc to line up for the attack run. He approached from the Northwest and began a shallow dive. The aircraft slowed suddenly as the ripple of rockets left the tubes and smoked their way towards us. I hugged the ground. Multiple explosions shook the slopes around me as the ordnance detonated in a welter of orange and grey smoke. He was over us and away.

The air around me evaporated and the ground shook with an earthquake of unimaginable violence. My ears felt as if they would burst their drums. My whole body was lifted from the earth and then slammed back into it, driving what little breath I had from my screaming lungs. I clawed the ground and sobbed uncontrollably, promising my maker everything if he would just let me live. The terrifying violence was replaced by a calm spooky silence, a short-lived respite, the eye of the storm. I curled into a ball again and willed myself to become as tiny a target as possible. In a useless gesture I pulled my woolly hat down over my ears and eyes, before covering my head with the hood of my smock, like a child woken from a nightmare pulling the bedclothes over his frightened face.

The aircraft dived again. Cannon shells began exploding across the LUP, sending shards of razor-sharp rock and red-hot shrapnel whining into every corner of our refuge. Shaking uncontrollably and babbling like a lunatic, I prayed for the terror to end. I had never felt so exposed and vulnerable in all my life. I dared not look up to see if we had taken casualties. Listening was futile. All I could hear was a loud ringing in both ears. There was a metallic, bitter-tasting acrid smoke stinging my eyes. My mouth was full of scorched soil. My back hurt.

Suddenly it started again. Chaos and mayhem! Flying splinters of rock and steel, copper-jacketed lead and high explosive sucking the life out of the atmosphere in a frightening cacophony of noise and earth tremors. Just as suddenly, God hit the mute button and the uncanny silence returned. Huddled in my hiding place I waited in terrified anticipation for the next attack. It never came; it was over. I was alive!

I began to take in my surroundings and assess my condition. Apart from the pain in my back and some minor splinter wounds, I appeared to be okay. My groin felt warm and wet and for a fleeting moment I thought I had been hit, but no, my bladder had eased its discomfort sometime during the attack. I raised my head and looked across to Yorkie's position. At first nothing seemed to register and then slowly I made out the shape of a leg tucked tightly into the crevice in the rock. It began to move and close to it a face appeared, grinning stupidly from ear to ear. The grin articulated and the mouth began moving rapidly, though no sound came out. I had been deafened by the bombardment. Blood was oozing from a gash on his cheek, but he seemed otherwise okay. Crawling to meet each other we hugged like a pair of schoolgirls. Yorkie's expression changed. He stopped grinning. He was staring into space over my left shoulder. I turned around to follow his gaze. The only rocket to land inside the LUP had scored a direct hit on Jock's position. A blackened smoking crater was all that was left. Charred, blasted rocks, smoking fragments of steel and uprooted sods of turf littered the ground. I noticed a boot lying on the edge of the crater. It was trailing blue smoke with the remains of a leg sticking out of it, shattered white bone clearly visible.

From somewhere to the left came a series of loud profanities. The earth moved and shaking off his shroud of turf and soil, Wheels struggled to his knees before pitching forward onto his face.

Spanner rushed across and turned him onto his back

'Wheels, speak to me. Come on, mate. Come on.'

The still figure flinched, blinked and his lips moved.

'Some bastard's going to pay for this,' said Spanner.

'Wheels, you twat! You okay?'

His eyes didn't register. He put his hands to his ears.

'Can't hear. Can't hear anything. Can't hear myself.'

'You hit anywhere?'

Wheels shook his head and struggled to sit up.

'My rifle. Where's my rifle?'

'Here' It was Yorkie. It's working. I checked.'

It was at that moment they noticed the crater. There was silence for several seconds until Yorkie shouted.

'Over there.'

Sixpack was lying on his back, motionless. There was a lot of blood around his groin and what was left of his face was the colour of old putty. He was not dead, but he soon would be.

'Watch the door!' Spanner barked, kneeling beside his friend. In the elation of discovering we were still alive, we had forgotten our predicament. I raced back up to my position, hot on Yorkie's heels.

20
Firefight
East Falkland, p.m. Saturday 22nd May 1982

Crawling to my position I eased myself slowly forward until I could see down the slope. There was no sign of the enemy. I glanced across at Yorkie. He shrugged his shoulders. Turning again to the slope I began scanning the ground through my binos, starting at a point on the left of my arc of fire and six hundred metres out. Working from left to right, I slowly swept the ground until I reached the limit of my arc, at which point I reversed the process sweeping back over the same ground much quicker until I reached the start. I then dropped my gaze to a point where I could repeat the process overlapping the first run. This method not only ensures that all the ground is covered twice, but sweeping back swiftly helps to pick up any small change from the first sweep that might indicate a target. Yorkie would be doing the same, but starting close to our position and working towards the enemy. He always worked outwards and I inwards. After twenty minutes, I was having serious doubts about my skills when on a backward sweep I picked up a slight change in the terrain and upon closer inspection satisfied myself that someone was moving very slowly in my direction. Whoever they were, they were damn good and extremely well camouflaged. What surprised me was how close he had managed to get.

They had moved up under the cover of the air attack and were now less than three hundred metres away. I reached into my webbing and retrieved the magazine I had left there, checking that it had the strip of red insulation tape around it, indicating it had thirty rounds of tracer ammunition. I removed the magazine from my rifle and working the bolt to eject the live round from the chamber, I put on the fresh one, and took aim at the clump of grass that was still moving almost imperceptibly towards me. I adjusted my sights to two hundred and fifty metres and nodded to Yorkie. I held two fingers of my right hand then five fingers spread, then finger and thumb joined to form a circle. Yorkie nodded and looked out to two hundred and fifty metres. Slowly and deliberately I squeezed the trigger once; twice. Two glowing red tracer rounds rocketed into the turf where the movement had been. A few seconds later there was a loud report as Yorkie's SLR spoke once. Before I could observe any results, a machine gun opened fire from somewhere to the left of my target, the rounds striking the slope just below and left of my position.

These boys were good. They were no conscripts but experienced regular infantry at the least, possibly even Special Forces. Things had definitely taken a turn for the worse. Outnumbered six to one. Two men killed: one-third of our strength. With Jock we had lost the grenade launcher, leaving us with just four rifles to defend our position against a well-trained enemy. They had at least one, maybe two machine guns and as we were painfully aware they also had air support. On the plus side, we still had the radio. Wheels had been patiently trying to raise someone on the net after re-rigging the aerials, but with no success. There was just a chance we might be able to slip away after dark, if we could hold out until then. The machine gun stopped and all was silent again.

I risked a look through the binos but could see no sign of movement. Then in the distance a dot appeared just above the horizon. In less than a minute it revealed itself to be a Huey helicopter which swept in low and landed some two hundred metres beyond the enemy, behind a low rocky outcrop. It remained on the ground for some minutes, its rotor blades clearly visible above the rocks. I had a bad feeling about this and looked to Yorkie for comfort.

'Mortar team,' he said.

'I was afraid it might be,' I replied, my stomach churning. If we were right then we were in deep shit. We could not engage the enemy as we could not see them, they could bombard us at will and with little or no overhead cover we could not escape serious casualties. If, as we suspected the Argies had an OP on the mountain above us and they were in radio contact with our friends down the slope, they could direct the mortar bombs right on to us.

Sporadic firing broke out to our left. Fortunately this was ineffective but as no target presented itself we did not reply, ammunition conservation being a priority.

'Spanner, we're going to start taking mortar fire any minute. We should move now.' Said Yorkie.

'I'll decide when we move. Watch your ...' He was cut off in mid sentence by the sound of an exploding mortar bomb impacting the slope about fifty metres in front of Yorkie's' position. Our worst fears had been confirmed. I began frantically trying to dig into the ground with my Boot knife, a hopeless task — solid rock being just below the surface. Three more rounds landed within a couple of minutes, the last one close enough to shower my position with debris. I hugged the ground and prayed for life as hard as I knew how. There was a lull for some five minutes or so, then another four rounds exploded. They seemed to land all around us. There was no warning, we could not hear them coming, which played havoc with my nerves. During the bombardment I shook with fear and foreboding, all the while praying and offering to sell my soul for earthly salvation. I just wanted to get home to my family. My mind was flooded with images of my children as babies and toddlers and adolescents with Carol's face swimming between them. This was not how I had thought of war. I had been trained by the best to be the best, to take the fight to the enemy and all I could do was curl up like a hedgehog on the M1 and wait to be splattered. I felt so helpless; nothing in my training had prepared me for what was happening.

Between salvoes we called out to one another for reassurance. Miraculously some twenty odd rounds fell without inflicting serious casualties. The nearest landed in the centre of the saucer, which was very soft ground. The bombs penetrated deep into the peat before exploding, the ground, absorbing the force of the explosion. The next round landed on a boulder behind spraying my legs and buttocks with flying splinters. I felt the impact but mercifully no pain. Seconds later another explosion shook the ground beneath me. The lights went out. I came round to the sound of small arms fire crackling around me and the by-now-familiar ringing in my ears. My face and neck were wet with what, on further examination, turned out to be blood and my left leg was painful, though it was bearable.

'Tony! Tony! You okay?' I heard from somewhere far off just before the lights went out again. The next thing I recall is Yorkie leaning over me with tears in his eyes, shouting at me.

'You're okay! You're okay! Just flesh wounds. You're okay! Can you move your legs?'

'I think so but my face hurts. I'm bleeding' I began to get alarmed. 'It's nothing. It just nicked your ear. You're fine, honest!'

'You sure?'

'Positive'

'Is it over? The mortars?'

'For now. Come on We've got to move! The Argies are almost on top of us. Come on!'

I automatically reached for my bergan.

Yorkie grabbed the rucksac and dragged me out of the position. Crouching low, we jogged across to the far side of the saucer, where Wheels was stuffing the radio into his Bergan. He worked frantically to make ready for flight. Spanner was kneeling next to him covering us. Yorkie turned to face the way we had come and as he did so Spanner's M16 burst into life, quickly followed by the louder bark of Yorkie's SLR From the corner of my eye I glimpsed two figures on the far rim of the hollow with weapons raised. In less time than it takes to draw breath they, were catapulted backwards in a hail bullets. Wheels slapped my shoulder.

'Move!' he yelled, rising to his feet and sprinting towards the rim of the saucer five metres away. He dived over it with me right behind. Before I had even landed, he was giving covering fire to the others, and by the time I had joined in they had reached us. Breathing heavily, I fired a few rounds at the rocks around the rim in the hope of discouraging pursuit.

'Anybody hit?' Spanner demanded, his voice charged with adrenalin.

'Just splinters' I said.

Wheels failed to answer, but he looked okay.

At that moment a burst of automatic fire from the rim sent rounds zipping over our heads. I clocked a brief movement in the rocks to my right and instinctively swung my M16 onto it, squeezing off two rounds. To my utter amazement both rounds hit the target. The Argie was no more than ten metres away and I clearly saw my bullets strike his face, knocking him over backwards behind the rocks, like a fairground coconut. For the next few minutes pandemonium reigned as we became embroiled in a fierce exchange of gunfire. At one point we were in danger of being outflanked on the left until Spanner drove the threat away with phosphorous grenades. The enemy withdrew, leaving at least five killed or seriously wounded, one of whom screamed continuously throughout the firefight.

'Ammo check!' Spanner called during the lull. His voice was excited but had a grim edge to it.

'Four mags,' was Wheels' reply.

'Five,' said Yorkie

I was relieved to find that Yorkie had picked up my mags and stuffed them in my pockets. A quick check revealed I had three full magazines and a further one hundred rounds in a bandolier, one hundred and ninety rounds in all.

'Listen in!' commanded Spanner. 'It'll be dark in half an hour. We'll bug out at last light, Tony lead scout; me, Wheels. Yorkie, you bring up the rear.'

'Tony,' 'Yorkie.' First name terms all of a sudden! The situation <u>must</u> be desperate. Truth was Wheels was still deaf and would be no use in the lead and as patrol commander Spanner needed to be in the middle to keep control. The frantic activity had died down enough for the cold to be felt again. Although there was little wind, it had begun to drizzle with rain.

My injuries were only superficial, just splinter wounds probably from rock fragments rather than shrapnel. There was very little blood on them, which was more than could be said for my face, the left side of which was caked in dried blood. My ear lobe was missing. Worst of all were the splinters in my backside, which made sitting or lying on my back very painful. Taking advantage of the lull to reload and take a drink from my water bottle, I speculated on our chances of survival. My optimism was fading. I was resigned to the fact that I was going to die. We started taking fire again. I hugged the cold ground and looked along a fissure in the rocks towards the enemy positions, just seventy metres away. I could see the occasional muzzle flash, but no clear target presented itself and the fire was too accurate to dare raising my head. Somewhere to my left one of us at least was returning fire when suddenly it all went ominously very quiet. The Argies had withdrawn, but why?

'Move now!' someone shouted. I rolled away from my position to see Wheels scurrying away and Yorkie yelling at me. I rose to my feet and legged it as fast as I could, up the slope, towards the next cover, some four hundred metres away. It was the longest four hundred metres of my life. My legs were leaden but my brain was in overdrive 'weave, damn it, weave, don't give them an easy target.' I don't know if I was saying it out loud, to myself, or just thinking it. I ran on, stumbling under the weight of my equipment, grimly hanging on to my sleeping bag and weapon, desperate to reach cover. Every lung bursting, heart pounding, stomach churning stride was like running in treacle. I strove with all my might, desperate to reach the next ridge and relative safety, expecting a bullet in the back any second.

The bullet never came and I tumbled over the ridge in an exhausted, excited heap. I made it! At that moment mortar rounds began exploding on our previous position. I lay on the ground, gasping for air unable to move, my lungs burning. Another mortar round burst some distance away as I became acutely aware of my own mortality. I was very scared. My hands were shaking and my whole body started to tremble. I was sure I was going to die. 'Crump!' Another mortar round landed, followed by two more in quick succession. I hugged the earth and prayed out loud. I hardly noticed the rain, which was now falling steadily. The darkness was creeping in. I quickly rolled up my sleeping bag and stuffed it into my bergan

'Smoke,' yelled Spanner. I reached for a grenade, pulled the pin and hurled it towards the Argies. Spanner's and mine cracked almost simultaneously. After a few seconds a thick white cloud cloaked us from the enemy. We ran up the slope, pursued this time by a ragged fusillade of ineffective small arms fire, which thankfully caused no injuries. Unless that is you include the bruises to my over-tightened ring-piece. Reaching another low ridge we got lucky. Just behind it was a gully, which was out of sight of our pursuers and hidden also from the summit by a rocky crag. It ran east around the side of the mountain, following a sheep track before dropping down into the gathering gloom. The mortars had stopped and only the odd angry small arms round zipped over our heads.

'Everybody okay?' Spanner asked.

'I'm okay.'

'Yes.'

'Fine.' Came back the replies.

'Listen up! We are going down the gully, I'll set up a couple of claymores to slow them down. Tony, you lead off, Wheels, me. Yorkie, bring up the rear. Okay lets do it!'

Spanner was setting the claymore mines as I turned to lead Wheels into the gully. I looked at Yorkie lying behind a rock; his SLR trained towards the enemy's last known position. Our eyes met briefly.

'Fuck off!' he said.

'Watch the claymores.'

'Fuck off!' he repeated.

I fucked off.

It was almost dark and climbing down through the narrow gully was far from easy. We were all knackered, wet through, chilled to the bone, nerves jangling. I thanked the Lord my injuries were slight and for all the training I had been through over my career. It was this that had seen me through. Above all I thanked him for the worsening weather which would neutralise the enemy's night vision aids to a degree, thus improving our chances of escape. It was almost dark. We had a chance.

For the first time in what seemed like ages, I allowed myself the luxury of believing I might live through this nightmare. This proved to be a mixed blessing, as with hope comes fear.

When you abandon yourself to your fate and place your trust in God, calmness comes over you. You accept death as inevitable and a kind of inner peace reigns. Your anxiety and fear dissolve. It's when you believe that you might beat the grim reaper that fear returns.

21
Escape
East Falkland
Dusk 22nd May - Noon 23rd May 1982

Picking my way through the rocks I stumbled down the hillside, my legs trembling. Whether with fear, exertion or both, I neither knew nor cared, I just wanted to get away from the danger as fast as I was able. The gully was narrow and I silently cursed as my bergan kept snagging on the rocks. As if that was not enough, pain from the splinter wounds in my legs came and went in waves. Fear-fuelled adrenalin kept me going. Every few metres I twisted my head around to check that Wheels was where he should be. This was a difficult manoeuvre, as the weight of the bergan forced me to walk hunched over and the steep slope combined with the confined space made it almost impossible to see upwards past the hump on my back. It was whilst attempting this contortion that Wheels ran into the back of me.

'Get moving!' he hissed through clenched teeth. I started to react, in what seemed to me slow motion.

I turned, took two steps and froze. An Argie appeared out of nowhere less than ten feet away. He looked as surprised and scared as I was. Time slowed down dramatically as I took in the details. He looked very young, eighteen at the most, his rifle pointing directly at my guts. My brain was racing but my body had shut down. It would not function.

We just stared at each other, neither knowing what to do. Slowly I began to react, I started to raise my M16 up to waist level. I just knew I was not going to make it in time.

His eyes narrowed as his grip on the weapon tightened, black gloved finger on the trigger, squeezing up the slack. Bang! Bang! Bang! I felt the blast of hot gases in my ear as the drum burst.

The head in front of me disintegrated like an exploding melon, as three rounds of high velocity copper jacketed lead, ripped and smashed their way through living flesh and bone.

'Move it!' said Spanner, his rifle barrel still smoking beside my ear. Stunned and shaken to the core, I stumbled on in a daze, without looking back. After a while the gully widened and the landscape opened up. The wind hit me with its icy blast as I emerged from the shelter of the rocks and I pulled my woolly hat down over my ringing ears. It did not prevent me from hearing the explosions behind me as the claymores went off.

That should discourage them, I thought, more in hope than belief. It was now fully dark with cloud obscuring the moon. Cradling my rifle in my arms, I ploughed on, head down, arse up following a rough bearing across the barren landscape as fast as my exhausted body could carry me. I did not consider the possibility of more enemy forces ahead of me I just wanted to put as much distance between me and the last contact. I felt more like a frightened rabbit than one of Britain's super soldiers. I just wanted to reach the warren and curl up in my burrow. After several minutes – ten or maybe twenty, I really had little idea, I stopped and turned to see if we were all together. Spanner was right behind me and without a word he too turned towards the rear. Wheels came striding heavily out of the darkness, moved past us without a word and took up watch on the route ahead. There was no sign of Yorkie.

Time stood still as we waited, staring into the cold black night, straining to hear any sound of his approach above the roar of the wind. We waited for what seemed an eternity when a swishing lumbering sound could be heard above the wind and before anyone had time to react, Yorkie's square frame shot out of the darkness and he was on top of us. Not a word said, we grinned at each other and turned to Spanner who led us off onto our original line of march. The elation at seeing my old mate safe again soon faded, as the grim task of battling through the freezing wind and rain became my main focus. We struggled to keep close contact, knowing our survival depended upon us staying together.

For three hours we plodded on, sometimes in darkness and sometimes in surreal, silver light, as the clouds cleared the face of the moon. The ground underfoot was rough grass, wet with the rain, punctuated by rocky outcrops. My face stung as the wind lashed it with icy fingers, making my eyes water so badly I had difficulty seeing. My morale began to steadily ebb away. I was so tired I just wanted to lay down and go to sleep, but I knew not to give in to temptation. At long last, Spanner called a halt. We gathered in a huddle around the map, to try to establish our position from time and distance travelled along the compass bearing. I was numb from the constant battering of the icy wind and virtually exhausted. The others looked no better. Unless we got some rest and shelter soon, we were going to be in serious danger from hypothermia.

We finally agreed that we had travelled about seven K since the contact and that we were now at a point where we should swing west towards beaches where our main landings would take place. I struggled to my feet, silently cursing as the bergan straps bit into my red raw shoulders, I removed the magazine from my M16, and exchanged it for a full one. For the next three hours we plodded across the sleet-swept landscape, stumbling on with heavy heart and leaden feet. Occasionally one of us would fall hard then curse and strain to regain his familiar head down arse up attitude. I began to argue with myself under my breath. *Just pack it in and get your bag out, you could just snuggle down and slide into the lovely warm haven of sleep. Bollocks, just keep going, just put one foot in front of the other, just like on Selection, you can do this. Selection! That was years ago, you can't keep this up like you could then. For Christ's sake you're forty-two not thirty-two Get a grip, pillock and stay focused Damn it I need sleep, I must sleep.* My mind began to wander and I started to imagine myself at home on the sofa in front of the fire with a steaming mug of tea. The boys and Carol kept swimming in and out of my consciousness, but no matter how hard I tried I could not see their faces clearly.

Suddenly I was brought back to the present as I collided with Wheels who had stopped and was staring ahead into the darkness. Yorkie appeared alongside my shoulder

'What's up?' He whispered in my ear.

I could only grunt in reply

'Tony? You okay? You look fucked'

'We're all fucked.' I croaked.

Spanner loomed at us out of the gloom.

'We going to lay up here and reassess the situation at first light. There is a bit of a depression in the peat up ahead, it's not much but it will have to do. Ninety-minute stags, I'll take first, Wheels, Yorkie then Tony last. Okay lets get to it.'

I could not believe my luck, I was going to get some sleep at last; more than four hours with a bit of luck.

Spanner was right. The depression did not offer much cover but I was past caring. It looked as good as a bedroom in a five star hotel to me. What I could see of it, that is, in the dark.

The rain had now mercifully eased. Yorkie and I stretched out a poncho on the bare peat and put our bergans against the bank which was just under a metre high and almost vertical on the windward side, dropping to less than half a metre on the leeward, about three metres away. We tied a second poncho to the bergans and pegged it to the ground, to form very small shelter, just long enough to squeeze us both into, but with enough room at the sides to accommodate our weapons and escape kit. We covered this with a cam net but it was more a token gesture than anything else. We were exposed and we knew it. There was no better cover to be found.

Somehow we got ourselves under cover and into our bags after first stripping off our wet clothes and changing into the one spare set of dry ones we each carried inside our kit. The wet clothes were put in bin liners to use as pillows. The hardest job was getting our boots off and getting dry socks and trainers on, but we finally managed it after many muffled curses. In the darkness we struggled into our bags in the cramped space and settled in to our LUP (lying up position). I was asleep almost before my head hit the bin liner.

I awoke from a bad dream in which rats were gnawing at my stomach and blinked through the gap between my feet and the poncho at the first glimmer of light beyond the horizon. I turned my head towards my comrade in arms and was gratified to see he was awake and watching over us. I was numb with cold and inactivity.

'Well, how's the Sleeping Beauty then?' Yorkie's humour was a tonic and it brought a smile to my cracked lips.

'Fancy a brew, mate?" he asked straight faced.

'If only' was my longing reply. Our days of cold rations had really begun to take their toll and as I lay back beside him I began to hallucinate. I could detect the distinct smell of burning Hexamine. It became so vivid that I began to sniff the air loudly.

'For Christ's sake blow your nose!' Yorkie hissed.

'I can smell hexi. I swear I can.'

'Well, how else am I going to make the coffee, muppet?' Yorkie replied in a tone you might use to a child.

'But...' Yorkie cut me off before I got going.

'Spanner gave us the go while you were asleep. You know, for a regular he is surprisingly on the ball. We wouldn't have lasted much longer without something hot inside us.'

It was the best coffee I had ever tasted and it saved my life. I put a brew on myself and filled the thermos. Even better it was followed by curry and rice which was passed around, missing out Spanner, who was deep in slumber, buried inside his bag. I tried to wake him but he lashed out with his fists beating me on my arms and spilling the precious scoff.

'Wake up you, noisy bastard!' It was Yorkie's voice, not mine. 'What was going on?'

'Wake up. They can hear you in Port Stanley.'

I stirred and rubbed my eyes, mumbling apologies as with a sinking heart I realised it had all been a dream; the brew, the curry, waking Spanner; all of it.

'You were really putting them away Tony. I thought I was never going to wake you' he hissed, regarding me with mock concern.

'I was in the middle of a lovely hot curry and a brew and you just buggered it up.'

'So sorry but it's your stag mate. Get this inside you.'

'Gee thanks pal,' I responded taking the oatmeal biscuit and processed cheese with my grimy black hand. I looked at my fingernails. I wondered if I would ever manage to remove the dirt of this far flung field from beneath them. It had invaded the intimate parts of my body, as efficiently as the Argentine Forces had invaded these once peaceful islands.

I used the last drop of water I had in my bottle to swallow the two Benzedrine tablets I had been issued. I hated taking medication but this was different. I knew my limits and I was reaching the end of my rope. I needed a chemical boost to keep me going and I knew the most effective time to take them was when you were well and truly fucked, which described my condition to a T.

'I'll get out and see what I can do to improve the camouflage before it gets light enough to be seen from any OP on the high ground.' I relayed my intention to Spanner, calling across the few metres to their Basha.

His reply was remarkably affable.

'Okay, it needs a bit of work, but be quick! You got around twenty minutes tops.'

He was right. This was a job which would require all my artistic skill and experience.

'Get on with it then,' Yorkie urged 'you're the artist, nature boy. I'll keep watch.'

'Here, you'll need these.' I tossed the binos to him as I eased myself out into the cold damp air and set about my task with an urgency born of the will to survive. I set to work stripping and relaying the cam net, weaving grass into the mesh, taking particular care to ensure that the blades all lay in the same direction as the prevailing wind. The time taken was worth it as the result was good enough to conceal all beneath from anyone further than twenty feet away.

Satisfied I could do no better, I lifted the camouflage at the side of my bergan and slid underneath, my feet finding their own way into the sleeping bag. Settling down beside Yorkie after carefully replacing the cam net, I peered through the verbiage at the world outside. It was a clear morning with the beginnings of a blue sky and no sign of rain or snow; in short the worst possible conditions for our situation. We could now only trust to luck and our camouflage skills. The wind eased while a watery sun rose to shine weakly through the early morning haze. I eased myself onto my elbows and reached for my binos to scan the area. We were seriously exposed in the middle of bare-arsed grass tufted 'moon country.' On the plus side there was no sign of the enemy, the weather had improved and with this, morale had lifted. Wheels called over to us.

'We are going to try to get comms back so we can arrange Heli to pick us up, so keep your fingers crossed.'

He was quite chummy. The attitude towards us had changed considerably since we first came under fire. I wondered if perhaps like us, this might have been Wheels and Spanner's first time under fire. They had almost certainly served in Northern Ireland, but might not have had more than an odd sniper take a pop.

The first couple of hours were spent resting and watching, Yorkie and I taking it in turns, half an hour at a time. This suited us better than the ninety minutes each we were allocated. It kept us more alert and by late morning we were both awake. The Benzedrine had kicked in and I was sharp as a razor and hyperactive. I broke the silence.

'I could murder a good fry-up'

'You and me both, mate. If we get out of this I will buy you the biggest fried breakfast in Yorkshire.'

'I'll hold you to that.'

'Don't worry we will get out okay, its not the first time we've been in bother. Remember the time we lost Johnny in the snow on Pen y Gent? We got out of that okay.'

'By the skin of our teeth.'

'Maybe, but we did it and the weather was a lot worse than we have seen this trip so far.'

'You're tempting providence you reckless bastard.'

He was right though, we had come through worse conditions in training. We had even evaded the *'enemy'* whilst doing it except that this time the enemy was real and using live ammunition.

I began to daydream, escaping from the reality of my current situation the only way available to me. My mind drifted back to the Yorkshire Dales and a dark, snow covered landscape lit only by the light of a crescent moon. I relived an episode from my peaceful training days. We had had a simple task to perform; that of retrieving a message from a 'dead letter box' at the side of a stile. The letterbox was a small cigarette tin, the stile was on the summit of Pen-y-Ghent. It was a freezing night with a sharp wind, which increased in intensity with altitude. We left Johnny on the lower slopes to watch our bergans and made the climb in belt order wearing issue windproof smocks over heavy-duty pullovers and woolen shirts.

We had no issue waterproofs, just civvy kagoules from Millets. They were far from perfect but the best we could afford at that time. We reached the summit about two a.m. to find the snow up to our waists. We abandoned the search for the letterbox after half an hour and decided to make our descent, struggling through waist deep snow to the trig point to note the number as evidence of our presence in case we were doubted at the debrief.

It began to snow and within five minutes we were in the middle of a blizzard. It was a complete white out and we very soon became disoriented. More by luck than by judgement, we found the dry stone wall and felt our way to the stile. We huddled together and debated whether to descend or wait for the weather to ease, quickly coming to the conclusion that we were not equipped to survive at altitude without our sleeping bags. Thus began our nightmare descent. Clambering over the stile we took it in turns to lead after first linking ourselves together with a length of Para cord attached to our belt kits. After twenty minutes or so, the snow was only up to our knees, but we had only travelled around two hundred and fifty metres. How we made it down that track I will never know. About half way down, the snow turned to sleet and then freezing rain, driven at high velocity into our right sides, which had the bizarre effect of making my left side feel warm. My face was numb and I was soaked to the skin. We were both suffering badly from the effects of exposure when we reached the pasture and had to resort to signalling with torches. The filthy weather however rendered this futile and we were beginning to get seriously worried for our health. We eventually got into Horton in Ribblesdale and sought shelter in the gents toilets in the car park where, wet and exhausted, we got our brew kit out of our escape belts and made tea on the floor of the urinals. It saved us but it was a close call. We linked up with Johnny around noon. He looked really worried.

'Christ, I thought we would going up to bring you down in body bags this morning. You scared the shit out of me.'

We walked up the track and into the field to retrieve our bergans and as I shouldered mine I looked up at the peak and felt very small. I had learned a valuable lesson in respect for the forces of nature.

A sound like tearing fabric brought the present screaming back into focus, as a fast jet rocketed past our position at a rate of knots. It was very low and gone before I had any chance to see it let alone identify it as friend or foe.

'Jeez that was low!' I exclaimed. 'Ours or theirs?'

'God knows,' Yorkie replied. 'How's the legs?'

'Not too bad thanks. Just a bit stiff. Those mortars were a bit hairy though. I was shitting myself.' As soon as the words left my mouth I realized that the fear was greatest after the event, here and now. Now that the adrenalin had drained away and we were no longer actively engaged in a frantic fight for survival, I had time to consider the possible consequences of the actions. My imagination brought on a sudden cold sweat and I began to shiver.

'Sure you're okay, Tony? You don't look so

good.'

'Fine, just cold' I lied without conviction. I was having difficulty seeing a way out of our predicament.

'Think they'll have any luck with the radio?' I asked by way of diverting attention from my thoughts.

'They'd better or we are in for a long tab and I don't know about you but my feet are hammered. We are running low on rations too. What I wouldn't give for that big fry-up and a hot shower.'

'I'll second that.'

'We did okay out there today Tony, we did okay.'

'Well enough, I suppose. The training really does take over when the shit hits the fan doesn't it?' It was more a statement of fact than a question. I was relieved that all the hard work over the last ten years or so had paid off. No amount of training, however, could have prepared anyone for the aftermath of the Pucara attack. I could not shut out the memory of the casualties we had taken. Graphic images of the smoking black remains of Jock's last position in the LUP kept swimming into my consciousness. I'd always been blessed with a vivid imagination. Blessed! Cursed would be a more appropriate word. I wondered if the Pilot of the Pucara was one of Ramon's squadron. I wondered where he was now, how he was.

Had he not been shot down, Ramon could easily have been the pilot that had wreaked havoc and death upon us. I was not sure how I would have reacted if he was still with us. The pilot just did his job, but the consequences had been awesome.

'What do you think our chances are mate?' I asked my solid, dependable friend.

'We've got food, water, ammo and the radio. What more do we need?'

I could have kicked myself for being so pessimistic. It was obvious from his tone that he was not going to allow me my negative attitude.

'We'll be back on the ship this time tomorrow, you'll see,' he continued, 'and we will be itching to get back out here and get on with this war.' I admired his optimism, even managing a wry smile as I reached into my bergan for my reserve water bottle. I opened the flask and before taking a swig offered it to Yorkie.

'It's brews that have kept the British Army going since it was formed you know' he mused between gulps. Brews, whores and bitchin' about the situation the squaddie finds his self in at the time.'

'Bitching I can manage, brews – we have the means but circumstances preclude us from making them. Shame about the whores.' I was lightening up in spite of my self.

'Good old Yorkie' I thought to myself. 'I can always rely on you when I need you.'

'That Puraka is a scary bit of kit, mind. I hope we don't meet any more of them!'

'Pucara' I corrected.

'What?'

'Pucara, it's a Pucara.'

'Pucara, Puraka, whatever you call it with your fancy University education, it's a really nasty bastard and if I never see another one it will be too soon.'

'That makes two of us pal.'

Yorkie wriggled onto his side, taking care not to disturb the netting and began to strip his SLR ready for cleaning. Taking my cue I got out my empty Magazines and began to fill them with bullets from the bandolier. This relatively easy task proved anything but in the cramped conditions with the cold biting at my fingers. Immediately Yorkie's rifle was reassembled, I stripped and cleaned mine. I then attached a full magazine but did not cock the weapon, leaving the chamber empty.

22
Lying Up
East Falkland, p.m. Sunday 23rd May 1982

There was little to do when not on stag, so we caught up on much needed sleep or simply lay quietly with our own thoughts. I was pleased that I had not let the side down so far, but apprehensive of going into action again now that I had seen death at first hand. I felt bad that I had not let a dying man have his prayer book. At the same time a part of me wanted to make him pay for Sixpack and Jock. After all he was the enemy, and yet I wondered if Ramon made it okay. Part of me hoped so, for I had no personal quarrel with him or any other Argentinean for that matter. My brain was like a revolving door, with conflicting thoughts entering and leaving at high speed. 'The insanity of war' I told myself

'No use getting stressed over a damn book.'

'What in God's name are we doing here?' It was just a thought really, I had not meant to voice it out loud, so I was somewhat startled, when a tired voice beside me replied.

'Just following orders and doing our job. Bit late to be having second thoughts now.'

'I was just wondering what I was I doing on the

other side of the world waging war on people I have never met?'

'Your doing what you get well paid for. You volunteered for the Regiment remember? If you didn't want this why did you join?'

'Do you really want to know? I'll tell you why,' I continued, without waiting for an answer. 'When I was a kid my Nan had this crush on Tyrone Power, the film star. She used to try to make me look like him. He had jet black wavy hair. Mine was black, but it was straight so she plastered it with this thick green goo. "Amami" setting lotion it was. She made it into waves with her fingers and held it in place with a hair grip. She sent me off to school like that. Trouble was, I was too much of a wimp to take it out in case she got cross. The other kids teased and bullied me. I was the smallest kid in the class, skinny and too sick with asthma to play rugby or do PT I was in short trousers until I was almost fifteen! Scared of violence, scared of taking risks, terrified of heights, afraid of my own bloody shadow. I was always getting beaten up, too scared to retaliate. I joined because I had to. I needed to prove to myself I wasn't going to live my entire life as a coward.'

Yorkie was clearly taken aback by my opening of the floodgates

'You've waited a long time to get that off your chest. I had no idea it was that bad. I don't know what to say. That's a big rock you have been carrying around in your bergan all this time. Feel any better now?'

'You know, I do believe I do.'

'I've known you a long time. You always lacked

confidence in the physical side of the job but it's s all in your head pal. I've met a lot of guys in my time, in the Para's, civvy street and the Regiment, but I never met anyone with bigger balls than you. You're no coward. You've faced the things you're afraid of and always conquered them. I know you were scared sick in the balloon cage. I know what it took for you cross that dam in the dark in pissing rain. You underestimate yourself. You've got more guts than I have.'

'That's bollocks.'

'No, it isn't. I'm too dumb to be as scared as I should be. That takes imagination and intelligence. You get really scared but you work through it. I don't think I could do that.'

'I look up to you Yorkie. You are the only real male role model I've ever had, you must know that?'

'Sure, same as I look up to you. I've always admired your intellect and knowledge. Something I will never have. Look what you've gained.'

'What do you mean'

'You are impressed because I can handle myself, yes?'

'You know I am.'

'Well, after the way you handled Spanner, do you think any of those kids who bullied you at school would chance their arm if they were here now? No chance. You think too much. All that education's fried your brain.'

I didn't know what to say, so I said nothing. I quietly tried to digest all that he had said to me.

After a while, I turned to my companion and proffered a pearl of wisdom. 'Education is over -

rated you know. Margaret Thatcher is far better
educated than me and yet she hasn't found a way to
settle the argument over the Islands without young
lads hardly out of school killing each other.'

Yorkie looked sternly into my face as if searching for
clues. I had touched a nerve.

'What the fuck has got into you Tony? We're
here to kick these Spicks off the islands. They came
uninvited, invading sovereign British territory,
terrorizing women and kids and shooting up the
place.'

He was in full flood now and boy was I glad we
were on the same side.

'The bastards want taking out and I intend to
twat every one I come across'.

It was just vintage Yorkie. 'Taking out!' I hissed.
'What's that about? Are you buying them dinner and
then taking them dancing? You mean kill them, snuff
out the life of some poor conscript kid who doesn't
want to be here. A kid who just wants to go home to
his mum and dad, his sister, girlfriend whatever.
Taking out, that's army speak; a euphemism to make
it easier for us to do the politician's dirty work. Work
no sane man would ever contemplate. I know it's our
job and we will do it because we're trained to, but I
can't help thinking that the Argies are here same as
us, so some bloody politician can improve his status.
If spilling some of his country's blood on foreign soil
is what it takes, fine. Just so long as it isn't his. A
squaddie is a squaddie whatever colour his uniform. I
just don't see the sense in blowing away a
complete stranger because he is wearing a different
uniform. Take Ramon, he was...' I did not get to

finish the sentence.

'Ramon? So that's what this is all about. I thought you were getting a bit cosy with him.' Yorkie's tone was accusational.

'It's not that. It's just that I could see myself having a beer with him, discussing life and such if we were not at war. I quite liked him.'

'That Argie Rupert was a pilot,' *Was a pilot,* I thought. Yorkie has already written him off for dead, 'and not just any old pilot, but a Puraka pilot. Have you forgotten what his mate did back there to Jock and Sixpack?'

He was the boy from the council estate, with a secondary modern education. I, for all my years at a top grammar school and fancy university degree could feel myself losing the argument. It was one thing to have this kind of debate over a pint in the local but quite another under present circumstances. I knew he was right. We had a job to do. A job that involved taking human lives, the lives of strangers, young men whose job it was to stay alive by ensuring that we did not. I had not expected this level of moral dilemma when I embarked on my journey. I had to learn to suppress my feelings and get on with it if I wanted to see my home again.

'Of course I haven't forgotten. I will never forget that experience as long as I live.'

'Here have a boiled sweet and concentrate on keeping warm.' He winked at me and tapped my shoulder in a gesture of friendship. He looked older than I remembered. I felt better for airing my views, but still a little uncomfortable with my chosen occupation. Even though I loved the life and at last knew I could handle the job for real, I was torn. I got a real buzz from testing myself and at last having a chance to prove just how good the training had been. All the years of exercises and schemes, courses and classrooms, not to mention the cold and wet had paid off. We were not just holding our own, we were doing our job and doing it well. The dilemma was that to do it well meant killing people. The enemy had been an abstract concept, until my encounter with Ramon had given it a human face and a personality.

I wanted to survive and get home when this was all over, but I was not comfortable with the thought that I might have to kill again to achieve this. Training for a war is exciting, one big adventure. The real thing is something else entirely.

'Why don't you get your head down?' I said at last as I surfaced from of my sea of reflection.

'I'm okay for now You have a kip if you like.' Yorkie replied.

'No, I'm fine.' I lied. The Benzedrine was keeping me high and whenever I closed my eyes I saw a slow motion replay of the Argentine soldier tumbling backwards behind the rocks as my bullets hit him. It was always in close up, just like a scene from one of Sam Peckinpah's movies. I could see the face clearly, not the face of a stranger, but Ramon's. Ramon whom I had grown to know and like despite the circumstances and our short acquaintance. His expression was one of disappointment and accusation, melting into fear and surprise, before finally dissolving into a bright red mist. I tried to justify my action at first (doing my job, etc.) and then tried to convince myself that he was not hit but had simply dived for cover. Maybe he had been hit by fire from one of the others. Deep down I knew. I saw the rounds strike. I knew that I had shot and killed a man. Ramon's accusing eyes swam up to meet me whenever I closed mine. I was not comfortable with what I had done, not comfortable at all. It seemed odd that this affected me more than the carnage I witnessed after the Pucara attack. Nothing in my training prepared me for the weight of my guilt. I would have given anything for a bottle of Scotch.

Spanner appeared and squeezed under our cam net.

'We have a problem,' he said. 'Wheels is still deaf. I need to command the patrol.' He looked really uncomfortable. I knew what was coming. 'Either of you...'

'He is,' said Yorkie, nudging me. 'Best signaller in the Squadron. Shit hot.'

'You want me to swop places with you for a while and get Wheels to fill me in?' I asked.

He nodded, clearly relieved at my offer, while embarrassed at needing to ask.

Wheels passed me the code books, cypher pads and frequencies. He satisfied himself that I knew what I was doing then allowed me to take over his precious radio kit.

Later back at my basha I quizzed Yorkie. 'What did he have to say then?' I asked.

'Not a lot. I told him you were a damn good signaller. He seemed happy at that. I don't think he wanted the patrol commander's job. He knows he's stuck with it.'

I hate to admit it but I've had worse.'
'Me too.'

23

Evasion
East Falkland,
Sunday May 23rd p.m −Monday 24th p.m.

Since the low flying jets, all had been quiet. The sky was clear blue with scattered clouds and best of all the sun was shining. I had no luck with the radio, but the weather, sleep, food and drink had done wonders for morale. We had established our exact position and felt more confident that we would be extracted once we got through to the task force. I pushed my dark thoughts to the back of my mind, sucked on a sticky green boiled sweet and took my turn on stag which did not even involve me getting out of my bag. I just eased myself into a half sitting position, and surveyed the ground though the cam net. Nothing stirred. All was at peace in the cold green windswept landscape. In the middle distance the ground rose gently at first and then more sharply towards the summit of Mt. Simon and to our right lay open ground to the lower slopes of Ball Mountain. Any keen-eyed observer on either of these peaks would enjoy an excellent field of view for miles and could call artillery rounds from any battery in range, reporting corrections at the click of a prestle switch, until the rounds found their target.

Since there was nothing I could do about it I banished the thought to the place where my darkest demons now resided and got back to work. For an hour I scanned the ground across our front. Simultaneously, Spanner or Wheels would be covering the other arc to our rear. Yorkie slept soundly and peacefully alongside, while the only notable occurrence was a skein of geese heading West at altitude in a large V formation.

My legs were hurting more than usual and I could not seem to get warm even in my bag. I was slowly deteriorating from lack of hot nourishment and found myself increasingly preoccupied with thoughts of food. Plates of hot curry, sausage and mash smothered in steaming onion gravy, my imagination knew no bounds, but all I did was torture myself. The day passed uneventfully in a cycle of observing, eating and trying to raise the task force on the radio. In the late afternoon it was decided by mutual agreement that we would move out at last light and tab towards the west coast to try to contact friendly forces. Wheels having had to give up the radio, was uncharacteristically in a foul mood. The strain was getting to all of us and he and Spanner had been out in the field for a lot longer than Yorkie and I. They had also lost two close mates in action.

Shortly after last light we packed our kit and prepared to move. Having established an emergency RV on the map, we set a bearing and headed off towards our objective some twenty-two map miles away. We had limited intelligence as to the enemy forces in the area and what we did have was almost two weeks old, so of little use. Spanner put Yorkie as lead scout with himself close behind followed by Wheels. I brought up the rear. For once the wind was not too strong and there was enough moonlight to navigate by without exposing us too much. Apart from the sore feet and legs and the constant rubbing from my bergan straps I did not feel too bad. Once we got on the march I didn't even feel too cold. Acclimatization they call it. Remarkable, considering we had not eaten any hot food for days with the temperature hovering around freezing.

We made good progress at first and had covered nine K in the first four hours, but then the terrain got tricky with a number of obstacles, not the least of which were a number of streams flowing with freezing cold water. Crossing them slowed progress, and sapped morale as our feet, which were already suffering, became numb in our waterlogged boots. At least it allowed us to fill our water bottles. An hour before dawn with twenty K still to go it was time to find our next LUP We found a spot overlooking the 'road' to Douglas above a feature marked on the map as Bombilla House. We had no idea if this was inhabited, but from a map appreciation we thought we should have a good view of the area once it got light. We settled in to the usual routine, now second nature.

The next day passed uneventfully and we were able to get plenty of rest. I spent the time between stags treating my poor feet as best I could and trying to dry my boots. My teeth felt as if they were covered in mildew, my stomach seemed like it was being gnawed by rats. We were running seriously short of food.

My body clock had been thrown into chaos by

suddenly switching night into day. Despite years of practice I never got used to it. On a Friday afternoon at five o'clock I would leave the museum and report to the barracks for training. I would join the rest of the Squadron for parade, classroom briefing followed by individual patrol briefings, a signals briefing, drawing rations and equipment from the quartermaster stores issuing weapons and pyrotechnics, etc. By the time we reached the exercise area it would be around midnight and we would then have to tab across country until just before dawn just as now.

The rest of the weekend typically followed a pattern of lying up observing and sleeping by day and moving at night. Breakfast at teatime and lunch at suppertime – your stomach never knew what time of day it was. I always made sure I had plenty of Rennies in my kit!

There was no sign of life from Bombilla House and indeed no sign at all of any 'friendlies.' When darkness fell and it was time to go, we were glad to be on the move. I experienced some difficulty getting going. My legs had become very stiff and numb with the inactivity but gradually I managed to pick up the pace as we tabbed into the gloom under a cloud filled moonless sky.

24

Ambush

East Falkland Dusk – Dawn 24th/25th May 1982

The night was still and cold, with a stiff breeze as we trudged across the soggy terrain towards where we supposed our lines to be. The ground underfoot was spongy. I was at the sharp end, Yorkie tail-end-Charlie. Lead scout had always been my favourite position in a patrol, but that was in peacetime. This was different. Eyes and ears straining for any sign of friend or foe I picked my way along between the peat outcrops and grassy tufts. Dry mouth, palms sweating inside my gloves, gripping my weapon and staring into the darkness, glancing frequently at the ground for obstacles, sweeping my gaze from side to side. The strain was really beginning to tell, and when, after a couple of hours Spanner tapped my shoulder and called a halt, I was mightily relieved. We took up all round defence and had a ten minute break while Spanner and Wheels checked the bearing and consulted the map. The latter was of limited use owing to the fact we could not see very much of the ground around us. Yorkie and I switched positions and he led us into the night while I brought up the rear. I had abandoned all hope of us raising anyone on the radio and had resigned myself to the fact that we would walk back to the task force. My bergan rash was killing me, my feet blistered and sodden, but I was alive. As the night wore on, the weather took a turn for the worse and visibility dropped to only a few metres. The bitter cold was dreadful, sapping my morale. I had to fight against my wandering mind to keep focused on the task in hand.

I wondered how the others were managing. I began to hallucinate, seeing of all things, a caravan serving hot dogs and burgers just a few yards in front of me. I shook my head vigorously and the caravan disappeared. *Just grit your teeth and keep going, I told myself.*

A blinding flash. I was flying through the air. A deafening bang. My body collided with something, crumpling on impact. I tasted dirt and cordite. Another tremendous explosion. Tracer rounds were buzzing overhead like demented fireflies. The unmistakable crackling tinder-wood sound of small arms assaulted my ear drums, punctuated with the blasts of exploding grenades.

Being blown off my feet was a curious blessing in disguise, as the air above my prostate form was ripped asunder with red tracer, right where I had been walking. With my ears ringing and gasping for breath I began to react to the threat, hugging the earth and blasting off rounds in the direction of the tracer. Someone was shouting but I couldn't hear what, because of the ringing in my ears and the clamour and crackle of the firefight. The noise was unbelievable; they were right on top of us. My sphincter was shut tight as a hatch on a submarine and the muscles in my forearms on fire with adrenaline. Another loud bang and then another, as grenade exploded near by.

Shouting, screaming, flashing tracer, utter pandemonium. I had no idea how or where the other lads were, although they could not have been more than a few feet away. The fire was still heavy and uncomfortably accurate. Above it all there was this terrible screaming, a truly awful sound that clawed through my gut like an eagle's talons ripping into a frightened rabbit. Someone was hurt real bad.

I tried to crawl backwards but my bergan forced my head into the ground. My instinct was to roll over and over to escape the killing zone but with a bergan on my back it was a nonstarter. Rounds began singing and whining as they struck the rocks behind me and I tried desperately to make myself small and at one with the earth. I banged off a few more rounds until the magazine was empty and tried to clear my head. I yelled Yorkie's name to no effect and tried to get at my magazines. Apart from the tracer and odd muzzle flashes there was no sign of anyone or anything. The air was heavy with smoke, stinging my eyes, the metallic taste of cordite in my mouth. My nostrils burned as my throat choked on phosphorous fumes. I reached for a fresh magazine, disoriented, cursing and swearing while praying at the same time. After what seemed an age I succeeded in reloading the rifle when a burst of gunfire close to my right was followed by a thudding blow to my back knocking me sideways.

'Oh Jesus! I've been hit!' I screamed. My mind went into overdrive but all seemed to be happening in slow motion. I felt the blood in the middle of my back and I started to panic. There was no pain just cold wetness along my spine. 'I'm hit! I'm hit!' I yelled. 'Help me. For God's sake help me!' It must be bad I thought. My mind went to my children, worried I might never see them again. I thought of Carol and my mother. I wished I had been a better father, husband and son. I made up my mind that this was it. My time had come. This was what I had been sure would happen to me; my premonition that I would become a casualty of war.

Someone was screaming in pain close by, so close at first I thought it was me. I took the last phosphorous grenade from my belt and then thought better of it as I was not sure where the rest of the patrol was. The firing seemed to have slackened and I was aware of movement to my left quite close by. I turned my rifle to face the threat and held my breath. The screaming continued to send a chill through me and I prayed it would stop. It was the most frightening thing I had ever heard.

'Tony! Tony!' I heard, just audible above the din.

'Here!' I shouted. 'Over here!'

Seconds later, Yorkie appeared as if by magic. Never had I been so pleased to see him.

'I'm hit! I cried,' vaguely aware of the bedlam around me and the flashing tracer arcing overhead.

'Where?' He demanded.

'My back! My back!'

Rounds were still whining and cracking over head and my eardrums felt like they were going to burst as Yorkie's SLR exploded into life alongside my head. After ten or twelve rounds of rapid fire he turned his attention back to me, yelling into my face. I could see his lips moving ...at that moment a grenade exploded somewhere behind him with a terrific bang which fused all the lights.

25

Rescue
East Falkland
Tuesday 25th – Wednesday 26th May 1982

A loud whirring in my head, wind tearing at my face through the blackness. Bitter cold, struggling through a strange dream from which I could not awaken. I tried to force my eyes open. I tried so hard, but could see only black until a sharp pain in my legs made the blackness dissolve into a dark spinning disc with rainbow edges. The pain came again, stronger this time and a window of vision opened in the disc, just like someone had cut away a slice of a cake to reveal a Wedgwood plate. It was a piece of blue sky and something slicing across my limited window of vision like a giant scythe. The grim reaper had come to claim me. I was being lifted, carried; there were voices a million miles away, then the pain began to ebb and I was drifting on a calm sea ruffled only by the scythe slicing the air above me. My nostrils were invaded with the familiar smell of aviation fuel and then all was black.

The bright white light above was swinging from side to side. It was too close and far too bright to be the moon, I was sure. A searchlight perhaps?

'Easy, mate. You are going to be okay.'

I turned my head in the direction of the voice, but after staring at the bright white light, all I could see was blackness peppered with dancing red lights.

'You were brought in last night.' The voice said. 'You'll be transferred to a hospital ship soon I expect. The Doc's done a good job on you; your war's over. You'll be going home.'

'We've landed?' I asked, my situation beginning to dawn on me.

'Five days ago.'

'Where...?' he cut short my obvious question with a soothing tone.

'This is Ajax Bay field dressing station and as soon as we can, we will transfer you to...' He was cut short by an outburst of firing from several machine guns including the unmistakable drumming of a big fifty calibre Browning.

The sound of fast jets fused with the furious crackle of triple A (Anti Aircraft Artillery), as the aircraft screamed in at ultra low altitude to unleash their bombs.

'It's okay they're after the ships out in the bay'

'Where?'

'San Carlos. San Carlos Water,' he replied in a very calm voice placing his hand on my shoulder in a gesture of reassurance.

'Got to go. They will be needing me.' With that he disappeared.

I never did see his face. I must have blacked out again because the firing had stopped and all was quiet, except for the hum of a generator somewhere nearby.

I had a drip in my left arm and was lying on a camp bed, inside what I surmised was some kind of agricultural building. Sunlight streamed through a multitude of holes in the corrugated tin walls, the results of earlier air raids or possibly our softening-up bombardment before the landings. I was not alone; casualties lay on both sides and opposite. Some were very heavily bandaged and were quiet and subdued, as a result of shock and sedatives I guessed. To my right, just an arms length away, was a young lad no more than seventeen. His face was ashen and he lay on his side, his breathing very shallow. His eyes were open but they were not registering his surroundings and he had the look of a lost soul without hope. I could see no sign of injury anywhere but he was clearly very ill. I was in no pain now and felt comfortable. More than that, I was really happy in a detached, floaty kind of way. Morphine does that to you. As my current situation began to dawn on me, memories of the last few days swam into my consciousness. Yorkie, where the hell was Yorkie? What had happened to him and the others? I remembered the firing. Tracer stabbing through the dark, grenades exploding and shouting; lots of shouting. I wished I was at home with Carol and the boys. I really missed them.

What seemed like hours passed before I saw anyone, but it was probably much less. Another orderly came in and stood at the side of the bed.

'You hungry?' he enquired.

'Yes, I am.' I replied, shocked at the weakness of my own voice.

'I'll see what's on,' he said.

'Yorkie?' I said sounding distant.

'Say again mucker.'

'Yorkie, my mate Yorkie. Is he okay?'

'You were brought in on a Heli. Just you. I don't know about anyone else. Sorry.'

'Can you ask for me? I need to know he's okay?'

'I'll see what I can do but things are a bit fluid at the moment. Now I better see about some scoff for you.'

I thanked him and he disappeared from view. He was soon back with a mess tin of airborne stew and a couple of slices of bread. Hot scoff! It had never tasted so good.

'Cheers mate!' It seemed so inadequate but it was all I could come up with.

'No sweat, mucker. I'm Nobby by the way. I'll fetch you a brew later.'

Nobby the orderly returned as promised with the brew and a couple of pills.

'Here. You need to take these'

'What are they?'

'Antibiotics,'

'How bad am I?' I asked.

'Shrapnel in both legs, but the Doc. got most of it. As long as we keep the wounds clean and keep the infection at bay you should be up and about in a couple of weeks. You were concussed too but nothing too serious. You should have some nice scars to impress the women with when you tell them about your heroic deeds.'

'My back what about my back? I was hit. I

remember being hit, the bleeding...'

'Your back's fine mate. You must have dreamt it.'

He winked and grinned at me like I was a refugee from the funny-farm.

'The Padre will be round later. You can ask him about your mate and get him to let your family know you're okay.' With this good news and my full stomach, I lay back and fell asleep.

I awoke suddenly some time later in a cold sweat. The nightmare was back. Ramon's face dissolving on the impact of my bullets.

My legs were hurting and I struggled to bend so that I could reach down and feel below my knees but before I managed to do so a soft voice close by said.

'Sorry, did I wake you?'

He spoke with quiet West-country lilt, and as I turned I could see his cheery face beneath the cherry-red Para beret. He was dressed in camouflage combats, apart from the white dog collar around his neck.

'Padre...' I started.

'Nigel, call me Nigel.' he urged. 'Is there anything I can do for you?'

'Do you have any cigarettes?' I asked.

'Here you are, have one of these.' He smiled and placed an Embassy tipped between my lips. He produced a black Zippo with a silver cross engraved on the body and lit me up. I inhaled the blue smoke whilst idly thinking. 'He doesn't look like a Nigel. He looks just like one of the lads.' I told him about Yorkie and he promised to look into it as well as getting a message through channels to let my family know I was okay. We chatted for a while and he told me we were making progress, consolidating the beachhead and that in spite of losing some ships, including two Frigates, we were doing okay. As he got up to leave I noticed that the camp bed next to me was empty, the young lad was gone. I looked first at the bed and then at Nigel.

'He is in God's care now,' he said. He looked suddenly very tired. It occurred to me I didn't even know the lad's name, didn't know if he was a soldier, sailor or marine.

'Is there anything else I can get you?' said Nigel as he made to leave.

'I would like to write home,' I said

'No problem. I will bring you a letter form and pen next time. Oh, I almost forgot. These are yours,' he said producing a green poly bag with a brown luggage label tied round the neck.

'Your personal effects.'

He placed them on the ammo box which served as both seat and bedside table and wishing me God Bless he moved on to comfort others in need.

The bed on the other side was occupied by a Royal Marine in his early twenties. He had a broken leg and cracked ribs sustained in a fall while transferring from ship to landing craft. The others were wounded during an air raid but Nobby insisted they were all going to be fine. Nobby was a real optimist. Tommy, the broken leg and cracked ribs, was full of bravado and macho bullshit. He couldn't wait to be up and at the Argies. Was *he* going to kick some ass! Kick ass! Too much television and too many all-American hero videos. I prayed he would not see any fighting.

26
Bad News/Good News
East Falkland Thursday 27th – Friday 28th May 1982

Wheels looked desperately tired, and he seemed to have aged dramatically. In spite of this he still managed a thin smile as he stood at the end of the camp bed.

'How you doing?'

'I'm okay. Got your hearing back okay?'

'Yeah, fine now thanks'

'What about the others?'

He looked down at his boots.

'I'm really sorry. He was a good bloke, your mate.'

At first it just did not register. Then, slowly it sank in. I suppose I had been half expecting it, but it hurt. It hurt like hell.

'How?' I asked with what felt like a golf ball stuck in my throat.

He stepped forward and sat on the now empty bed beside me.

'Grenade. He took the full force. If he hadn't you wouldn't be here.'

'Did he say anything?'

'Too quick mate, he never felt a thing'

We both knew it was a lie, a well-intentioned and kindly lie. I wanted to probe him for more info, but had the sense to realize what a futile exercise that would be. I passed. I had learned enough to know that a quick and merciful death is a rare luxury in our business.

Our business. I had come a long way from the dusty museum archives. My weekend hobby, had become my life. I had survived, shaken and bruised, most likely changed forever, but alive.

It was then that I noticed the bandage on his right hand. 'You okay?' I said nodding towards his injury. He held up the bandaged limb and waved it theatrically.

'I'm sound mate. Just don't have a little finger any more. Didn't even feel it at the time.'

'Spanner?' I asked tentatively

'Not a scratch, jammy bastard. He told me to say you did a good job; both of you.' He looked all serious.

'You are pulling my pisser.' I replied.

'No way, we all had reservations but you proved us wrong. You did okay. You both did.'

'Thanks. I know that would have pleased Yorkie. You "22" guys were his heroes, not that he would have ever admitted it. It was our first time in action.'

'Yeah mine too, and Spanner's'

I studied his face for clues. Was he winding me up? 'I did wonder ....'

'Jock had seen a lot around the globe. Sixpack had his share in Northern Ireland, but me and Spanner no. Just exercises and some live ops no one ever shot at us before.'

'I had no idea.'

'Yeah well,' he said apologetically, 'there you go.'

'What happened anyway? Who got me out? What about the Argies?'

He did not reply for what seemed like a very, very long time. When at last he did speak his voice was shaking with emotion.

'There <u>were</u> no Argies. They were ours, Marines. It was Blue on Blue. An S.B.S. (Special Boat Service) recce patrol. Fucking war. Bastard fucking war.'

I couldn't find a thing to say at all. I felt like someone I had smacked me in the guts with a shovel. I shook my head. More bloody insanity, damn the war, damn the politicians, damn them all. I was choked but could shed no tears. Not now, later perhaps. Recent experiences had hardened me, taught me to keep my emotions under wraps, something I would have thought impossible a month earlier. I was naturally an emotionally open person, used to showing my feelings. This was, I believe, a by product of my Spanish blood. It had caused problems in relationships when I was younger until I found Carol, someone who could not only deal with my emotionally open way but even liked me for it.

We fell silent for a time, locked in our own thoughts. After a while he filled me in on the detail. It seemed that the SBS patrol leader ordered a cease-fire after hearing shouting and yelling in English and had challenged us to surrender. Spanner was nearest and managed to convince them we were on the same side. Two of their guys were hit, both by seven point six two millimetre which could only have come from Yorkie's SLR One was badly wounded in the shoulder, the other just a flesh wound in the arse! The weather was so bad we could not be picked up and anyway helicopters were rare as rocking-horse shit. We spent the whole day being looked after by the able bodied until late morning on Wednesday. A Gazelle picked us up in three lifts; the two wounded marines and I going in the first. Thanks to my old comrade, concussion from the grenade and a bit more shrapnel in my legs was all I had in the way of injuries. Physical ones that is. My emotional wounds were something else. I was suffering the effects of exposure but I had not gone down with hypothermia. As for the life threatening wound in my back it was nothing more than a burst of rounds hitting my bergan and going through a water bottle. No blood just water. No wonder it was so cold. The irony is, it wasn't just any water. It was Ramone's urine. I got shot by my own side while the enemy simultaneously pissed up my back! Quite literally. I wondered if God was trying to tell me something.

Wheels got to his feet.

'Got to go. Things to do,' he smiled that thin smile again. 'Oh I almost forgot. The intelligence guys seemed well pleased with the intel you got. Spanner filed the report for you at the debrief.'

'Great. Tell him thanks'

'Sure.'

He turned towards the way out.

'Before you go just satisfy my curiosity will you?'

'How's that'

'Spanner and Wheels, where did the names come from?'

'Simple enough, Spanner's a mechanic, his parent unit is REME [Royal Electrical and Mechanical Engineers] and I'm a petrol head, always messing with cars. That's how we got together. He's really a good bloke Spanner, you know.'

'Yes, I reckon so. Tell him take care okay? You too.'

We shook hands and said all there was to say with our eyes. He turned and walked out leaving me to try to make some sense of it all – this chaos.

Talk about history repeating itself; first the Royal Navy kill my father and now my best friend is sent to meet his maker courtesy of the Royal Marines. I was hurting badly from the loss of my comrade but glad to be alive and thus able to hurt at all. I went through the angry stage next; angry with everyone, the politicians, the army, God and most of all myself, for it was me that brought him here to this windswept boil on the arse of the world. The poor bugger had not even heard of the Falklands until I stuck my oar in. Had it not been for my selfishness he would be still in UK and we would be looking forward to a reunion piss up upon my return. If I had not been such a wimp, calling out when I thought I was hit, he would have stayed put and might still be alive.

Nigel dropped by with cigarettes and a sympathetic
ear, which I bent cruelly in my anger at God for
allowing his children to slaughter each other for no
good reason. He was a wonderfully patient man and a
great help to me as I struggled to come to terms with
my feelings of guilt. Good as he was though, he could
not make them go away altogether. The feelings
festered away like a wound that would not heal.
Nobby gave me the news that I was to be transferred
to a hospital ship in the morning, news, which, under
normal circumstances would have lifted my spirits but
which now hardly raised a glimmer. Nigel talked a
while with me and urged me not to lose faith and to
pray to God to show me the way out of the black
hole into which I had stumbled. I promised I would
try but I really did not believe myself when I said it.
He left to tend to his duties. I took some more pills
and then slept for a couple of hours or so, waking
in a cold sweat when my slumber was invaded yet
again by my recurring nightmare.

Lying awake with a kaleidoscope of images
whirring around my head only served to make me all
the more restless. The pain in my legs became a
welcome distraction from the turmoil in my mind, the
search for answers I knew I would never find.
Answers that I knew did not exist. I was wracked with
guilt for denying Ramon his prayer book. How could
I refuse comfort to a dying man, what sort of man did
that make me? I missed my old friend. I missed my
wife and family and could not wait to get back to
them, but I was scared of how I had changed. I had
read enough war memoirs to be aware of the dangers
associated with returning from conflict to the bosom
of the family.

Fortunately my war had been brief and although bloody in parts it in no way compared to that of men in the First and Second World Wars away from home for years, fighting in appalling conditions. Eventually tiredness overcame me and I fell into a deep sleep, not waking again until Nobby roused me with my medication and a brew.

'I need to change the dressings on your legs so you'll be all ship shape when you transfer out of here.'

'Any idea when that will be, Nobby?'

'Later this afternoon I reckon. We are going to need the space.'

'When can I get up and walk about?'

'Patience patient,' he said taking great care to enunciate each word to make his point.

The day wore on into late afternoon with no word of any transfer. I dozed and ate a little and spent a lot of time reflecting on the past week or so and how events had changed me, probably forever. I began to sink into depression as the morphine wore off. The lamps were lit and I was aware of the generator humming away in the background. Outside, the light was beginning to fade. Suddenly there was frantic activity and the air raid warning sounded. My body stiffened involuntarily as I braced myself for the danger. *They'll be after the ships* I told myself; *we'll be safe here.*

Automatic gunfire crackled across the bay as the air defences sprang into action, their sound mingling with the rush of air as the Skyhawks screamed across the bridgehead. The sound of exploding bombs followed the shock waves, which made the ground beneath us tremble. One bomb at least came quite close, shaking every thing around us. We could do nothing but lay where we were. I felt naked and helpless yet again. Without warning there was a loud crash and a sound of tearing metal, like a head on car smash. To my horror a bomb tore through the roof and out again hitting the ground outside with a thump like a medicine ball striking the drill hall floor. I stopped breathing and waited for the explosion and my inevitable death. *How could this happen?* I thought. *Had I survived close contact with friend and foe, been shot at, bombed and rocketed, only to die in bed?*

There was no explosion, no violent bloody death but, I almost died from forgetting to breathe. When I finally did I looked around to see a few looks of utter disbelief, followed quickly by total relief. I began to pray furiously, for the first time since my anger at God for all the killing. Someone began laughing hysterically, which broke the stunned silence. The raid ended as suddenly as it began. Nobby came to check for casualties. He calmly announced that we had taken hits by three, 'bloody big bombs' but not to worry they had not gone off. Like we would not have noticed if they had. Outside, a fire had been started quite close to us by one of the bombs that had exploded. It spread to stockpiled ammunition. The first we knew of this was when mortar bombs and Milan anti tank missiles began exploding alarmingly, just a hundred metres away. Exploding small arms ammunition added to the noise. It continued throughout the night, but we soon got used to it and mercifully no one was hurt, in spite of the shrapnel whizzing through the air.

27

A Shock to the System
Hospital Ship S.S. Uganda, 29th May - June 1982

The following morning I bid farewell to Nobby and along with several other inmates, I was carried out on a stretcher to the makeshift heli pad to await transportation to the hospital ship. Wessex and Sea King helicopters clattered overhead with netted loads dangling beneath them, ferrying ammunition and equipment from the supply ships, taking the wounded out on the return trip. The place was alive with men and machines loading and unloading munitions, food and other vital stores. The scene reminded me of an anthill whose top had been suddenly sliced off, everyone frantically working to put it right. The ammo dump was still smouldering and on the surrounding high ground, the Rapier batteries and .50 calibre air defences were combing the skies for enemy aircraft. Below them the ground was peppered with men digging slit trenches on the steep slopes. Bulldozers were clearing paths and building roadways, closely followed by engineers laying steel track-ways for the heavy vehicles to run on. At the water's edge two landing craft disgorged their cargoes of fully laden trucks.

While we waited for information I looked out over San Carlos Water at the big ships at anchor with their escorts. It was an impressive sight, especially the massive Cruise Liner Canberra, dwarfing the attendant dull grey Royal Navy frigates. Rumours passed back and forth among the casualties and I learned more of the ships that we had lost: Frigates Ardent and Antelope and HMS Coventry, a type 42 Destroyer. Most worrying of all, was the loss of the merchant vessel Atlantic Conveyor, which was rumoured to be carrying most of our helicopters.

My destination was the hospital ship Uganda and when our turn came, the transfer from shore to ship was smooth and uneventful. I found myself in another world. A world of beds and bunks, clean sheets and soft pillows. A warm, dry, luxurious world far removed from the one I had recently known and very welcome it was too. We were processed immediately and allocated berths. Unable to walk as yet, I was carried to mine and laid gently on a bed with my kit, such as it was, deposited in the bedside locker. Beside the bed was my kit bag, testament to the Navy's efficiency. I immediately retrieved my wallet and took out the photos. It felt so good to see my family again. The green poly bag with my other personal effects, I placed on top of the locker. How many of us were in that sick bay I have no idea, but it seemed a lot. Orderlies and other medical staff busied themselves, moving from casualty to casualty assessing and documenting, tagging and flagging. I was examined by a naval doctor and later carried to the showers. Upon return to my bed I was able to shave with a razor and bowl of hot water thoughtfully provided for me. I felt better than I had for what

221

seemed an eternity. We were fed decent grub and mercifully left unmolested by the Argentine Air Force. I wrote a long letter to Carol and the boys, deliberately leaving out almost all the significant events of the past week or so. I wrote half a page on the weather and made up some bits about penguins and stuff. There was no way that she could understand the nature of things down here. I finished the letter and placed it on the locker.

I longed for mail from home. Still troubled by my feelings of guilt, I became increasingly withdrawn, taking little or no active part in the socialising of my fellow patients. They were, for the most part, just kids in their teens and early twenties. We had little in common.

Early in the evening I spotted a familiar face moving from bed to bed offering comfort to the sick.

'Fancy meeting you here.' I remarked as Nigel grinned at me from the foot of the bed.

'Well, I'm one of you now,' he said, indicating the crutch tucked under his left arm. 'Picked up some metal in the last air raid and they sent me packing. Tried to get out of it but they said I would be needed here with the wounded. Moral blackmail of course, but orders are orders eh? So how are we then?'

'Okay' said I, without a trace of conviction.

'Hmm, that bad. Say, you don't play chess by any chance do you?'

'Chess?' I was caught off guard by this remark. 'Er, yes, I do, a long time since I have but yes, I do.'

'Excellent!' he replied a twinkle in his eye and sitting himself on the bed produced a small wooden box from his pocket. He opened it to reveal two opposing armies in miniature on a chequered battlefield.

'You're white. Your move,' he said in a firm friendly tone. Before I knew it we were playing. He beat me the first two games but in the third I gave him a run for his money. It was a clever ploy. It took my mind away from my troubles for a time and forced me to concentrate on what was, after all, only a game. As Nigel was setting up the board for another game, gently he inquired as to how I was coping.

'Sleeping okay are you?'

'On and off, you know how it is. I keep seeing stuff and it wakes me up. It's too real. I had this prisoner, he was wounded and in a bad way, he knew he wasn't going to make it. All he wanted was his prayer book. I wouldn't let him have it. Needed to break him you see. Then it was too late. How could I do that to a dying man?'

'It is never easy, the conflict between human instinct and duty. I doubt God will judge you as harshly as you do yourself.'

'You reckon?'

'I am sure of it. Did he say anything before he died?'

'Don't know, last I saw him he was being evacuated on a chopper.'

'So he may have survived?' His voice optimistic.

'I doubt it. He was in bad shape.'

As Nigel set the board up for another game, I reached across to the locker for a mug and some water. In so doing I accidentally knocked the green poly bag with my personal effects onto the deck spilling the contents.

'Damn!' I cried.

'Okay. I've got it,' said Nigel, kneeling down to retrieve the bits and pieces, which he heaped on the bed. My wallet, watch; stopped at 02.30, tobacco tin, empty but for half a packet of Rizlas, the Zippo Yorkie had given me for my birthday, my Silva compass and an Ivory coloured prayer book with a painting of Christ on the front.

'This the book?'

'Yes, that's it'

'Your family?' he said picking up a photograph from beside the book.

'No, must have fallen out of the book. I guess it belonged to the prisoner. Here,' I said, reaching for my wallet, 'this is my family, my wife and two boys. This is my mum and dad.' I passed the treasured snapshots to him. Nigel took the photograph and looked at it then looked again at the picture that had fallen from the prayer book. He studied first one and then the other scrutinizing them closely. He looked up at me with a puzzled expression and then back to the photographs.

'Remarkable,' he uttered at last, 'quite remarkable!'

'What's remarkable?' I asked.

'Where is your father now?'

'He was killed before I was born. They're both dead, my Mum and Dad. Killed in the last war.'

'You've not seen this photograph, have you?' He said. It was more a statement of fact than a question.

'I haven't. No,' I answered, baffled. 'I put the book in my pocket and forgot about it. Why?'

'Here,' he said, passing me the picture. It showed an attractive young girl in her early twenties with dark hair and a lovely smile. She was dressed in a wedding gown and next to her stood a handsome young man of about thirty in a dark suit. My heart stopped. I looked up at Nigel. He was holding out the other picture. The one of my parent's wedding. I took it and held them together. The handsome man in the picture; it was the same man. My father. How could this be? My mind was turning somersaults. It's him, it must be him, but it's not possible. He's dead. Being wedding shots they were both quite clear and both taken in good light from the same angle. Surely there could be no mistake.

'November 1942.'

'What?' I said still in a daze.

'November 1942' repeated Nigel, it is written on the back of the picture.

I turned it over and there in faded pencil was written

'Rosario November 1942.'

'Are you all right, Tony?' He placed his hand on my forearm.

'I don't really know; it is the same man, isn't it'

'Well, I would not like to say for sure, but there is an uncanny resemblance.'

'But he was killed in 1939. At least that's what I have always been told. This cannot be happening.'

'If this man is your father...'

'No. This is too bizarre. These must be

Ramon's parents. Wake me Nigel please.'

'You are awake old man. It could just be coincidence, a doppelganger.'

I looked him straight in the eyes.

'Stranger things have happened. Let's look at it. How was your father killed?'

I told him what I had been told since a small boy, my head spinning.

'He was a prisoner on a German battleship. The Graf Spee. She was attacked by Royal Navy cruisers and he was killed by a shell. He was in the Merchant Navy.'

'This would have been The Battle of the River Plate, the one they made a film about in the fifties?'

'That's right.'

'Gomez, that's a Spanish name right? Your father, he was Spanish?'

I was in a daze. 'Yes.'

Nigel, God bless him, was a rock. He was logical and methodical and together we analysed the evidence. The date was right, my dad was the right age for the man in the photo; everything fitted. We both knew something of the of the Battle of the River Plate having seen the film starring John Gregson and Peter Finch. In 1939, when the German pocket battleship Graf Spee was surprised by three British cruisers and suffered damage in the encounter, her captain headed for the nearest neutral port for emergency repairs. This was Montevideo in Uruguay. Once docked, the prisoners were disembarked. Uruguay is next door to Argentina and for a Spaniard to cross the border would not have been difficult. It was easy to see what might well have happened. The question was 'why then not send word home? Why the disappearing act, or was it all an incredible coincidence and a case of two look alikes?' We concluded that the latter was most unlikely. I stared in disbelief at the two photographs, trying to get my head round it all. If all was as it appeared and he was still alive, then I had a father back from the dead, my former prisoner was my half brother and my father had a son he knew nothing of. Assuming he was still alive that is. He would not have even known my mother was pregnant or that she had been killed at the tender age of twenty-four. Moreover it was likely, that I had other siblings.

I had no idea where Ramon was or even if he was alive. Nigel promised he would make some enquiries for me through official channels and others not so official. As he got up to leave, I thanked him.

'Think nothing of it,' he replied, 'this is fascinating. I'm intrigued. Just try to take things calmly, Tony, and I will see what I can find out.'

'You're a star Nigel and a mean chess player. Take care out there my friend.'

'You too, my boy.'

With that he was gone and I was left with two pictures, many unanswered questions and an ache in my heart that I could not make go away. What a week! I felt as if I had aged ten years. I might have gained a brother but I had lost one too. Yorkie was gone forever. Yorkie my rock. Never again would we curse and laugh together at discomfort and adversity. No more would we swap lies at the bar, or tell the same stories of derring-do, for the umpteenth time, embellishing each re-run with exaggerated and fanciful 'recollections.' I was going to miss him.

28

Connections
Hospital Ship S.S. Uganda June 1982

Like the giant Canberra, which weighed just short of 45,000 tons, the Uganda was a peace time P&O liner, although at just under 17,000 tons she was considerably smaller. Launched on Clydeside in January 1952, she started as a passenger liner operating on the East Africa service. When this closed, she switched to educational cruising, carrying youngsters in her dormitories and a number of passengers in the first class section. She was cruising with many school pupils on board when the call-up was received by radio from her owners and the Ministry of Defence. Following conversion into a hospital ship, Uganda sailed to the South Atlantic to await orders from the Royal Navy task force. This was the vessel that I found myself aboard, wrapped in clean sheets lying in a hospital bed on a deck just above the waterline.

I had not seen Nigel since the day after the transfer. I soon settled into the routine and even became a little sociable, although this involved more listening than talking. News that the Paras had taken Darwin and

Goose Green, was greeted with cheers throughout the ship. There was a large influx of wounded from these battles, some of whom were in pretty bad shape and the medical staff was kept very busy over the next few days. As I looked around the ward, my feeling of waste and futility was further fuelled by what I saw. Young men in the prime of life, missing arms and legs, others with faces obscured by bloody dressings. *Would this be my sons' fate one day I wondered? Would their blood be spilled in the corner of some foreign field in some misguided adventure at the whim of Downing Street?*

It was a sobering thought. As child growing up in the aftermath of the Second World War, I often saw men on crutches with a trouser leg held fast with safety pins below the stump of a limb and others with an empty jacket sleeve tucked into the pocket. Artificial limbs were not so readily available in those days. They are so good now that the effects of combat are effectively swept under the carpet.

Remembering Nigel's advice, I tried to find something positive to hang on to. I reflected on my present circumstances, searching for the positive. The weather outside was good for the time of year at this latitude. I was beginning to regain my strength. Another plus was the grub, which was not bad and we were warm and comfortable. Listening to the survivors of Goose Green put my experience of action in perspective. It seemed trivial by comparison. I really should have been happy to be alive, but I just couldn't shake off the black cloud of guilt over what had happened to Yorkie, Ramon and the Argie I had killed.

For two days I wallowed in self-pity, a guilty self indulgence. Nigel reappeared on the third. There was no news of Ramon, despite his best efforts. We played chess again and I even managed to win a couple of games. On Monday, May 31st the doctors allowed me out of bed for the first time. I felt a lot better and could walk a few steps with the aid of two sticks. I asked if I could get back to duty, maybe as interpreter or interrogator, but the doctor dismissed the idea out of hand. I had the crazy idea that I could maybe get some information about Ramon if I could only speak to the prisoners. In any event under the terms of the Geneva convention any combatant treated aboard could not be returned to operations on the Islands, so it was not to be.

On Tuesday morning Nigel came for a chess game. He sat down, placed the board on the bed and it being his turn to be white, made his opening move. I replied with standard king's pawn to king's pawn two. Without lifting his head from the game he addressed me quietly.

'The Ambulance ship Hecla is on its way to Montevideo with a load of wounded prisoners for repatriation. Ramon Ramirez is on the passenger manifest.'

I could not take it in at first. He lifted his head and nodded. I saw the truth of it in his eyes and felt a surge of energy pour through my veins. I felt alive again for the first time in days.

'Is he all right?'

'As far as I know and anyway he is in the best hands. We should pray for him, it is the best we can do right now.'

'You're a star Nigel, a real star. Thank you.'

'Glad to be able to help my boy,' he said smiling. 'I have been in touch with a friend in the Red Cross and she will try to get a message to him if you wish. Before you say yes, think carefully what you are going to say, you don't want to hit him with too big a shock if he is not well.'

I spent a long time drafting a letter to Ramon and much later when I had finished, I read it to Nigel. It would perhaps have been better if he had read it himself but as he did not understand Spanish I had no choice. He made a couple of suggestions, which I took on board and eventually produced something I was happy to send.

Ramon: Please read this. It is important. Please do not show this to your family until you have digested the contents.

Antonio Gomez,
Sergeant, British Army.
South Atlantic   *June 1st 1982*

Dear Ramon,
I sincerely hope that you are getting better and will soon make a full recovery from your wounds. You must be wondering why I am writing to you and in truth it is hard to know how or where to begin. Like you my war is now over and I find myself with time on my hands. I still have your prayer book, which I promise I will return when I can be sure it will reach you. I also have the photograph that was inside and this I will also return but for the moment I wish to keep it for reasons which shall, I

hope become clear. I also carry a photograph of my parents taken on their wedding day in 1939. I never knew my father. I believed him to have been lost at sea before I was born. He was reported missing, presumed killed, in 1939 at the Battle of the River Plate. He was, an officer in the Merchant Navy as you will see from the photograph I enclose. It has been a comfort to me as I am sure yours will have been to you. Please take care of it, it is the only one I have.

Forgive me for presenting you with what I believe to be evidence of a link between us, but if it is true, I could not allow this chance to pass. I have no wish to cause you or your family any pain or distress. I believe it was fate that brought us together and hope you will forgive this intrusion and find in your heart the will to reply to the address at the bottom. I am glad to have known you, despite the awful circumstances of our meeting and regret very much that our countries' leaders were not able to settle their differences peacefully. It is my earnest hope, that in spite of the war and our different upbringing we can be friends and that it may be possible to meet again someday when this war is over.

Antonio Gomez
36 Mill Lane
Farsley
West Yorkshire
England

I slipped the photograph inside but did not seal it. I debated with Nigel whether it would pass the censor. In the end he just took it from me, winked and tapped the side of his nose with his finger. 'My Boss,' he said lifting his eyes toward heaven, 'has connections.' I crossed my fingers and in spite of mixed feelings towards God, offered up a silent prayer for the safe delivery of my letter. Having done all I could for the time being, it was back to normal routine and just hoping that something would come of it.

29

Homeward Bound
S.S. Uganda/RFA Princes Royal, June 1982

I spent the rest of my war aboard ship, acting as unofficial interpreter with the wounded Argentine prisoners while I remained aboard Uganda. Early in June I received news that I was to be transferred to another ship for the trip home. Nigel and I played chess for the last time, exchanged phone numbers, as you do, knowing that this was not 'au revoir' but 'goodbye.' At the last minute he pushed a plastic carrier bag into my hand. Inside it was a bottle of Scotch.

'For the journey: God may be with you but he might need some help.' I vowed not to open it until I reached U.K.

'Let me know how things pan out with your brother?'

I promised I would as I shook his hand and thanked him for all his help, both practical and spiritual. We did not seem to have much else to say and I felt a big sense of anti climax.

When news of the surrender of Port Stanley reached my ears on the 15th of June, I was already well on my way home aboard the RFA Princess

Royal, the vessel in which Yorkie and I had travelled
south, what seemed like an eternity ago. It had in fact
been only one month since we had sailed from home.
There was cheering throughout the ship and a party
atmosphere sprang up instantly. We were a mixed
bunch of walking wounded and other odds and sods
and we were all eager to get home. I was now able to
get about quite well and my strength had returned to
some degree, although I tired easily and my legs were
still quite painful. This was dulled somewhat by
the application of alcohol (internally of course) as we
celebrated not the victory, but the end of the fighting.
We had all seen too much violence and its dreadful
consequences. We wanted it to stop before mates still
on the Islands were added to the casualty list.

We docked at Ascension Island on June 18th where
we received mail from home. This was the first for
me as I had been moving around so much it was
always playing catch up. There were six letters, all
from Carol, each of which contained a page from the
boys. The effect on my morale was tangible. It was
wonderful to read about ordinary domestic life. The
boys were doing fine apart from Mark, who had lost a
tooth playing football. Carol had been out with her
mother to the local working men's club and had won
fifty quid at bingo. They had both got drunk on part
of the winnings. The rest of the news was mundane,
but mundane was what I needed to counter the
extraordinary events I had been living through. I read
the letters over and over, filling my head with
thoughts of my homecoming. For a while all was well.
Full of hope for the future, I allowed myself to
imagine everything returning to how it was before,

except that, God willing, in time I would forge a new relationship with my brother. As for my father, if he was still living, I did not know what to think. I had mixed feelings and many unanswered questions. I was hopeful I would get a reply to my letter, but it was by no means certain.

Sitting in the shade of one of the containers that made up part of the deck cargo, I watched the heat haze shimmering over the ocean. *'What a contrast to the cold wet war zone down south.'* I thought. It was then the doubts began to creep back in. How could anything be the same after what I had seen? I marvelled at my mother's generation, who had endured six years of war and just got on with life, apparently as if nothing had happened. They lived with bombing for years, spending night after night in the damp dark Anderson shelter sunk into the vegetable patch. My next door neighbour in Leeds had been in the infantry and had married his childhood sweetheart on embarkation leave in January 1940. He was sent to France four days later and in June he returned with just the uniform he stood up in after being evacuated from Dunkirk. He had a week at home and was then sent to North Africa to fight first the Italians and later Rommel's Afrika Corps. Finally posted to India to take on the Japanese, he did not see his wife again for six years. He never spoke in detail of his experiences but I once saw a photograph of him in uniform, a stocky young man, in contrast to the wiry little chap who now weighed eight stone, dripping wet. His wife explained that he had suffered with malaria in the jungle and it had emaciated him. He had never been able to regain his weight. How, I wondered, does a human being handle such trauma and stay sane? I felt ashamed of myself for being upset at my comparatively minor experiences.

I missed my family badly, but was apprehensive about seeing them again, scared that they would not know me. I was irrational, but convinced the changes I felt inside had altered my appearance, or at least the way they would perceive me. I felt no better when we set sail for home and by the time we docked in Portsmouth in early July, I was not fit company for anyone.

It was late in the afternoon when we tied up at the quayside and were confined to the ship until the morning. It was not at all what I expected, now that I was back in the UK. Allowed one phone call each we were escorted off the ship to the pay phones in groups of six. When my name was called I joined the queue with all the others. We were told to keep it brief, as there were just two phones and more than twenty of us. When my turn came and I eventually picked up the receiver, my hands were shaking so badly it was all I could do to stop myself from dropping it. Carol's voice was full of excitement and at first I could not get a word in, then when at last she paused long enough for me to speak I froze. Eventually I managed to open my mouth and tried to reassure her I was okay, then the boys came on, wanting to know if I brought any Argentine guns back with me as souvenirs. Things got a bit emotional. I struggled to keep control. I told them I would be home in a couple of days at most, I hoped. Finally the money ran out and I had to pass the phone on. 'I love you all!' I shouted down the receiver just before we were cut off.

The following morning we rose at 06.00 and after a breakfast of bacon banjos we were visited by the ship's doctor who bade us farewell. We walking wounded disembarked and lined up in very un-military fashion on the dockside, before shuffling into a warehouse where a couple of army clerks were seated behind two trestle tables. I gave my name and number to the first and was issued with a rail warrant to Leeds, a small white cardboard box containing a packed lunch of cheese sandwiches, biscuits and an apple and told to report to the movements officer for transport to the railway station. We had a pay parade just before I left the ship, so money was no problem and miraculously my civvy bag was waiting for me at the transport.

The army can get things right sometimes, I thought as I boarded the civilian coach. As we set off for the station, I wondered why we were not in military transport. Although it was not uncommon to hire civilian vehicles my cynical mind concluded the MOD had chartered the coach rather than use a military one in order to keep the return of wounded troops low profile. It would never do for the public to discover what the war was doing to 'their boys' now, would it? I arrived at the station in jeans and T-shirt, my feet once again in my comfortable old trainers. My legs were now well on the mend and the dressings were gone, although I needed a stick to take the weight of my right leg, which was still giving me trouble. My civvy bag was not too heavy, having only few essentials like shaving kit waterproof jacket, socks, etc. My uniform had been lost along the way and the tracksuit I had been issued while in hospital left with the transport officer for return to stores. There were about a dozen or so other Falklands lads dropped off with me, but not in the mood to mingle I headed straight for the news stand, where I bought forty Bensons, fuel for my Zippo and a copy of the Guardian to hide behind. I had an hour to kill.

Entering the buffet with the idea of getting a cup of tea I opted instead for a mug of coffee. *Whisky goes better in coffee. God bless you Nigel,'* I said to myself as I took the bottle of Grants from the carrier bag and poured in as much as the mug would allow. I browsed the paper, not really taking in any news, just going through the motions. By the time I boarded the train I had drunk three mugs of coffee, heavily laced with half the contents of the whisky bottle. A warm glow spread throughout my system as I made my way along the half-empty carriages to the buffet car and ordered a McEwan's Export. I sat alone at the end of the carriage and stared out of the window alternately sipping Scotch and guzzling beer. I have no idea how much I drank but it must have been a lot. Sadly it was not enough. Try as I might I could not escape the pictures in my head. I was too scared to sleep in case I woke up screaming. The journey was long and unpleasantly stuffy in the buffet car, which had become very popular with the usual mix of holiday makers, businessmen and women and a group of squaddies who, like me, were on an alcoholic mission. They seemed to be having more success than me it seemed, as their banter grew louder and the obscenities increased in number and frequency. I bought another McEwan's and one for backup and made my way towards the front of the train, wobbling along on my dodgy pins. I eventually found what I was looking for – an empty First Class compartment. Some time later when the ticket collector entered and I handed him my Second class one, he looked at the stick and my Army issue watch and asked,

'Falklands?'

I nodded.

'Good job. I was in Korea with the Gloucesters.'

He studied my face for a couple of seconds.

'You'll be wanting some peace and quiet,' he said. An old soldier, he had been in harm's way. He understood.

The rest of the journey was uneventful. When we pulled into Leeds I was so stiff from sitting so long I had difficulty standing. I managed to get myself and my bag onto the platform and steadily shuffled across to the steps then painfully descended into the subway and up the other side. By the time I passed through the barrier I was knackered.

The sensible and logical thing to have done would have been to get straight into a taxi. I could have phoned Carol, but she did not know I was home, as I'd had no idea of transport arrangements when I called her from Portsmouth. Instead I made my way out of the Station, slowly worked my way down the steps to the street below and crossed the road straight into the Scarborough Taps. I glanced at my watch. It was 7.30pm. The bar was quiet. I found a perfect spot on a barstool at the end of the bar and ordered a large Scotch, Nigel's farewell gift being left on the train, empty of course. Several cigarettes later, mercifully the drink began at last to do its job. At closing time, I staggered out of the pub and by some miracle found myself at the Taxi rank outside the Station. The next thing I recall was the room spinning and my head down the toilet bowl. Carol must have put me to bed at when I had finished throwing up, for I awoke in the spare bed the following morning with the mother and father of all hangovers and a raging thirst. Not exactly the return of the conquering hero, but I was home.

30
Aftermath
Yorkshire 1982

Carol was wonderfully understanding and did not get on my back over my drunken state or the fact that I had not warned her when I was coming. I finally made it down to the kitchen at mid day and was surprised to find her waiting for me with coffee and Alka Seltzer.

'I rang in and booked a lieu day,' she said. 'How are you feeling?'

'I've been better,' I replied with my fur coated tongue.

She stepped forward and placing her hands on my shoulders leaned into me and kissed my cheek. We wrapped ourselves around each other and hugged for what seemed ages until I broke away and reached for the coffee.

'I am surprised you didn't bring Yorkie with you, it's not as if he has got any family to go home to.'

I could not bring myself to look at her.

'Tony, he is all right isn't he?'

'He is still on the Falklands.'

'Oh. When is he coming home then?'

'No hurry.'

'What?'

It was a rhetorical question. She knew from the tone of my voice that she would not see him again but I answered anyway, surprised at the matter of fact tone in which it came out.

'He was killed on the 24th of May.'

'Oh Tony I am so sorry.' There was a long pause before she asked the question. 'How did it happen?' 'What bloody difference does it make,' I snapped, 'he's dead.' I instantly regretted my outburst. I was full of anger but had no legitimate target for it.

'I'm sorry love,' I said at last, 'I didn't mean to take it out on you.'

'I know love. It's okay, just take it easy on the boys eh?'

'Yeah, sorry. I'm really sorry.'

We spent the rest of the afternoon catching up on what I had missed and no more was said about what had happened on the Falklands. When Mark and John got in from school they were surprisingly gentle with me, more so than I deserved. I guess she had briefed them before school whilst I had been sleeping it off. It was wonderful to see them, to be a family again. They filled me in on what had been happening at school and with their friends. It was so good to spend time with them. I made a promise to myself to be a better father and husband. I really meant it too. Unfortunately things were not that simple.

As the weeks passed my anger got worse and I suffered huge mood swings. I found it impossible to settle back into normal life. I saw my doctor who referred me to hospital as an outpatient for treatment to my legs, and I was signed on long term sick. I called the barracks and arranged to see the OC I avoided going on drill night. I was not ready to meet the lads just yet. He offered me his sympathy over the loss of my best friend and a transfer to the signals store until my retirement date was up. He asked if I would pass on any lessons learned from my experiences to the rest of the squadron, when I was ready, of course. I said I would, but only for the sake of appeasement; I could not think of anything I would less like to do.

I began to spend a lot of time during the day either drinking at home or in the pub. I deliberately avoided my local, where I was well known, but instead used those which I did not normally visit. I began frequenting the seedier rough dives where I was among serious hardened drinkers. It was not long before I began to feel at home. One pub in particular became a favourite because the beer was cheap and the clientele kept themselves to themselves. The more I drank the more I needed, but try as I might and boy did I try, I could not banish my demons. I am by nature a very tactile person, openly affectionate in normal times and always craving affection in return. These were not however normal times, at least not for me. I shunned any form of close physical contact with Carol and the boys and in spite of their understanding, things began to slide badly. I could see our relationship crumbling before my eyes and yet I felt powerless to stop it. Communication broke down between us and I became more withdrawn. In early August Yorkie's body was brought home and on the

18th we gave him a grand send off at York Crematorium. I was one of the pallbearers and laid his belt and beret on the casket. Most of the lads turned out and we sang the squadron hymn 'Jerusalem.' The local branch of the Parachute Regiment association sent a standard bearer and bugler who sounded the last post while the standard was lowered. His sisters and mother were in attendance and after the service we retired to the pub and drank to his memory.

By mid September I was still on the sick and rarely sober. I could feel everything I cared about slipping away but could do nothing to stop it. In my darker moments I flirted with the idea of suicide. The only thing that held me back from the abyss was my family. I could not bring myself to cause them any more pain than they had endured already, even if it would mean an end to mine. I had by then given up all hope of any reply to my letter to Ramon, of which I had still made no mention to Carol. One evening in October, I was propping up the bar of my favourite bolt hole when Carol walked in and ordered a pint of lager.

'Celebrating are we?' she said sarcastically. 'You should be,' she continued before I could reply. 'but I doubt you can remember what.' She was seriously pissed off.

'Do you know what day it' is she asked?

'Saturday. I might have had a couple but I can still tell you what day it is'

'Saturday, October the 16th. Your son's thirteenth birthday you pathetic bastard.' She picked up the pint of lager, threw it in my face and left.

I did not even have the sense to go home. I returned late that night drunk as usual to find an empty house. A short note cellotaped to the TV screen said 'Gone to mum's not coming back.' I just sat in the chair and stared at the wall. The same wall greeted my eyes when I opened them some eight hours later, stiff and aching in my limbs, but no trace of a hangover. I didn't get hangovers any more. I was never sober long enough. Struggling to my feet I made my way to the bathroom emptied my bladder and doused my face in cold water. I regarded my reflection in the mirror with contempt. I hated myself. How could I forget Mark's birthday? How could I do that? He was now a teenager!

I headed downstairs in search of a drink. I opened the fridge looking for a beer but I had drunk it dry. I rifled through the cupboards but there was no booze to be found. I was on my knees cursing and swearing surrounded by the cupboard's contents. I did not hear the front door open. I turned around still on my knees. John was standing key in hand, looking down at me shaking his head from side to side.

'Look at yourself Dad, just look at yourself.'

My hands were shaking. He looked all grown up, fifteen going on twenty-five.

'Hello son I didn't hear you come in?'

'Come on Dad. Let's get the kettle on.'

He took charge like a mother hen, made me sit at the kitchen table and drink coffee. Two mugs of coffee. What I really wanted was a large Scotch. I was feeling sick.

'You have to stop Dad. If you don't you'll kill yourself.'

'I'm fine' I lied 'I just need it to steady my nerves. I'm okay.'

I wasn't fooling either of us.

'How's Mark?' I asked changing the subject.

'How do you think?'

There was real anger in his voice. Anger with a bitter aftertaste. 'He says he's not coming round anymore. Mum says you need to see the doctor.'

'The doctor can't fix me son. There are no pills for what I have'

'Then fix your fucking self you selfish bastard.' he yelled, fighting back tears.

By the time I had got over the shock of him swearing at me, he was through the door slamming it so hard behind him the mirror fell off the wall, smashing into a hundred pieces on the hall floor. Staring down at the shattered glass I saw my reflection in the pieces. Fragmented like my life had become. Was this a sign? Was God trying to nudge his way back into my life? Whatever it was, it was something. For the first time in months I took a long hard look at myself. I was in a real mess. What happened to the Tony Gomez who had faced the balloon cage and conquered it? Tony Gomez who kept going through two selection courses. The Tony Gomez who once was looked up to by his sons. I had reached the bottom and I knew I had only two ways to go. Salvation or oblivion. I resolved there and then to seek help.

I made an appointment with my GP for the following morning. I needed something to focus on, a short term achievable goal. I would clean the house. I set to with a will. Like a man possessed, I spent the next several hours tidying, Hoovering, scrubbing and polishing. I chain smoked my way through the day. At eight o'clock I rang the takeaway and ordered Chicken Madras with rice and chips. I had not had a drink all day. My hands were still shaky but strangely I was not craving alcohol as much as I expected. At ten o'clock I ran a bath and threw in a liberal dose of Radox crystals. As I lay in the warm water, I began to formulate a plan to get my life back together.

My doctor gave me a thorough examination, asked loads of questions, prescribed antidepressants and referred me to a consultant at the Hospital. He told me I had the classic symptoms of something called Post Traumatic Stress Disorder.

When I got home I rang my mother in law. After a long chat she agreed to meet in town for a coffee. For the second time in twelve hours I had a bath, shaved and splashed on aftershave. I put on a clean pair of jeans and a polo shirt and set off to walk the mile and a half to the town centre in my desert boots. There was an autumnal nip in the air as I strode along, my hands deep in the pockets of my Barbour jacket. I was early but Liz was already sitting with a coffee and a Kit Kat when I arrived. She greeted me warmly, and as I sat down, I was pleased to see she noted the change in my appearance. I explained as much as I could about what the doctor had said.

'This post trauma thing, it's like depression then?'

'Yes, that is exactly what it is. It is what they used to call shell shock. He's given me pills to calm me down and I have to see this trick cyclist at the hospital and go to some form of regular therapy.'

'How long for?'

'God knows. As long as it takes I guess. Look I'm really sorry for my behaviour since I had got back. I've been a complete twat I know. I didn't mean to cause such hurt to everyone. I know it is asking a lot and I will understand if you say no, but would you ask Carol if she will see me. Give me a chance to explain, make amends.'

'I will try, but she is very hurt you know, especially about the way you've been with the boys.'

'I know but if you will just try to put in a word. Tell her I am getting help. Please.'

'I'll do what I can, Tony. I can see you are trying, love. Don't think it will be easy though, my daughter knows her own mind and she is seriously pissed off with you. You have some mountain to climb.'

I was under no illusion as to the task ahead but I had taken the first step. God bless my mother in law for agreeing to help me begin the long climb out of the pit into which I had fallen, or was it jumped. It took a couple of weeks before Carol would agree to see me. She sensibly wanted to wait until the pills had had time to start working and to see if I could stay off the booze. I had a tearful reunion with the boys. We went to McDonald's and then the pictures to see E.T. All they wanted to know was when would we all be together again. All I could say was. 'Soon, I hope.'

Carol wisely declined to move back at first, but came around during the day at weekends until eventually she stayed overnight, once a week at first and then more frequently. The boys then stayed over also and gradually some semblance of normality began to return. I kept on with medication and counseling fully aware that I still had my mountain to climb. It was not all plain sailing, but the drugs kept my anger under control and gradually the therapy began to work. There were times when I retreated to the shed and buggered about with bits of wood or sharpened tools just to keep myself focused, but these gradually became less.

Christmas was a relatively quiet affair but we splashed out and bought the boys new bikes. I gave Carol a silver necklace and matching ear rings. She bought me a new duvet coat to replace the one destroyed by the Falklands episode. The boys, bless 'em bought me a small transistor radio so I could listen to music in the shed. We saw in the New Year at Carol's parents. I drank red wine, in moderation, with Carol's blessing, the first alcohol I had touched for months. The nightmares that I had been experiencing since my return were still vivid, but were not waking me quite as often. Things were far from perfect, but I felt we were on the right track. The episode with the mirror had re kindled my faith and I was now praying again.

One morning early in the new year as I sat eating my toast, Carol walked into the kitchen with the post. She had a puzzled expression on her face.

'You have a letter, love. Looks like it's from Argentina!'

I took the envelope and looked at the stamp

and postmark. I did not dare to open it, turning the envelope over and over in my shaking hands.

'What is it Tony? What's the matter?'

'Sit down love. I have something to tell you.'

So it was that for the first time I told her about Ramon. I explained how I made the discovery, about Nigel and how he had helped me aboard Uganda. I kept it very specific and did not mention what took place on the Islands. She listened intently without comment until I had brought her up to date. Speaking about it was difficult and I became emotional and had to stop from time to time with the result that it was almost lunchtime by the time I had finished. All the while the envelope lay untouched upon the table.

'Well, you had better open it,' she said when I had finally finished.

I carefully slipped the letter opener into the corner and slit the envelope open. I removed the single sheet of blue airmail paper. In blue black ink written in a neat hand with what I guessed was a fine nib fountain pen, was the reply I had longed for.

Casa Fortuna
76 Calle Lateral Del Río,
Al Oeste Central
Rosario
Argentina

Dear Antonio,
Forgive please the delay for writing this reply to you. My name is Maria Consuela Ramirez and I thank you for what you did

to help my brother Ramon. He speaks of you with a kind heart and says you are a good man. The war was a terrible time. We lost my youngest brother who was just seventeen years old, a sailor on the Belgrano. Since the war Ramon is not a well man and much troubled and so it is me who writes but with his permission. Your letter was great shock of course and we have taken time to discuss much of it. Our mother is very strong and has spoken with father on this and we are all agreed that because you helped Ramon we must tell to you what has happened. This is a great surprise to me and Ramon and to mother also.

Our father was put in the hospital in Uruguay in 1939, for long time. He was hurt in the battle and could not see. Our mother was nurse in hospital and she became his friend. She is Argentine. It is long time for our father to be well almost one year and then they fall in love.

They come to Argentina in 1942 and they are married. But now of course this is no marriage because our father is married already in UK.

Our mother is of course upset and our father also but the love is strong. They talk with the priest and next month will marry again for the first time. I hope this is good news for you and you will be happy for us. This is very strange but please write again.

With affection

Your sister, Maria.

I showed her the letter.

After reading it carefully twice she looked up at

me and smiled.

'You will write back won't you?'

'Damn right I will. I have some good news for them.'

'What good news?'

'Maria's mother has no need to be upset. There is nothing wrong with her marriage. My mother was killed on the 2nd of October 1942, that's at least four weeks before they got hitched. I am not sure I can get my head around all of this you know, it's like something off the tele.'

She leaned forward and kissed my forehead.

'Don't worry it will all turn out all right in the end love. It's fate, that's all'

Fate? Divine intervention perhaps? Who knows? All I knew was I had one more reason to get back to a normal life. I had something to focus on, a long term goal: to be reunited with my brother and to meet my father. Unreal!

I spent the next couple of days composing a reply which ran to four pages; quite something for me. I wrote about us as a family, especially John and Mark as these were as I far as I understood it my father's only grandchildren. I told Maria the news about her mother being married after all and finished with the wish that one day we might all get together although I knew it was very much a remote possibility.

31
Pen Pals
Yorkshire 1983 - 1992

I finished with the Army for good and in the spring concentrated all my spare time on gardening. I was at my best when working physically, especially outdoors. I had secured a job at a local Garden Centre through a contact I had in the Squadron. It meant a substantial drop in income, taking into account the loss of TA pay as well, but we could manage – just. The work was quite physical and mostly in the open air, which was a beneficial contrast to the museum. I continued with my therapy and my psychiatrist recommended that I keep myself busy and also, curiously, to keep up my physical fitness as this would help me in the fight against my demons

'What do you think about a pond?' I asked one morning over my bowl of Weetabix.

Both boys were all for it and Carol acknowledged that a project would do me good.

'How are we going to afford it?' Carol said. We're only just managing as it is.

'I'm going to give up smoking and get a bike, and I can get all the gear at the garden centre with my staff discount.'

'Come on mum, please!' the boys said in chorus.

'Only if your dad keeps his word and stops smoking.'

'Radical.' Mark said, obviously delighted. I had no idea what he was talking about.

Over three days Mark, John and I dug a hole three feet deep roughly fourteen feet in diameter.

'Are you sure it's big enough love? Carol asked taking the proverbial. Look's more like a boating lake than a pond. We'll have nowhere left to grow flowers.'

'We'll grow water plants in the pond. I'm going to take the boys out to the canal and collect seed from the yellow flag irises. There's all sorts of other plants we can collect and it won't cost a penny. One of the guys at work has promised me a water lily too.'

'That's good of him.'

Yeah. We're sorted. Could do with a hand with the liner this afternoon, if you're around.'

'Okay, just give me a shout.'

We all worked together getting the rubber liner installed and finally we were ready to fill it.

'I'll get the hose Dad,' Mark shouted.

'No, me Dad.' His brother pleaded. While I was trying to settle the dispute, Carol appeared from nowhere, several steps ahead of the game and blasted me with cold water from the trigger gun on the end of the pipe. It all descended into chaos, wonderful happy chaos. We all got soaked.

I went off with the boys to the canal where we collected plants, insects and other creatures to stock our pond. This activity brought us closer and reminded me of my own childhood, collecting frog spawn and catching newts. The main difference was that I had done all my playing about in ponds on my own. I regretted not having had a dad to help me when I was young, although I was by no means alone in this. Many of the kids I grew up with had lost their fathers in the war.

I exchanged many letters with Maria and eventually Ramon put pen to paper. We traded birthday and Christmas cards and developed a good pen pal relationship, which was all very light hearted, the war not being mentioned, except in passing. I bought my bicycle which helped on the economic front. I would not accept help from the state I would have regarded that as failure, I had to do this myself. Things started to come together and we became a real family again, spending quality time together. We went walking in Wensleydale and I became a regular on the touchline when the boys were playing football.

One Saturday morning as I was raking up the Autumn leaves Carol called me from the kitchen doorway.

'Tony. You have a visitor.'

I went in to find a dapper sixty something man wearing a well tailored suit sipping coffee at the table. It was the secretary of the Regimental Association

'Tony. How are you keeping?'

'Fine thanks. To what do I owe the pleasure?'

'The pleasure is mine and it is the Regiment that is in debt; to you. He took an envelope from his inside pocket and offered it to me. The Association would be pleased if you would accept this small token of our thanks, for your efforts during the campaign in the South Atlantic.'

Inside was a generous cheque.

'I can't take this I said.'

He sighed. 'That is what everyone says. Don't give me a hard time Tony. We owe you this. You have paid your dues so don't be a prat and take it.'

How could I refuse?

'Take your charming wife and family on holiday. It will do you the world of good.'

I was deeply touched.

We booked two weeks walking and fishing in Scotland for the following August. It was good to have something to look forward to and when the holiday finally arrived, we were full of excitement, especially the Mark and John. I was still on medication, but with a reduced dose and the boys and I had become close again. They were so understanding it made me quite humble. I had not touched alcohol since the New Year celebrations, but on the first night of the second week we had a lovely family meal at our rented cottage and I had three large glasses of wine, Carol even more. Later that night we made love for the first time since before the Falklands. Lying in the dark, our bodies entwined, I felt relaxed in a way I could hardly remember.

'Was it really awful?'

'The war?'

'It might help to talk about it. You know I am a good listener.'

'I remember the cold mostly. We were always

freezing cold. The food on the Islands wasn't up to much and that was all cold too.'

'But you had your little stoves?'

'We couldn't light them. It would give our position away.'

'The Argies, were they near to you then?'

I didn't answer.

She squeezed my hand and kissed my cheek.

This was the beginning of my audio therapy as I liked to call it. My wife, best friend, lover and now psychotherapist. I talked to Carol about what had happened on the Islands. Small stuff, at first. Insignificant stuff she already knew, but it was a start. The last barrier had been breached. Over the coming months I gradually opened up and went into some detail although I spared her the graphic gore. This, the best form of therapy in the world, began to free me little by little from some of my guilt.

I was one of the lucky ones. I knew from my group therapy that those who had no family or worse still, family lacking in understanding and compassion, had a real really hard time. Some, like me, turned to drink or drugs, while others fell foul of the law. Violent antisocial behaviour, saw a number of good men end up in prison. I thanked God for my family. Their love was my lifeline in the cold and hostile ocean in which I was still treading water.

The holiday was the best we had ever had. John and Mark had both caught decent-sized trout for the table, which put a permanent grin on their faces. It all ended too soon, but the long drive home was a pleasure, the weather glorious and the traffic was free flowing all the way.

Sitting at home together on the sofa that night mugs in hand, mine tea, hers black coffee, I felt at peace.

'How can you sleep after black coffee last thing at night?' I asked.

'Easy love, clear conscience and a happy life,' she replied, a twinkle in her eye.

'I'll drink to that.'

Over the next several months many letters were exchanged between the Ramirez household and ours.

'Breakfast is ready.' Carol shouted from downstairs as I came out of the bathroom, the smell of grilled bacon spreading a smile across my face.

'You've another letter from Argentina.'

My smile broadened into a silly grin.

'Maria's working as an administrator for the Red Cross,' I said, chewing a mouthful of smoked streaky.

'Ramon can't get work because of his injuries. His dad's packed the sea in, but he's still working at home.'

'Your Dad, love. He's your Dad too.'

'Yeah of course. I just haven't got used to it yet.'

'They have a bar-cum-restaurant overlooking the Parana River. Small, but popular so Maria says. Her Mum works in the bar, in fact they all do it seems. She says Dad does all the cooking for the bar and he is very good too. Ramon's legs are weak from of infection getting into his wounds. The doctors apparently discussed double amputation as an option at one stage. Anyway they dropped the idea and he now walks with a stick, so that's not too bad is it?'

'I suppose not.'

I spent hours in the library reading up on Argentina, an activity which, I found both therapeutic and rewarding. My ultimate goal, was to be reunited with Ramon and to meet my father and sister. Pie in the sky really, for we were struggling financially and anyway, relations between our countries made it next to impossible, for the time being at least. Even so, it gave me a valuable focus on the future which, coupled with the support of my family, became the cornerstone of my recovery.

Over the next few years, the nightmares came less often and I learned to deal with them better. The anger was still there and I could not watch politicians spouting their lies and propaganda without swearing at the television and more often than not, storming out of the room. I got particularly angry at news stories of British troops going into action around the world with inadequate equipment and at the millions of pounds of taxpayers money wasted on poor, unsuitable kit.

When I 'went off on one,' everyone just left me alone until I calmed down. I was still angry with my father for deserting my mother, but could not bring myself to confront him. Somehow it did not seem appropriate by letter.

In 1985 we received photographs of Maria's fortieth birthday party. One was a group photograph with Ramon and Miguel in a smart grey suit, between Rosita and birthday girl Maria. Miguel was still recognisable as the man at my mother's side in my dog-eared photograph. His hair was grey and yes, he was older, but it was still him. In his hands he held a cream coloured Panama hat. Rosita was small and dark with her hair drawn back tightly into a bun. She was wearing a plain navy blue dress with no obvious waist, but she appeared quite slim. Maria reminded me of the film star Linda Cristal. She was very attractive, with a slim but shapely figure shown to advantage by her well-cut white dress. Her hair was coal black with curls that danced around her shoulders. Even the boys were impressed. We replied with a similar group picture although it was very difficult to get Mark to stop clowning long enough to get a decent shot. Over time we exchanged more photographs of key moments in our lives, but gradually the letters became less frequent. It was only to be expected and by my fiftieth birthday in 1990 we were down to three a year plus Christmas and birthday cards.

It was an eventful year, Mark had his twenty-first birthday and was studying in London at the Royal College of Art, while John was in his third year at Manchester University reading Engineering. Both had girlfriends, but nothing serious as far as I could tell. We got on well when they came to visit and I had much cause to thank God for how my life had turned around. That is not to say it was trouble-free, for even after nine years I still struggled from time to time with the fallout from my Falklands' experience. It had waged a war of attrition on our marriage. Now that the kids were independent and I was probably as well as I was ever going to be, Carol felt that she had done all she could and finally announced that she was moving out. I was too tired too argue and we parted amicably after more than twenty years together.

One weekend when the boys came for a visit we told them. They were sad but not surprised. Mark said at the time, 'at least you are still friends.' John's reaction was much the same. As for Carol and I, love had died slowly and almost imperceptibly over nine years, just another casualty of the war. Love had done its' job, it had been strong enough to hold the family together through the worst and it had given me back a life. Christmas 1990 was a sombre affair and the New Year was depressing.

I struggled with my anger at the government again in January, as once again Britain became involved in war. This time it was Kuwait and Iraq. I was sorely tempted to take to the bottle again but some how I hung on. In July I received a letter from a firm of solicitors in Cardiff. My father's sister had died suddenly. Always a strange one, she had been living as a recluse for as long as I can remember. I only recall seeing her about three times in my entire life, in spite of her living a short bus ride from my gran's where I was brought up. Being the only relative able to make the journey, I travelled to Cardiff to assist with the funeral arrangements.

She died, unaware that her brother was alive and well and living in South America. I had kept this from her at his request, although I am not sure she would have cared. I had never heard her speak of him and somehow held the impression they did not get on. I guess Miguel did not want to get any deeper into his past than he had already, but I wrote to tell him. In the end I could not bring myself to post the letter.

Her death changed my circumstances significantly. She died intestate which presented a problem. Her closest living relative and therefore beneficiary was Miguel, but officially he was dead. I of course, knew different, but if I kept quiet I could receive a tidy sum, as the house alone was worth £75,000. I would be able to pay off my mortgage and would be able to afford a visit to see my brother and sister and meet my father at last. I was sorely tempted but my morals got the better of me and I wrote to the solicitors explaining the situation giving them Miguel's address.

In late October I received a letter from Ramon. Inside the letter was a cheque.

Dear Brother,

We have long wished for an opportunity to meet again and this will now be possible. Thanks to you we now have much unexpected money. Please accept this gift as thank you and use it for an airline ticket. I look forward to seeing you soon, with affection.
Ramon.

At long last my chance to meet my father was about to become a reality.

32
Pilgrimage
Falkland Islands, March 1992

Over the next few weeks, letters zipped back and forth between the UK and Argentina, and dreams of a reunion with Ramon slowly morphed into reality. It was a time of high excitement tinged with anxiety. Early in the new year of 1992, I booked a flight to the Islands with the RAF I confirmed the dates and flight times, picked up the phone and dialled long distance. It seemed to ring for ages before the receiver was picked up.

'Hello' said a gruff voice at the other end.

'I would like to speak to Rory Walker if I may please,'

'You are,' came the sandpaper reply, 'who is it?'

'Tony Gomez, Rory. Remember me? Penguin Tony.'

'No kidding. It must be thirty years.'

'Thirty-seven, to be precise, 1964. So, how are you?'

'I'm right as rain, laddie, but you didn't call from the other end of the world after all these years for chit chat now, did ye?'

Straight to the point, that was Rory. It was comforting to know he had not changed.

'No, Rory, I need a favour. I'm coming down for a couple of weeks. Can you recommend somewhere to stay?'

'Your room is still empty, Annie does her sewing in there when she's a mind to, but the bed's still there. New mattress.'

'Terrific. Thanks so much.'

'What else, laddie?'

I must have shown a touch too much emotion in my voice. He still knew me well after nearly forty years.

'It'll keep until I see you Rory.'

'Whatever you say. Give me your flight details and I'll be there. Annie will be tickled pink.'

I gave Rory the information and we said farewell. His last words before the line went dead were. 'Bring me some St. Bruno.'

In March I embarked upon my pilgrimage to the Falklands. It was my wish to travel alone. The boys drove me to RAF Brize Norton and bid me an emotional farewell at Passport Control. It was nostalgic from the start, as I had flown from Brize several times with the Squadron; to Germany and Denmark mostly, for exercises overseas and to annual camp. As well as its' operational transport squadrons, Brize Norton is home to Number One Parachute Training School the unit that trained me to be a parachutist thirty years before, when it was based at Abingdon in Berkshire. The base is also home to the RAF's air refuelling fleet. The flight, long and tedious, was uneventful, but the Lockheed Tristar was more comfortable than I remember the VC10 to have been when I last flew from the airport. It was more conventional, in terms of passenger accommodation as the seats faced forward and not backwards as they did in the VC10. I say airport, for that is what Brize is, the RAF's own international airport with flights covering most of the globe. We stopped off at Ascension Island to refuel, disembark personnel and take on passengers before continuing on our long journey south. As I looked out of the window at the aircraft and kit dispersed around Wideawake Airfield memories stirred at the back of my mind.

Eighteen hours after we lifted off the runway at Brize, I looked out of the window to see a Tornado aircraft, complete with sidewinder missiles, flying on a parallel course half a mile distant as we began our descent into Mount Pleasant Airport. The big jet touched down at 10.17 local time, thirty minutes late but with a silk smooth landing that raised a murmur of approval and a round of applause from the passengers.

Point. It was here that members of the Regiment called down artillery fire and directed attacks on Argentinian positions during the advance on Stanley.

'Well, that is one hell of a story, laddie. One hell of a story.'

'Wait 'til Annie hears this. So you want to go back to where you lost your friend?'

'Yeah, it's just something I need to do. I have the grid reference. Got it from the flight record of the Heli I was casevacced on. It'll mean a walk.' I said apologetically.

'Don't trouble yourself. It might not be as far as you think,' he said patting the dashboard. 'Not so many places Bess here cannot go.'

'I am really grateful...' I began.

'Hush now, 'tis we that are grateful for you coming to our rescue in eighty-two. It's no a nice thing to be invaded.'

'I guess not.'

The rest of the drive we just swopped small talk until we drew up outside a freshly painted white single storey house with a green corrugated iron roof. It was only the second building we had encountered since we left the Stanley road. Annie rushed out of the front door and clapped me in a bear hug the second I set foot on the land.

'House look's lovely.' I said when I was able to fill my lungs.

'She insisted I give it a coat of paint in honour of your visit,' moaned Rory in jest.

'Ignore him and come on in, the kettle's on.'

While Annie brewed the tea, I sat at the beechwood kitchen table. The mouthwatering smell of roasting lamb filled the room. I looked out of the window to Estancia settlement, half a mile away across the inlet. Rock Cormorants were diving for fish in the cold waters, while steamer ducks dabbled in the shallows. The view was wild and breathtaking.

Rory joined me at the table.

'Your gear's in your room. You'll no' believe this Annie love, no' at all. You tell her laddie, tell her what ye told me.'

I repeated my story for Annie's benefit. She was more shocked and surprised than her husband, her green eyes widening with every sentence.

'Mercy me,' she kept saying, 'mercy me,' all the while fidgetting with the overlong sleeves of her hand knitted arran jumper.

When I had finished, she sat in silence trying to digest what she had heard.

'I am taking the laddie out to Bombilla House in the morning. We are going to leave a marker.'

'That reminds me,' I said, and I excused myself to fetch some bits from my rucksack.

'There you go Rory,' I announced as I put half a pound of St. Bruno Flake on the table with a litre of Malt Whisky. 'And for madame...' I plonked a bottle of gin and a large tin of Quality Street in Annie's lap with a flourish.

'My favourite sweets! You remembered, Tony.'

'Thanks Laddie.' said Rory caressing the bottle of Glen Morangie.

'My pleasure, enjoy 'em.'

Later that evening, full of Annie's roast dinner and relaxing in front of a peat fire, Rory, and I slowly demolished the bottle of Malt while Annie knocked back Gin and Tonic. I was more relaxed than I had been for a long time and it was not just the whisky. There was something about Island life, like stepping back in time to my Nan's day when everyone knew everyone else and nobody locked their door. Just being here was a big step forward in the healing process. At ten o'clock Annie got up and announced she was off to bed.

'You too,' she said, looking at us like the schoolteacher she once was. 'Early start in the morning.'

The smell of frying bacon wafting from the kitchen stirred me from an untroubled sleep. I broke my record for morning ablutions by several seconds and presented myself at the kitchen table. I was touched by the way I had been welcomed back after such a long time and I made a promise to myself to keep in touch with these good people. Annie set a plate full of eggs, bacon and fried potato in front of me which I demolished. Rory was already outside checking and loading the Land Rover.

We set off on our journey across the wild expanse of East Falkland at 8 a.m. heading towards Douglas settlement as the sun began to climb. The gravel road was wet from the overnight rain, as we approached the second of three small bridges over the creeks which fed into the inlet. In contrast to the flat shores on our right, the limestone crags of Smoko Mountain dominated the landward skyline. The windswept vista was one of wild beauty that truly was a joy to behold. We passed Teal Inlet settlement just before 8.20 and twenty-five minutes later we turned South onto a grass track below Douglas Station. We trundled along the rough track until we were about a mile and a half from Bombilla House, at which point Rory wheeled right onto a barely discernible track.

'Not far now laddie'

'Four K I reckon,' I said, studying the map.

'Two and a half miles, you bloody European'

'Okay have it your way.' I replied as we banged

and bounced our way towards the place where the lights in my world were suddenly extinguished ten years ago. My stomach began to knot. Rory pushed the vehicle to it's limits, up and down banks, through streams and across rough pockmarked slippery slopes. Ten minutes later we ran out of track and Rory expertly guided the Land Rover, slithering across the undulating ground for another five, until he finally stopped on a flat plateau fifteen feet above a point where a stream entered a river.

'Well done, Rory. Spot on.'

'This is the place I reckon.'

'Yeah, this must be where the Heli landed to casevac me out.'

'You want me to come down with you?' Rory asked looking across to the far bank of the stream.

'Yes, I would, if that's okay.'

'Of course, laddie.'

With that, he disappeared round the back of the 'Rover and fished out a narrow canvas bag about five feet long and slung it over his shoulder.

'Wait and see,' my companion said as I opened my mouth. I closed it without utterance.

I grabbed my rucksack and we walked to the edge of the bank and scrambled down it's steep, slippery grassy sides.

'I'm getting a bit bloody old for this,' Rory observed as we waded across the stream and climbed onto the grassy bank.

'Well, laddie?'

'I am not sure. Somewhere here. It was dark, we were knackered. I was so tired I remember hallucinating at times.'

Rory took the canvas bag from his shoulder, unclipped the top flap and drew out an entrenching tool and an old ex-army mine detector.

'We'll soon know,' he stated confidently, as he put on the head phones and switched on. In less than ten minutes he hit the jackpot and dug up seven expended M16 cartridge cases confirming we were in the right place. He handed me the treasure and tactfully backed away.

'I'll be down by the river if you need me, son.'

Nodding acknowledgment, I opened the rucksac and removed three lengths of aluminium tubing. Screwing the sections together brought the memories swimming back, as the simple cross took shape. Engraved across the horizontal bar, the words...

Cpl. Matthew 'YORKIE' Barnes
Brother in arms B. 31.03.1936.
Killed in action 25. 5. 1982

I pushed the cross into the soil, hammering it home with the entrenching tool. Stepping back, I looked down at the memorial to my fallen comrade.

'Well, mate, this is just au revoir. I know we'll meet again even if you don't. I never thought I would see this place again. To be honest, old pal, I was scared of coming here, but now I don't know why at all. It is beautiful here, un-spoilt and peaceful. God be with you my brother.'

I walked slowly away towards the river, where

Rory was sweeping with his detector. For the first time I noticed the complete absence of wind. The Falklands without wind, it was like Morecambe without Wise, strawberries without cream – unheard of. I looked up to the heavens, was he trying to say something?

'Over here with that entrenching tool, laddie.'

Rory was standing at the edge of the river, hovering the detector over the lip of the bank. I handed him the tool and a couple of minutes later, he removed a metal object the size of his hand from the dirt. He washed it in the river, then held it up. I recognized it instantly. My question was answered, Yorkie was talking to me from beyond the grave. At this point I broke down in tears, tears that I had waited ten years to shed.

Rory put his arm around my shoulder.

'It's his. It's Yorkie's,' I said.

'It's a rifle magazine, it could be anyone's laddie.'

'No, it's Yorkie's. It's from an SLR. Only Yorkie had an SLR we all had M16s, even the Marines that fired on us.'

'Souvenir,...er... memento I mean' said Rory awkwardly offering me the rusted metal.

'Thank you.' I drew my sleeve across my eyes to wipe the tears.

As I took the magazine, I felt a powerful sense of connection with my lost comrade, as if he was looking out for me still. A sense of peace settled on me like a warm comfortable blanket and I climbed the bank like a twenty year old on Benzedrine. I felt happy.

We arrived back at the farm mid afternoon, to the smell of mutton stew simmering on the stove and a big mug of strong sweet tea. Being with Rory and Annie again had given me a new perspective. In 1982 we came to fight to preserve a way of life for good honest hard working folk, who did not have the means to defend themselves. In itself it was a noble act, but one that was launched for political reasons. I would never lose my anger towards the politicians for not finding a negotiated settlement, but at the same time I was proud we gave the country back to the Islanders.

Slowly, I was learning to accept that I would never be completely comfortable with that part of history. It was hard, but I knew if I could just accept it, I might be able to move on. My pilgrimage was working. Bit by bit I was coming to terms with things in a way I never could have, 8000 miles away in England. It had been a satisfying day, a good day. I hoped and prayed tomorrow would also be a good day, the day for reunion with the living. I was nervous, but then I was nervous about revisiting the ambush site and that had been in the end a very positive experience. I had at last got the closure I needed with my old comrade. At long last I felt forgiven for bringing him to the war that took his life

MIGUEL

33
Reflection
30,000 Feet Above the South Atlantic 1992

The early morning sky was overcast with light rain falling, as Ramon, Maria and Miguel settled into their seats aboard the LAN Chile Boeing. The engines were running and the aircraft slowly began to move along the taxiway towards the runway for take off. The control tower at El Tepual gave the pilot clearance and the jetliner lurched down the runway gathering speed until she lifted off and climbed into the grey Chilean sky. The connecting flight from Argentina had been Miguel's first experience of air travel. He was apprehensive about the trip, but not just because of flying. He was nervous of his son's possible reaction when he finally came face to face with the man who's mother he had deserted.

It had taken many weeks of work by Ramon and Maria to persuade him that it was the right thing to do, to travel to Las Malvinas, to make his peace with his son. The enterprise had involved much planning between the two families at opposite sides of the world, but gradually it had all come together. They would be spending a week on the Islands, staying at the Uplands Goose Hotel in Stanley, very different from the accommodation Ramon experienced during the occupation in 1982. He and Maria also were apprehensive, wondering how they would be received by the locals, how Miguel would handle meeting his son for the first time and for Ramon, what memories might be triggered by return to the Islands.

As he settled into his seat and tried to relax for last leg of the journey, Miguel's thoughts were of the happy times when he and his young Argentine nurse were getting to know each other and the love that blossomed between them. The smile these memories brought to his eyes slowly faded as tiredness gradually overcame him. The early start and the long journey from Buenos Aries had left Miguel exhausted. Closing his eyes he slipped further back in time to a long forgotten world before the war. Not the Falklands War, but the Second World War; his war. With misty eyes, he recalled the day he met Alice.

34
Looking Back
Cardiff, July 1937 – September 1939

It was Saturday evening and Miguel had been ashore for six days having recently returned from Singapore. Not tall, he was however, undeniably dark and very handsome, cutting quite a dash in his new uniform. He had just been promoted to Chief Steward. This was no mean achievement for a twenty-five year-old son of Spanish Immigrants, who began his career as a fourteen year-old cabin boy.

Leaving his parents' house in Barry, he made his way down the hill to the railway station in the warm afternoon sunshine, nodding to the Co-op bread man who urged his horse up the gradient. Walking briskly, black kid gloves in hand, Miguel stopped briefly to buy a newspaper from the vendor on the street corner, and only just managed to catch the local train to Cardiff. Finding a seat he took out a silver cigarette case and extracted from it a Players Navy Cut, which he placed carefully between his lips. Fishing around in his pocket he produced a Ronson lighter and lit up, making a mental note to trim the wick as he observed the black smoke and strong petrol smell as he worked the action. The paper was full of gloom about the situation in Czechoslovakia and the possibility of war with Germany. Lord Runciman had been appointed as mediator by the British government in an attempt to find a way out of the crisis. He wasn't going to let anything cast a cloud over his day, however and so he turned to the sports pages to pass the rest of the short journey.

The train pulled into Cardiff General Station, hissing to a halt in a loud cloud of steam. Miguel stepped down onto the platform and made his way towards the steps through the crowd, the smell of soot hanging in the air. In less than fifteen minutes, he was standing at the bar in the Merchant Navy club with a large rum in his hand, the first of many. Years at sea with little to do when off duty had given Miguel a taste for alcohol and a high tolerance to its effects. By eight o'clock he had drunk enough to send a normal man staggering, but he showed no sign at all of instability. He was, after all, used to carrying a tray of drinks along a pitching deck in heavy seas without spilling a drop. He made his way east along Queen Street towards the Connaught Rooms, strolling in to the sound of George and Ira Gershwin's 'Love Walked In.' The dance floor was half-empty, but it was still early. There were one or two other uniforms to be seen Royal Navy and RAF officers, most of the rest of the men wore lounge suits. As for the women, there were quite a few in small groups sitting at tables around the dance floor, all dressed to the nines and ripe for plucking.

Miguel headed for the bar, mentally preparing himself for the charm offensive he would launch later. Impeccable manners and a silver tongue were his stock in trade, combined with a dazzling smile and

Latin looks that many women found hard to resist. Once they accepted his invitation to take to the floor they were his, for he was a superb dancer, gliding across the floor like Fred Astaire. He set his sights at a pair of likely beauties occupying a table in a softly lit corner, approaching them with his flashing white smile, pouring on the patter. The darker haired of the two declined his offer, claiming not to be a dancer but added,

'My friend would love to, wouldn't you Alice? She is a great dancer,' the brunette added.

She proved to be excellent, as he led her in the quickstep. They moved well together and after three dances they were getting on fine, chatting away about nothing in particular. Nevertheless Miguel excused himself after escorting his partner from the floor and thanking her with an exaggerated bow. Taking his leave, he disappeared into the crowd that had now begun to fill the dance hall and made his way to the bar.

Forty-five minutes and several Rums later, he returned to ask Alice to take to the floor with him again, but had to wait as she was already waltzing with another young man. He stayed in the background, biding his time until at last she left the floor and returned to her seat. Moving in with charming intent Miguel launched into his patter and soon had the full attention of both women. By the time the evening was drawing to a close, he had made a lasting impression and taking Alice's hand he led her on to the floor for the last waltz. She was small and slim, no more than five feet two and yes, her eyes were the palest blue. Light brown hair fell just short of her shoulders, her dress was beautifully cut and looked expensive. He could not help but be impressed when she confessed to him that she made it herself. They all left together and Miguel walked the ladies to the bus stop and waited for them to board, though not before ascertaining that they would be at next week's dance. Waving them off, he turned and headed back towards the Merchant Navy club,whistling as he went.

Over the course of the next three weeks Miguel became a regular fixture in the Connaught Rooms and Alice hardly danced with anyone else. As he walked her to the bus stop, Miguel broke the news that he was sailing on the morning tide for Buenos Aires and would not be back for three months. Alice showed no emotion at the news but said she would be happy to see him when he returned. So it was that a pattern became established and over the next twelve months they spent as much time together as possible, whenever Miguel was ashore. They got engaged on November the 15th, 1938, Alice's twenty second birthday. They were married on Saturday September the 2nd 1939. After the reception held in the Park Hotel, they went away by train to Weston-super-Mare. The small hotel was cosy and they had a sea view from their room. After a light breakfast and a stroll along the front, they returned to the hotel lounge where residents and staff alike were gathered around the radio in total silence. The Prime Minister was speaking.

I am speaking to you from the cabinet room at ten Downing Street. This morning, the British ambassador in Berlin, handed the German government, a final note stating, that unless we heard from them by 11 o'clock, that they were prepared at once, to withdraw their troops from Poland, a state of war would exist between us. I have to tell you now, that no such undertaking has been received and that consequently, this country, is at war with Germany.'

Alice looked at Miguel. He squeezed her hand and smiled thinly. Alice saw apprehension behind his eyes.

'What will happen to us Miguel?'

'We will send the army to France, just like last time.'

'Those poor boys stuck in the trenches again. How awful.' Said Alice.

Miguel slowly shook his head.

'It will be different this time Alice. There will be bombing. Look what they did to Guernica two years ago.'

'Where?'

'Guernica. It is a littlel town in Spain, up in the North, only six thousand people. My Uncle lived there. The Germans bombed it. They sent their airforce to aid that scoundrel Franco in the Civil War. They killed one thousand six hundred innocent civilians. My uncle was one of them.'

'Miguel, I am so sorry, I had no idea. When was this?'

A couple of months before we met, Chiquita. April 26th. A date I shall never forget.

Later, over a roast beef dinner they discussed the situation further, not really knowing what the immediate future might hold for them. The honeymoon had passed by in the blink of an eye, or so it seemed to Miguel, as he watched the countryside rolling past the window to the clickety-clack of carriage wheels on steel rails. His thoughts turned to his next voyage and the fear of German submarines that would soon be prowling the sea-lanes, looking for fat merchant ships to send to the bottom. Excusing himself from his young wife's company, he made his way into and along the corridor to the toilet and locked himself inside. Leaning against the rocking window he put his hand deep into the inside pocket of his tunic and pulled out a silver hip flask, unscrewed the top and swallowed greedily.

Russian Vodka: not his favourite tipple but it had one great advantage; it left no telltale smell on the breath. Taking one last long swig, he pocketed the flask then swilled his face and hands before making his way back to the compartment.

Less than an hour later, they walked out of Cardiff General station, and in an extravagant gesture Miguel hailed a taxi to take them home to Alice's parents' house where they occupied the back bedroom. The first thing Alice noticed upon arrival, were the new blackout curtains that her mother had made. They gave the room a sombre air. There was much talk of the war over tea and jam sandwiches, as Miguel studied the Telegram ordering him to report to the Shipping line office immediately upon his return. Later that night, Miguels' last before he sailed, unknown to either of them Alice was conceived of a son. Miguel rose early and busied himself in the bathroom. Alice sat up in bed with the door ajar, the better to hear the beautiful sound of Miguel's singing as he shaved in front of the mirror. He was a fine tenor and rendered 'O Sole Mio' in faultless Italian.

Not that this was difficult, for Miguel had a natural gift for languages and was fluent in Italian, French, Portuguese and German as well as English and Spanish.

Without bothering to eat breakfast, he packed his case and with a sad-faced Alice on his arm, walked down the back garden path and out into the lane towards the bus stop. His last view of his new wife was her standing motionless at the roadside, clutching a small lace handkerchief, as his bus sped on its way towards the city. At Kingsway terminus, Miguel stepped off the bus and walked along in the shadow of the massive castle walls towards Duke Street.

He caught the tram to the docks, settling on the hard slatted wooden seat at the back of the lower deck. Looking out of the window as they rumbled across Wood Street Bridge towards Grangetown, he watched a group of young boys fishing from the bank of the Taff.

Seconds later, the power died and the Tramcar rolled to a halt. The roof-mounted pickup had come off the overhead power line, cutting the electricity supply. Jumping from the back the conductor pulled a long bamboo pole from its housing beneath the tram, and hooked the wayward arm back into position and they were on their way again.

Miguel did not go straight to the docks, but instead called at the Steam Packet to top up his alcohol level. It was late afternoon by the time he reached the offices of the Shipping line, where he was told to report to the Master of the Jamaica Carrier. She was loading cargo in Roath Dock prior to sailing for Buenos Aires, via Dakar in West Africa. The

3000-ton vessel, new to Miguel, had been requisitioned by the Admiralty. Just four years old, she was a mixed passenger/cargo ship whose peacetime run had been Cardiff/Rotterdam/Jamaica and back. This time, she was bound for Argentina laden with coal. Instead of bananas her holds would be full of corned beef and grain for the return journey: Kriegsmarine permitting.

35

Harbour
SS Jamaica Carrier
September 13th – December 8th 1939

The Jamaica Carrier slipped her mooring and made her way out into the Bristol Channel on the morning tide of Wednesday 13th of September, with a cargo of coal and twenty-three passengers. It was Miguel's duty to attend to the needs of these passengers, assisted by his two stewards and a galley boy. The voyage to Dakar was pleasant and uneventful, with the only sign of the war a lone Sunderland flying boat on patrol off the Irish Coast. The ship docked on October 10th, and remained at Dakar for three days during which time the crew had a run ashore. Miguel remained aboard, preferring to quaff rum in his cabin when not on duty. They reached Buenos Aires at the end of November and this time he took every opportunity to go ashore.

Hundreds of thousands of immigrants had poured into the city since the 1880s, mostly from Spain and Italy, its three million inhabitants now making up one-third of the entire population of Argentina. Here he felt at home, slipping easily into Spanish and blending into the scenery when out of uniform. Making his way down the gang plank in the noon day sun, Miguel reflected that he had not written to Alice as promised and he made a mental note to put this right when he got back to the ship. Miguel made regular mental notes, but was not in the habit of acting upon them, being easily side-tracked by his liquid mistress. Such was the case today, as he headed for his favourite bar to feed his appetite for alcohol. Wearing cream slacks and a white shirt with sleeves rolled up and pressed sharp, white canvas deck shoes and a Panama hat to shade him from the sun, he melted invisibly into the populous street. Strolling across the busy road, down a side street and into a narrow alley, he entered a small anonymous-looking bar.

Miguel addressed the large dark hulk behind the mahogany counter. 'Manuel, mi amigo. ¿Qué pasa?'

'Miguel compadre! ¿Bueno verle otra vez cuánto tiempo este vez?

Miguel called for beer with a rum chaser and shook his friend warmly by the hand. Manuel was at least twenty stone and moved awkwardly as he poured the amber liquid into a tall glass for his second customer of the day.

'To answer your question, I am here for at least one week because the ship has a problem with the engine. We shall have some more good times, my friend.'

'Bueno!'

'Well, how has it been? Tell me what I have missed these past months,' enquired Miguel as he passed his glass for a refill.

For the next couple of hours they swopped

stories and tit-bits of news, content in each other's company. The Bar was tired-looking and in desperate need of a lick of paint. In spite of this, it was spotless and the stone floor was worn from Consuela's scrubbing. Manuel's wife was the one who did the work, while he spent his waking hours sat on his fat backside, drinking the meagre profits and shooting the breeze with his customers. Miguel understood Manuel and vice versa. Totally relaxed, Miguel slipped into the situation as if he had never been away. Gradually the bar filled up with a mix of dockyard workers, sailors and a few local prostitutes relaxing before the night shift. Miguel thought of Alice and fantasized briefly about bringing her to settle out here. It was pure fantasy, for she would never leave home and as this realization dawned, he began to wonder why he had married her. She was way too good for him he told Manuel, as the drink robbed his brain of reason and melancholia set in. Consuela put a comforting arm around Miguel's shoulder and spoke softly in his ear.

'Hey encantador querido de Miguel para verle. ¿Usted va a darnos una canción?'

'Consuela my darling, of course I will sing for, you but only if you will play for me.' Miguel replied.

The bargain struck, Consuela placed her matronly figure at the piano in the corner of the room, while Miguel moved across the room to join her. Placing his beer and rum chaser on the piano, he whispered to his accompanist and without further introduction, launched into a series of standards and favourites to the delight of the clientele. The bar filled up and became quite crowded as word got around that 'Caruso' was in town and Miguel was fed drinks on a human conveyor belt by a captivated audience. Miguel worked his way through a comprehensive repertoire from Nessun Dorma and Una Furtiva Lagrima, to the popular Over the Rainbow. He was in his element, revelling in the attention, awash with free booze.

Later, when it was quiet, Miguel, Consuela and Manuel fell to talking about everything and nothing. Consuela was a good listener and his tongue loosened by drink, Miguel confided his doubts about his marriage to her. He had proposed in a fit of romantic madness, his judgement clouded by drink. He was wracked with doubt, not because he did not care for Alice, but because he was married to the sea and alcohol was his mistress. He knew that it was just a matter of time before Alice would try to get him to find a job ashore. Women were like that, always wanting you to settle down. He was hopelessly hooked on the freedom of sailing the seas and there was no place in his life for the shackles of domesticity.

Miguel left the bar in the early hours, depressed as only alcohol could make him. He made it back to the ship, drunk as a lord and wobbling up the gangplank, as he had so many times before. The passengers had all disembarked and he was not on watch until noon, which was just as well, for he cared not a jot as he fell face down into his bunk and swam into oblivion. The Germans could torpedo the ship and he would not have stirred, not this night. This set the pattern for the rest of the time in harbour when Miguel was off duty. When he was on duty however, it was a different story. He was sober and performed his duties with professional vigour, firm but fair with his subordinates. He would not tolerate slackness, drinking on duty, or anyone who could not give one hundred percent as a result of over indulgence the night before. He was, however, a compassionate man and dealt with sailors' personal problems with understanding.

The crew followed the course of the war in Europe through the BBC World Service radio broadcasts. Not that much was happening; the British Expeditionary Force manned static defences in France waiting to see what would happen next, while overhead the RAF were bombing the Germans with paper leaflets pointing out the error of their ways. The Germans replied by sending a submarine into the Royal Navy's anchorage at Scapa Flow in the Orkneys, where it torpedoed and sank the battleship HMS Royal Oak. This was the worst loss since the passenger ship Athenia was torpedoed on the day war was declared, with the loss of one hundred souls.

'Do you think the Germans have got subs out here in the South Atlantic Sir?'

Miguel looked at the cabin boy and smiled.

'Just you get on with your duties, Matthew, leave the Captain to worry about U Boats boy.'

'Why do they call them 'U' Boats Sir?'

'Underseeboot, it's German for submarine …under sea boat see?'

The boy stared back blankly. It was going way over his head.

Not the sharpest knife in the galley, Miguel thought, *but bless him, he works hard.* 'Good. Now away to your duties boy. Vamos.'

'Aye aye Sir.'

As the boy doubled away to his work, Miguel put down the requisition list and looked up at the porthole. It was a clear bright moonlit evening outside, perfect U-boat weather. They were safe enough in harbour, but would soon be crossing the Atlantic again, alone and unarmed, full of supplies that Britain needed to fight the war. Bully beef for the army and grain for bread.

In spite of the tropical night, a cold shiver ran through Miguel's body. He needed a drink but would not break his rule and determined to wait the two hours until his watch was over. He told himself that, as they had made it across the Atlantic unmolested, there was no reason to believe they would not reach British shores safely once more, hopefully without incident. After all it was a vast ocean and Hitler could not have that many U boats now, could he?

36

Panzerschiff!
Jamaica Carrier
South Atlantic December 9th – 13th 1939

The Jamaica Carrier weighed anchor on the morning of December 9th. The ship's log recorded the day as bright and sunny, the sea state as calm. Comforted by the engines' regular heartbeat coursing through the mahogany deck, Miguel had shaken off the gloom of his domestic fears for the time being. The repairs had been completed satisfactorily and it felt good to be underway again. A restless soul, he was always happier travelling in anticipation than arriving. He posted two letters to Alice before they left port and bought her perfume for Christmas, as well as a length of bright red satin, enough to make a lovely dress. He could not have known that Alice would never see her Christmas presents, or that he would never have to face her with his doubts. He was soon to be absolved of that responsibility, courtesy of the German Navy. The events of the next few days would change the course of Miguel's life forever.

It was mid afternoon on the 11th when the port lookout reported first smoke and then a masthead on the horizon. A short time later, a large warship flying the French flag could be clearly seen by the lookouts steaming towards them at high speed. The vessel closed to within two miles before the Carrier's captain realized that all was not as it seemed and by then it was too late. He just had time to alert the crew and throw the ship's code books over the side before receiving a signal from the battleship to heave to. There was no choice but to comply. Miguel watched as the French flag was hauled down and the German Ensign was run up in its place. The pocket battleship Admiral Graf Spee, one of the most feared ships in the Kriegsmarine closed up and sent a boarding party across by launch. Miguel made for the bridge, knowing his fluent German would be valuable to the captain.

The German officer was polite but businesslike. He gave the crew thirty minutes to gather essential personal items and muster on deck to transfer to the Graf Spee. Miguel went straight to his cabin and stuffed as much rum as he could find into his canvas grip then, job done, shepherded his flock to the head of the ladder, ready to transfer ship. Like most of the crew he was still in shock, but grateful not to have been sunk without warning. It was not what he had expected and not at all how he had imagined the war would be. No torpedo in the middle of the night; no thrashing around in shark infested water, clinging to a life raft, just a polite request to transfer to another ship. As they climbed onto the German Raider's deck the Graf Spee's three point five inch anti aircraft guns depressed their barrels and traversed to train on the British steamer. A tremendous bang which shook the deck and those on, heralded the delivery of the first of the five high explosive shells it took to send Alice's bright red satin to the bottom of the ocean. Why he had not saved it Miguel knew not, but it troubled him as he watched helpless from the rail. The guns boomed loudly again and the shells struck home just below the waterline. In less than ten minutes she slid beneath the water to her final resting-place.

'There goes our beer money boys' the First Mate declared. 'Bloody Jerries!'

'What's he mean Sir?' Asked a puzzled Matthew. Miguel put a comforting arm around the boy's shoulder. 'My boy, this is not the Royal Navy you know, the company will stop our pay from the moment the ship was lost. We get nothing until we sign on another ship– if we get the chance, that is.'

'That's not fair is it? It's not our fault the ship sank.'

'Fair or not that's the way it is, boy. Come on now, things could be worse, we could have gone down with her.'

'I s'pose so,' the boy muttered as they were taken below with the rest of the crew to join the crews of previous victims. They were allocated hammocks in what might well have been purpose built prisoner accommodation. Whatever, they would have to make the best of it and Tony gathered young Matthew and his stewards, making sure they were settled before stowing his bag and claiming a hammock for himself. Well, at least he was alive and unharmed – in excellent health in fact – so things could be a lot worse.

'What is going to happen to us, Sir? They aren't going to shoot us are they?'

'I seriously doubt it, Matthew,' Miguel answered. 'If they had wanted to kill us they would have sent us down with the ship. I expect they will send us back to Germany to a prisoner of war camp.'

'How long will that be for, Chief?' the boy asked wide-eyed with worry.

'Until the war's over, you dope,' chipped in one of the Stewards.

'Until we win the war.' Miguel corrected.

'We are going to win, aren't we Sir?'

'Of course we are boy. Don't you doubt it.'

Inwardly, Miguel believed that Britain would indeed be victorious in the end but he also guessed that it would be a long hard slog.

'Try to relax and settle in Matthew, we are going to be here for some time, I think. Just try to get used to it and count yourself lucky that we are being well treated.'

'Yes, Sir. Thanks, Chief, I er...'

'What is it boy? Spit it out!'

'My Mum...she is going to be worried. She didn't want me to go to sea you see.'

Miguel put his arm around the boy's shoulder and spoke to him in a soothing voice.

'Why don't you write her a letter and when we get to the prison camp you will be able to send it through the Red Cross? Let's face it, you have a lot to tell her. Here I have some paper and envelopes in my bag.' Miguel rummaged in his kit and produced the writing materials.

'Do you have a pencil?'

'Er no, Sir, I don't.'

'Here, Matt, use mine.' It was the Steward again.

'Ta very much.'

'That's all right. You just tell your mum all about your adventures on the high seas, eh?'

'I will, yes, thanks.'

The boy finally smiled, seeming to accept the situation and Miguel finally climbed into his hammock. Swinging lazily with the motion of the ship, pondering his fate, he was interrupted by the first mate calling from across the deck.

'Hey, Miguel. How about a song?'

'Aye go on, Chief, give us a song,' came a chorus from around the accommodation.

'It will be good for morale,' the Captain chimed in.

Capitulating, Miguel began softly to sing 'O Sole Mio' in Italian, the beautifully crafted notes rising to the steel plates overhead and slowly permeating the ship. The crew listened in respectful silence as Miguel worked his way through his extensive repertoire in English, Italian and Spanish. The sound of his voice carried through the ship to the delight of the German sailors on watch and even Kaptitan Langsdorf became aware of it by way of gossip among his junior officers. When not being entertained by Miguel's singing, some of the men slept, or swapped stories with other inmates from previous sinkings. Altogether there were crews from five other ships, whose experiences were largely similar to those of the Carrier's crew. Men wrote letters or joined one of the inevitable card schools, where they could gamble away their pay.

That night when most were asleep, Miguel lay in his hammock pulling on a bottle of 100% proof Jamaica Rum, until he slipped into the arms of Morpheus. They were fed breakfast of coffee and black bread with tinned ham and cheese. Their treatment could not be faulted and by evening all were relaxed as they settled down to eat the third meal of the day. Bratwurst and Sauerkraut were not to everybody's taste, but it was nourishing and wholesome. Miguel counted the hours until the men fell asleep and the deck was quiet enough for him to hit the Rum again without being discovered. He had absolutely no intention of sharing his hoard with anyone. When he deemed it safe he pulled a navy blue woollen pullover from his kitbag and without removing the bottle from it's hiding place in the sleeve, removed the top, put the neck to his yearning lips and let the fiery liquid run down his throat. When he was drinking Miguel felt more alive than at any other time. Rum was his life blood. It gave him the confidence that his natural charm, talent and looks should have, but did not. He slipped slowly into his private sanctuary en route to peaceful oblivion.

Sleep was shattered by the blare of a Klaxon and the sound of running feet, as the German crew answered the call to action stations. Miguel could not comprehend what was happening at first, indeed he was not sure where on God's ocean he was. Men were stirring in their bunks, someone shouted 'What the 'ell, turn the bloody thing off!

'Looks like they got another victim lined up for the kill I reckon,' the First Mate said.

'What time is it?' Miguel asked, rubbing his eyes as he raised his voice to make himself heard above the din. His watch said 05.54 and his head hurt. With no portholes to see out of they could only guess what was happening and the general consensus was that Graf Spee had found another merchant ship to add to its tally. At 06.00 the engine noise altered and the ship increased speed to what Miguel guessed must be nearing her maximum. The appraisal of the situation was abruptly revised at 06.17 when a thunderclap shook the ship.

'Bloody hell!' a disembodied voice exclaimed, 'That's her big guns! That ain't no merchantman, it's the bloody Navy. Gotta be.'

The vibration and shock wave was so severe that it loosened the paint from the bulkhead causing a shower of flakes like a mini snowstorm, with every broad-side.

Miguel was not amused. He did not relish the idea of being blown to bits by the Royal Navy. Why could they not just leave him alone, so he could spend the war out of harms way in an internment camp? For the next hour, the big guns boomed and even the secondary armament joined in, adding to the din. The noise was deafening and made Miguel's ears ring. Once there was a sound of an explosion as a shell hit close by, which caused some of the prisoners to cheer, while others cringed. The ship was now altering course frequently and sometime around 07.25 another near miss rattled the plates. Throwing caution to the wind Miguel reached for the bottle of rum and took a giant swig. It was to be his last for some considerable time. A direct hit on the galley next to the prison deck shook the ship. The explosion tore a hole in the steel bulkhead, the pressure wave shattering the bottle in Miguel's hand, driving shards of glass into his neck and shoulders as the blast slammed him into the deck.

37
New Beginning
Montevideo Uruguay
December 14th – 26th 1940

The sea was calm, the sky pure cobalt. He was gently floating on a snow-white raft, serenely drifting; at perfect peace with the world. This perfect world could not be any better, of that he was sure. Then he saw her. A beautiful dark eyed creature slowly gliding into to vision from somewhere behind his head, stopping to gaze down upon him. Her cherry lips parted.

'You are awake at last. This is very good, Dr Ferriera will be pleased.'

'Who are you? What am I doing here? Where is here?' Miguel's head was full of questions.

'Please calm yourself, you are in hospital, you have been very sick. You had a bang on your head and some nasty cuts on your face but you will be fine soon. You must rest.'

'Hospital. What hospital? You do not look like a German.' Miguel croaked, desperately trying to make sense of his situation.

'German? By the saints I am not. I am Nurse Rosita Gonzales. I am from Argentina.'

'Argentina? How did I...?'

She put her finger to his lips 'Shhh you must rest. I am from Argentina but we are in Uruguay; Montevideo to be exact. Esto es Hospital de Santo Maria de Las Rosas, the Hospi...'

'Hospital of Saint Mary of the Roses' Miguel interrupted.

'You speak Spanish?'

'Si senorita. Mis padres son de España, yo nacieron en Gran Bretaña.' Miguel's head began to swim and he felt weak as a kitten.

'You must rest now. I insist.'

She sounded like an elderly schoolteacher. She looked like a model on a magazine front cover.

'But...' Miguel began, only to be silenced once more in the same manner. Her fingers felt good on his lips, her dark eyes mesmerizing. The ache in his head was dull, the pain in his upper arm sharp, like a bee sting, then slowly his eyes began to close under the weight of their lids. He fought to stay awake for he did not want to lose sight of this lovely creature. The fight was short; the outcome inevitable. The sedative took hold and Miguel melted back into the darkness whence he came. The next time he swam to the surface of his black lagoon, Miguel was alone in the room. For the first time he was aware of the drip line in his arm and the bandages that covered his entire scalp. The small room was painted glossy dark ochre to waist height, topped off with a two inch band of chocolate brown. Above this, walls and ceiling were off white. There was a strong smell of antiseptic and bleach and through the window opposite his bed, Miguel could see a clear blue cloudless sky. He was surprised to discover he was hungry. After what seemed an age he heard footsteps in the corridor and his heart began to race in anticipation of seeing his little dark-eyed nurse. When at last the door opened, his disappointment was impossible to conceal. The new arrival was short, round and in her mid forties. She took his temperature then scribbled something on the notes attached to thclipboard at the bottom of the bed.

'Where is Rosita?' Miguel asked.

'Nurse Gonzales is not here today,' came the stern reply and before he could say any more the door closed and he was alone again. Half an hour or so later, another nurse brought him orange juice and chicken soup which she spoon fed to him. The orange juice he managed through a straw, after which he slept. He slept a lot and when he slept, the dreams came, invading his peaceful world. They were chaotic – jumping in and out of locations and situations in a confusing cycle. Alice's face kept appearing accusingly and disappearing into the red satin floating on the sea. Then there was noise and smoke, choking hot smoke, and gasping for air, he surfaced from the dream, coughing, crying and very afraid. The third time this occurred Nurse Rosita Gonzales was there to comfort him, her soft voice and cool hand like a life raft in a sea of troubles. So it was that as the weeks passed, Alice featured less and less in his thoughts, pushed out by the presence of Rosita Gonzales as she nursed him slowly back to health. No one from the crew came to visit; he assumed they had all been interned for the duration and apart from a brief visit from some lowly official of the British Consulate, he seemed to have been forgotten. Rosita told him that the Graf Spee had scuttled herself in the estuary rather than face the Royal Navy waiting out in the Atlantic.

'At least that is one less ship to worry about' was his reaction. 'What about the crew?'

'They came ashore in the launch. There was a huge explosion then several more. The sky lit up as the sun went down. It was very dramatic. Kapitan Langsdorf shot himself. It is very sad.' She looked upset.

Miguel lay his hand upon hers.

'War is a terrible waste,' he said. 'No winners; we all lose, yes it is very sad. They treated us well you know, the Germans.'

She did not move her hand and her eyes never left his. As he looked at her he knew that this was the woman for him. His wife got not a second thought, for he was selfish in pursuit of his own wants and needs. He had always had a firm following of female admirers and he took them largely for granted. Miguel was quite shallow in his relations with the opposite sex and well aware of it. This time though, it really was different. He could not get Rosita out of his head. She dominated every waking moment even invading his dreams, driving out the demons, replacing them with peace and tranquillity. She too was concious of becoming inexorably drawn deeper and deeper into his world. She resisted, desperately trying to behave with professional detachment, even as she saw the boundaries blurring before her eyes. It was the classic romantic situation: the pretty nurse, the wounded hero; except he was no hero, just a sailor far from home, albeit a very handsome one.

Nurse Gonzales withdrew her hand suddenly and composed herself. She saw the hurt in his eyes and knew she was losing the fight. She turned and left without a word, her mind a whirl of confused thoughts.

Miguel gradually regained his strength over time and after three and a half months of the finest nursing a man ever had he was on his feet again. By this time there was an unspoken understanding between them. Rosita's defences finally crumbled when he sang to her, Cole Porter's 'I've Got You Under My Skin.'

It was in the hospital grounds one beautiful sunny afternoon in April 1940 that nurse Rosita Gonzales finally surrendered to the charms of a charismatic rogue. For the first time in her life she threw caution to the wind and followed her heart.

She found Miguel a job with a friend who owned a restaurant near the hospital. Here he split his time between serving customers and singing for their entertainment. His long period of healing had separated him from the rest of the former captives and the authorities had lost interest in him. His Spanish looks and fluent tongue made blending in to the scenery a breeze and the bar owner paid cash, no questions asked. He soon developed quite a following of fans that filled the bar night after night to listen to him sing. He had a small room above the restaurant. Rosita and Miguel became 'a couple' in the eyes of the clientele and she soon demonstrated how strong a character she was.

Very early in the relationship she realized his weakness for drink, mainly because her father had died an alcoholic and she knew the symptoms. In spite of this she could not bear to be without him and vowed to change him. To prevent Miguel drinking all his pay away she took charge of the finances, banking cash for him and giving him a small allowance each night. He did not go short of alcohol though, as customers bought him so many drinks he hardly had to put his hand in his pocket. She negotiated more money for him, on the back of the increased custom he brought in and in a little over a year she had saved a tidy sum. In early 1942 they moved to Argentina, to live with Rosita's mother whose failing health prevented her from running the Bar which her late husband had founded in Rosario. Miguel ran the kitchen and Rosita the bar. She also took care of the books and with Miguel's singing breathing new life into the business, it went from strength to strength. Life was good, bringing them much happiness and in 1943 Ramon, the first of two sons was born. Maria followed in 1945 and finally Juan in 1965, unplanned but not unloved.

They had their ups and downs, but Rosita held the family together and kept Miguel's drinking under control. She had not succeeded in changing him, but instead had learned how to manage his habit. They watched their children grow and develop and all was well with their world until the Junta embarked on the insane invasion of Las Malvinas in 1982.

Had Britain any other Prime Minister, they might have got away with it, but Margaret Thatcher was a one-off. She was not called the Iron Lady for nothing. She was not one to let it go. A task force was hastily assembled and sailed eight thousand miles to challenge Argentina's claim to sovereignty over the

Islands.

Their beloved Juan was a seventeen year old sailor on the General Belgrano, flagship of the Argentine Navy. The twelve thousand ton cruiser was torpedoed and sunk on direct orders from the British cabinet. Juan perished in the freezing ocean, along with three hundred and thirty-three shipmates, leaving a devastated Miguel, Rosita and Maria to deal with the loss of a much loved son and brother. The family struggled to deal with the aftermath. They feared for Ramon, stationed on the islands, terrified lest they lose another son. When he heard the news he bore it with military professionalism while inwardly writhing in agony. At home it was Rosita's strength, once again that held the family together through this terrible trauma. Miguel coped the only way he knew; with the bottle.

38

Reunion
Falkland Islands March 1992

Miguel felt someone tugging at his arm. 'Rosita what is it?'

'Papa it's me Maria, we are go ing to land soon, you must fasten your seat belt.'

As the Boeing made its final approach, Miguel reached into his inside pocket and took out a packet of indigestion tablets. He popped two into his mouth and began to chew. Maria squeezed his hand and smiled at him. He managed a weak smile in return. The landing was without incident but not until the aircraft came to a complete stop did Miguel finally relax. After a short delay the passengers began to disembark down the steps and on to the apron. The ritual of baggage retrieval and document checks was accomplished in due course and the party made their way to the transport.

A little later, as they were on their way to the hotel in the minibus, Ramon turned to his father.

'This is a very strange day for us but we are all God's children and he will guide us through this, you will see.'

He was not sure he believed the show of faith

he had just proclaimed, but if it helped, then what did it matter?

They pulled up outside the hotel and got out in complete silence. Ramon helped the driver with the cases as best he could using his walking stick to support his weak left leg. Maria carried her own bags as she helped her father to the door. At Reception they were received with cool professional courtesy, the events of 1982 being still fresh in the Islanders minds. After taking a few minutes to register, they were shown up to their rooms. Miguel and Ramon shared a double while Maria had a small but comfortable room to herself. Tired from the journey both men elected to sleep, but not Maria. She wished to explore her surroundings. After an hour of sightseeing she returned, settling in the bar with a coffee, to write postcards she had purchased at the post office.

It was a fine day, mild, with a fresh breeze off the sea. The sun shining through the window made her feel pleasantly relaxed, until she began to contemplate the meeting to come. The time agreed for the reunion was eleven o'clock the following morning and she was not really sure how she felt about it. Excited and curious, she was also apprehensive, especially for her father. She had always been Papa's little girl, falling under his charming spell like all the others and she was fiercely protective of him. Ramon could look after himself, but Papa was frail and she must protect him. Who knows what Antonio might say when they met? After all he must be a little angry that Miguel did not come back to find him all those years ago. Papa was a good man, she reasoned, it was not his fault he had been hurt and put in the hospital. Mama says he very nearly died, he was hurt so bad. She looked up to see her brother smiling at her. He had shaved and changed into navy blue slacks and a grey lambswool sweater over a blue cotton shirt.

'Ramon you look much better.'

'I feel it now that I have had a sleep. Papa is still snoring bless him. I had to come down to escape the noise. Would you like some more coffee?'

'Thank you, yes.'

Ramon ordered coffee for two and sat down opposite his sister, gazing out across the sunlit, wind-swept water, lamenting the fact that they had not been able to hold on to the islands.

The barman brought the coffee and he settled back in his chair.

'What about tomorrow?' Maria asked. 'Are you nervous?'

'A little. You?'

'Yes, a little, but I am a little excited too. I want it to go well. You say he is a good man but he was your enemy and he did interrogate you. I know you never speak of it but I am not stupid you know. Just because I am a woman does not mean I do not understand. He must have hurt you.'

'He was doing his duty as I did mine, Maria. He looked after me. He carried me to the helicopter and put me on it. If it was not for that I would not be here today. He is a God-fearing Catholic the same as you and I.

'I am grateful for that Ramon. It is Papa. I worry Antonio will upset Papa, because of what he did to his mother.'

'I worry too, but it is right that they speak, for he is Papa's son too. Do not worry I will not let anything bad happen...to either of them. He is our brother remember. Now let us just enjoy the day. What shall we do?'

They spent an hour walking around Stanley which was all Ramon could manage before needing to rest, returning mid afternoon to find their father in the bar nursing a large rum.

'Oh Papa what would Mama say?'

'Mama is not here chiquita. Anyway I am too old now to worry. It is much too late for me, the damage was done many years ago. I am not long for this world now.'

'Don't talk like that. Ramon make him stop.'

'I can no more do that than make the wind stop little sister. Papa is Papa.'

'Do not be upset Chiquita my life has been good I have two fine children,' Miguel's eyes began to fill with tears,' and beautiful memories of my beloved Juan.' He picked up his glass and emptied it as Maria put her arms around her father and hugged him.

'Yes, and tomorrow,' he paused to compose himself, 'tomorrow, we will welcome a new one to the family.'

His positive outlook reassured Maria to some degree, but there were still nagging doubts gnawing away at the back of her brain. She was determined to protect her father from any unpleasantness come what may.

Miguel ordered another rum, wine for Maria and a beer for Ramon, then settled down for a 'session' before dinner. That evening after dinner, despite his daughter's protests, Miguel continued to drink until late. Unencumbered by Maria's rose tinted glasses, Ramon saw his father for what he was and had long since recognised that any attempt to reform him or curb his habit would be futile. Not that he loved him any less, for he had been a kind and loving father who always made time for his children. It was just that he drank. He drank all the time despite his wife's efforts to rein him in. He drank because he had to, it was a compulsion, one he did not know how to resist. Even he knew, as did Ramon, that if it was not for Rosita that he would be under the ground by now. She managed to slow him up just enough to keep him alive, but the clock was ticking.

Despite the liberal application of alcohol, sleep did not come easily to Ramon. His father went out like a light and was soon snoring his head off so loudly Maria could hear him in her room. She too struggled with sleep, trying to predict how the meeting might go. She lay awake running various scenarios through her head, rewinding and editing them trying to find the perfect ending until sheer exhaustion put her under and she slipped into the waiting darkness.

TONY

39
Family Matters
Falkland Islands, March 1992

I was sitting at the bar halfway down my second large Scotch and beginning to wonder if it would be wise to stop at that before I got myself in trouble, when a dark haired woman, in a figure-hugging black lambswool dress walked confidently into the sparsely-populated bar. Despite her forty-seven years, a few male heads turned to follow her path. She walked straight up to me, smiled and introduced herself.

'I am Maria and you are Antonio yes?' she said, her head inquisitively cocked to one side.

I stood up and offered her my hand. She reciprocated and there was an awkward moment as I tried to decide if I should shake it or kiss it. We shook.

'Delighted to meet you at last Maria. Would you like a drink?'

'Thank you. I would like glass of red wine please.'

We took our drinks to a corner table and sat down.

'My brother and my... I am sorry, our father,

will be here in a little while.' Her smile put me at ease, she was a real charmer and softened up by the Scotch I began to relax. 'I guess you are the advance guard sent to soften me up, yes?'

Humour flashed in her eyes.

'Will it be necessary to soften you up?' she said.

'Not any more' I replied, 'Not in such charming company.'

She flashed me an old fashioned look. 'Steady boy,' I thought, 'this is your sister, you are flirting with.'

The ice broken, we conversed more easily asking all the usual polite questions about the journey, health and such and half an hour passed in the blink of an eye as the barriers came down.

'Papa is not well,' she said regarding me intently, 'he is no longer a young man.'

'I am sorry to hear that.'

'You must understand it will not be good for him to be upset or put under stress.'

'I will try to remember that,' I replied feeling the barrier rise again a little. She was playing the protector. Her loyalty to her father was commendable and she was right to be wary, for I had serious questions to ask Miguel when the opportunity arose. I was aware however, that since I arrived on the Islands my feelings of frustration and anger had been diluted by what I had experienced, particularly after my visit to the spot where Yorkie had given up his life to protect me. It had been a humbling experience and one which helped me see things more in perspective.

We were discussing musical tastes when Maria stopped in mid sentence and her facial muscles tensed as she looked over my shoulder in the direction of the door. I turned slowly and got to my feet, at the same time stretching out my hand towards Ramon. He took it and shook it vigorously.

'It has been a long time, amigo.'

'That it has, my brother, that it has,' I replied turning my gaze to the small smartly dressed grey haired figure behind him. As our eyes met, thoughts of recrimination swam to the surface of my consciousness. We stood in awkward silence for what seemed like an age, neither able to speak. Miguel avoided looking directly at me. Maria came to the rescue taking her father's arm and mine, hugging them both with hers. The awkward moment passed and we sat down. Ramon ordered a round of drinks and we settled around the table. Conversation was neither easy nor comfortable, and Miguel took no part other than the occasional nod. It was not going well as far as father and son were concerned. After an hour we moved to the restaurant for lunch. As we sat down I reached into my pocket and took out a small jiffy bag and passed it to Ramon. 'What is this amigo?'

'Open it,' I said, and you will see.'

Peeling off the cellotape, he upended the bag and the Prayer book slid onto the table.

'Muchos gracias amigo this makes me very happy. It was for my confirmation when I was eleven years old. It is good to see it again.'

He opened it at the first page, scrutinizing it carefully for several seconds before slipping it into his pocket.

'I am only sorry it has been so long,' I said.

All through lunch Maria stuck to Miguel like

glue while he remained tight lipped. When the meal was over, we ordered coffee and Miguel spoke for the first time. In a faltering voice he asked to be excused as the journey had worn him out and he wished to retire. Maria volunteered to go with him, leaving Ramon and I to catch up on what had happened after we parted company all those years ago.

Ramon gave me an apologetic look.

'You will excuse father I hope, it is maybe too much for him today, but by tomorrow he will be fine I am sure'

'No problem' I assured him, trying hard to conceal my obvious disappointment at not being able to voice the questions burning away inside me.

Ramon got up and made his way to the gents as I ordered fresh drinks. When he returned he was beaming as if he had won the football pools.

'What are you grinning about?' I inquired.

'Later amigo, tell me about England.'

After doing my bit for the English tourist board we fell to talking in the way that old soldiers do, until inevitably we touched upon the war. The whisky had loosened my tongue and I began to really let go.

'You know what pisses me off the most? Well, I'll tell you. We came home after the war, docked in the dead of night away from any other vessels. They spirited us away on coaches and trains or to hospital wards so no one could see us. A bloody PR exercise, so Joe public wouldn't see lads on crutches or with burnt faces and hands. So no one could interview the traumatized teenagers. God forbid they should see the real cost of war. It makes me sick still.'

I felt my brother's hand on my arm. I put the

glass to my lips and savoured the whisky as it slid over my tongue.

'I know,' he said, 'It was the same for us. Our soldiers were told not to speak of what they had seen here. They were warned that their families would suffer if they did. We were sent to Malvinas as heroes but when we came home...' He shook his head slowly from side to side. 'We were treated as if we were lepers. I was so angry. You know what is strange? I did not feel angry towards you or any of the British soldiers. It was Thatcher. Thatcher and Galtieri. I wanted to climb into my cockpit and bomb those monsters, blow them both to pieces. We went to war for a lie just to keep those two bastards in power.'

I took another swig of whisky, but this time I swallowed straight away.

'It is always the politicians. They start the trouble and send us to do their dirty work. Bloody politicians every time.'

We had found a field of common ground which, as we carried on giving vent to our feelings brought us closer together. Ramon told how he had been sent to Montevideo on the Ambulance ship, although he did not remember much about it as he was so ill. When he got home to Argentina he was hospitalized for four months and then an out patient for another six. It had been a close-run thing. He too had suffered with nightmares but his were of his younger brother, who idolized him, drowning. We were somewhat drunk by midnight and Ramon was exhausted. I was about to help him up to his room when, with perfect timing, Maria breezed in.

'Now then, boys. Have you finished telling your war stories? I hope so because it is time for your medication Ramon.'

'We were just coming,' I said apologetically, rising unsteadily to my feet. We then both helped Ramon up and as we did so he put a drunken arm around my neck and declared to all and sundry.

'This is my brother. He is a good man, my brother. I love my brother' at which point his legs gave way and he collapsed back into the chair, much to the amusement of the dozen or so drinkers in the bar.

It took a bit of doing but we eventually got Ramon to his room and I bade Maria goodnight. I had taken the wise precaution of booking a room. Rory had promised to come for me tomorrow to give me time to get to know my new family. I retired to my room and went straight to bed. As I lay in the dark I could feel myself smiling. Not the stupid senseless smile of intoxication, but the satisfied smile of a contented man. True I had not managed to buttonhole my father, but my brother and I had got off to a great start. Even Maria was okay with me. The Islands were continuing to work their magic. I slept like a baby.

40
Closure
Falkland Islands March 1992

I rose early and went out for some fresh air. Crossing
Ross Road, I walked onto Victory Green, stopping
beside a large section of mizzen mast. This relic of
history had once been part of the first iron propeller
driven ship ever built; Isambard Kingdom Brunel's,
SS Great Britain. I turned up the collar of my duvet
jacket against the early morning cold, lit a cigarette
and looked out at the hulk of the Charles Cooper
lying in the shallows as it had done since 1866. After a
few minutes looking at the wreck I sensed a presence
behind me and turned slowly to see a heavily muffled
figure approaching. Miguel walked slowly over, stood
beside me and gazed out across the water. After a
long pause he spoke softly in Spanish.

'Last night I did not know what to say. Today I
do not know what to say. I only know that to say
nothing is not right. All my life I have told people
what they wanted to hear. I was young and I looked
good, I had confidence and the silver tongue. Now I
am an old man and I know that my silver tongue is no
use here. I have no excuses for what happened all
those years ago. I cannot even blame the war. It
played its part and it changed my life, but it does not

317

excuse what I did. If I could rewind the clock…'

I was caught completely off guard. I was expecting excuses, lies, blaming others, but soul baring confession no. I was not prepared for this. It is very disarming when you are ready to go for someone who has wronged you and they admit guilt throw themselves upon your mercy.

I asked myself; was he trying to manipulate the situation to his advantage? All I knew of him was what I had learned from my Nan, and from reading between the lines in the correspondence over the last ten years. My Nan was obviously biased so her view would be unreliable. I knew he had a drink problem, I had observed him in the bar sinking copious amounts of Rum with no apparent effect and there was no denying he had abandoned a young wife, although he may not have known she was pregnant. My cold, analytical, military head was mightily suspicious, but my Spanish heart was prepared to believe him. He was undeniably charming and, by his own admission in possession of a silver tongue.

'Your mother was too good for me my son. She was not aware of the ways of the world.'

'Then why did you marry her?' I asked without hiding the bitterness in my voice.

'We met at a dance. I have always been a dancer and in those days I was good, very good. She was the first girl who could match me on the dance floor. She was Ginger Rogers to my Fred Astaire. We just fitted together so well. Every competition we entered we finished in the top three and in most we were first. It was as if it was meant to be. She was so different to the women I was used to. She had very high standards, not really a sailor's woman. I thought I was in love. It was something I had not experienced before. I know this may not be what you wish to hear, but this is how it was. I was young and your mother was very beautiful. We were very happy but then the war changed things. This is not an excuse my son, it is a matter of fact. I am a man with weaknesses. You are not a fool. You have seen my need for the bottle. It is a sailor's comfort in the lonely weeks at sea without the arms of a woman.'

'Spare me the sob story. You left us without looking back. You didn't even write to let your family know you were alive.'

'I was in the hospital a long time, many weeks. At first I was too ill and then...then there was Rosita. The longer it was left, the harder it became. I told you, I am weak. Like Oscar Wilde I can resist anything but temptation. As for you, I swear I had no idea your mother was pregnant.'

'Would it have made any difference,' I asked, calmer now, but still angry.

'I do not know my son, and that is the truth as God is my witness.'

As I looked into his eyes I saw pain and genuine remorse but still it was not enough. I wanted retribution, I had travelled 8,000 miles for an explanation. I now realized how naive I had been. There was no explanation which was going to tie up the loose ends so we could all live happily ever after. Real life is just not like that. The death I had seen on these Islands had altered the way I looked at life.

Miguel was staring out across the water and I too stared across the sea, unable to look him in the eye, not knowing what else to say. I tried to imagine what my mother would have said to him but I could not. She was just a photograph to me, I had no tangible memory of her at all. She was like a ghost or a character from a book I had read as child. My Nan had filled the void left by my parents and filled it well.

'What about Nan? How in God's name could you let your own mother think you were dead? She was a good woman, how could you do that?'

'Tell him, Papa.'

I turned to see Maria staring at me, hostility burning in her eyes. Ramon was with her. He looked like he wanted to be somewhere else; anywhere else.

'No? Then I will tell him, Papa.'

'Maria...' Ramon began.

'He will not stop until he knows,' she cried. Maria planted herself protectively between us. She stared deeply into my eyes with the fire of anger in hers. 'My father is a sick man, he made this journey against the wishes of the doctor. He did not have to come.'

'Enough, my daughter. It is my life. I shall tell it. What does it matter now? Soon I shall have to answer for my sins before God.'

He gently moved Maria to one side and stepped forward until I could feel the rum on his breath, which, despite the early hour was no surprise to me.

'Your grandmother was old fashioned,' he began, 'a very strong Catholic. She worshiped the Church, it was the most important thing in her life. When I became engaged to your mother she disowned me. It caused many fights with my father. There were big arguments and he took to drink, so you see my son, it is in the genes. For me to marry outside the faith was for her a terrible sin. It was unthinkable. She refused to come to the wedding. When he died she did not write to tell me. I heard from his solicitors six months after the funeral.'

He looked relieved to have got it off his chest but it had taken it out of him. He was pale and trembling.

'Come Papa let us get inside,' Maria urged, taking his arm.

'Papa did not have to come. He came for you Tony. For you! Do you understand? It is a matter of honour. He wished to make his peace before it is too late. He does the best he can. He cannot change the past, so learn to forgive and move on. We cannot help you any more than this.'

With that she steered Miguel back towards the Hotel. Her passionate tirade rocked me back on my heels. I grudgingly admitted she had a point. Miguel could have stayed in Argentina and avoided the stress of a meeting. He had been man enough to face me. I realised also that it was his leaving my Nan that had hurt me the most. She had been mother and father to me. I now understood why I had been made to attend Church so often and why I had been so spoilt by her. I had been a surrogate son. I understood things better now. I lit a cigarette and began to digest and weigh the evidence. As I walked back towards the hotel my anger slowly dissipated. Maybe I had expected too much, some instant fix to cure my ills. This was real life, there was no definitive ending with all the loose ends neatly coiled and secured. What there was, was real people with human failings. None of us was perfect but there was good in each of us and I could not alter the fact that half the blood in my veins was Miguel's and blood, as they say, is thicker than water.

There was no sign of the others when I entered the hotel and I went straight up to my room to get my gear together ready to vacate after breakfast. At nine o'clock I walked into the dining room to find the rest of my family already seated. I approached tentatively and asked if I may join them. It was Miguel who spoke.

'It would give me much pleasure my son,' he said with genuine warmth.

'I should like to apologize to you all,' I began.

'There is nothing for which to apologize,' said Miguel, 'it is a strange situation to be in for all of us. It was bound to be difficult and not without pain. What matters is where we go from here. Whether we like it or not we are all of the same blood.'

Miguel was in philosophical mood but also making sense. I might not have chosen this man as a father but that was not the point. For the first time in my life I had a father. The void that I had lived with all my life was at last filled. So what if it was less than a perfect fit, the void was gone.

'You are right of course Papa. It is alright to call you Papa?'

There were tears in his eyes as he nodded. Ramon offered me his hand and Maria leaned across and kissed my cheek. I felt as if a huge weight had been lifted from me. The feeling I had always had that a crucial part of my life was missing simply vanished. The last piece of the jigsaw just fell into place.

My 8000-mile journey had revealed one simple truth. Mistakes of the past cannot be rectified. We cannot change history and to believe we can is not only foolish but it causes suffering and pain. Dwelling on the past is a barrier to the future.

I recalled what Nigel the Padre said to me aboard the Hospital ship.

'Think of life as a voyage in a small boat and all of your worries as ballast. The more ballast you take on board, the less seaworthy the boat becomes, slowing your progress until eventually it stops altogether. If you continue to take on emotional baggage the boat will sink and take you down with it.'

My pilgrimage to the Islands had helped me put things into perspective and to finally make some sense of it all. I took the last of my emotional baggage, heaved it over the side and let it drift away. I felt as if the world had been lifted from my shoulders. At last I could sail into the future without looking back. It is the future and what we make of it that counts. For better or for worse, the past is dead and the dead should be buried.

41

Post Script
Falkland Islands, March 1992

The next few days were spent visiting the war memorials and the Argentine cemetery as well as a trip to see where Ramon's aircraft had crashed, courtesy of Rory and his Land Rover. It was a very emotional experience for all, especially Ramon who insisted on walking right up to the sight despite his poor legs. Rory had got us as close as he could with the LandRover with the finest demonstration of off road driving I had ever witnessed.

At the site we recovered a small piece of the tail as a souvenir for Ramon to take with him back to Argentina. It was evident that this visit helped my brother to find some kind of closure to his experiences of the war, just as my visit to the spot where Yorkie had been killed, had done for me. The long drive back to Stanley was passed in complete silence, each of us lost in our own thoughts.

That evening we spent in the bar and the atmosphere was noticeably lighter and most convivial. By the time our last night had come around we had become totally relaxed in each other's company and had begun to feel like a family. Rory and Annie had arranged to stay with friends in Stanley so they could join us in the bar for our last night. It was quite a party and I had the best time I can ever remember. The genuine warmth of the company did more to heal me than all the pills and self medication on alcohol had ever done to date.

We all drank far too much, but none of us could match Miguel for volume. Annie and Maria were happy talking girl talk while Rory and Miguel were on a mission to work their way through the selection of malts behind the bar. Ramon leaned in towards me.

'Antonio,' he whispered, taking his prayer book from his pocket. 'Do you remember when you gave this to me the other day? Do you remember I excused myself and when I returned from the bathroom you asked why I was grinning?'

'You wouldn't tell me,'

'I did not want to spoil anything between us. I was not sure how you would be with me when you discovered my little secret.'

'What little secret amigo?'

'I shall show you. It is time I think.'

He took his prayer book and held it up to show the inside cover. It was in the form of a cut out window mount, framing a picture of the Virgin Mary. Slowly with the exaggerated care only a drunk would take, he slid the picture out of its frame and removed a tightly folded piece of flimsy paper from the recess behind it and handed it to me.

'Open it.'

I did as I was bid. Looking at the list of letters and numbers written upon the sheet, I knew their significance at once.

'So this is why you were so keen to get it back, you crafty bastard,' I said with a chuckle. 'Nothing to do with faith in God at all.'

'I am afraid not.'

'The information you gave me when I interrogated you?'

'Mostly out of date, just enough to make you believe.'

I looked again at the sheet of paper. The radio frequencies, call signs and signals codes neatly hand written together with passwords and grid references of Argentine observation posts. I had been in possession of an intelligence gold mine since the day I joined the patrol all those years ago, I just did not know it. I gave him back the sheet. I had to hand it to him, he had well and truly pulled the proverbial wool over my eyes. He carefully folded the sheet and replaced it behind the image of the blessed virgin then placed the book in my hand.

'For you, my brother, a souvenir.'

ABOUT THE AUTHOR

Stuart Pereira was born in Cardiff in 1945 just as the war in Germany was coming to an end. He trained as a Graphic Designer, and followed a career in museum exhibition design from 1965 to 2002. His short stories have won two international competitions. **South Atlantic Soldier**, his first novel, was published in 2012. It follows the fate of two members of the 23rd Special Air Service Regiment (TAVR) in the Falklands war of 1982. The author served for almost 12 years in 23 SAS in the 1970s and 1980s. Stuart enjoys clay pigeon shooting and plays golf very badly. Besides writing he paints vintage aircraft and wildlife. His second novel **Helter Skelter** is the first in a series of books featuring SAS sergeant Mark Skelter. Currently working on the final edit of the second in the series **Skelter's Vengeance**, Stuart is widowed and lives in West Yorkshire.

97861110R00186

Made in the USA
Columbia, SC
18 June 2018